Danny Mason

David Palmer

Danny Mason

Vanguard Press

A CIP catalogue record for this title is
available from the British Library.

ISBN 978 1 80016 974 6

This is a work of fiction. Names, characters, businesses, places, events, and
incidents are either the product of the author's imagination or used in a
fictitious manner. Any resemblance to actual persons, living or dead, or actual
events is purely coincidental.

*Vanguard Press is an imprint of
Pegasus Elliot Mackenzie Publishers Ltd.*
www.pegasuspublishers.com

First Published in 2024

**Vanguard Press
Sheraton House Castle Park
Cambridge England**

Printed & Bound in Great Britain

Foreword

Was Danny Mason a product of his environment? How often the question is asked among criminologists and the establishment. The age-old question that fascinates people, is it nature or is it nurture? His entire family from both parents were criminals, some were violent sociopaths, some were common thieves, all were in one way or another involved in criminality or had been at some time in their lives, that lifestyle was ingrained in them all, what chance did he or any of them have?

From his birth in 1964 right up to the present day, the odds of staying out of this lifestyle were stacked against him. Witness to his mother's brutal murder when he was just eight years old, sent to a children's home the same year, bullied by his peers to the point where it was either fight or be a victim, he chose the former and boy did he learn his craft well, with extremely violent tendencies and a spitefulness that were unprecedented in one so young he soon became a person to steer clear of, a person to fear, one social worker who was assigned the traumatised boy. commented "I've dealt with dozens of young boys from similar backgrounds, and most are manageable, but this boy is just cold, he just smiles when he's done something bad or violent and goes silent. He makes my blood run cold."

Danny had spent most of his early years in one institution or another from the age of eight until he was twenty-two, care homes, reform school, borstal, and prison, his descent into crime, violence and that way of life were a mere formality, however becoming a hired killer was not inevitable. It was a choice and one he embraced with genuine happiness, he enjoyed and wanted to hurt people.

By the age of thirteen He had killed his first person, it wouldn't be his last.

A chance meeting with Tommy Spillane a north London gangster while serving his latest sentence at Maidstone jail set off a chain of events that were irreversible and changed his life forever, his two uncles Jimmy and Harry Parkhurst, his mother's half-brothers, who themselves were violent and psychotic gangsters had come to visit him out of the blue in 1986, they knew Tommy Spillane well and at his recommendation had rekindled their connection with Danny.

During their visits they told him that uncontrolled violence was not the way and although violence was inevitable, especially in their world, there was a way to earn from it there was a way to refine it he could have all the things he dreamed about, money, women, cars fancy holidays and flashy pads, all he had to do was listen, learn and give his complete and total loyalty to them, that's all they asked. After all you are family,

Danny was never interested in money, girls or fast cars, all he ever wanted was to be accepted and loved, to be part of a family. He missed his mother, she was the only one who had ever shown him true love and he wanted that feeling again, his mother's facial features were etched in the faces of his uncles sitting opposite him and reminded him of her, he felt strangely angry in that moment, an indescribable rage that even he couldn't understand, all he knew is that he needed this, he needed to find some structure in his life and who better to provide that than family.

So he merely smiled at the brothers and nodded his head in response, he wasn't really one for small talk, they understood what that meant, they were banking on it.

"Watch out for false prophets, they come to you in sheep's clothing, but inwardly they are ferocious Wolves".

-Matthew 7:15

Chapter 1 Present Day 1995

Danny was fast asleep and dreaming.

His dreams hadn't changed much over the years and were usually ones of violence, mayhem and absolute terror, in these nightmares, he was always desperately trying to find an escape route. In this one, he was fleeing from an unknown assailant in the hallway of an old and derelict house who was hunting for him, he could hear him but not quite see him, the floorboards were loose and no matter how hard he tried he could never quite find his feet to run, almost like he was treading water. Whenever he reached a door it always led him into another room where the monster was waiting and not the exit he was searching for. Panic and desperation were the only real feelings he had during these dreams.

The person chasing him was definitely a man, that much he knew, however, he could never remember who or why it was chasing him, and he could never quite put his finger on it, no matter how hard he tried, the faces and places blurred and disappeared without a trace in those first few moments of consciousness.

When he eventually woke from these nightmares in a pool of sweat and panic while gasping for air, nothing remained, apart from the smell of burning, a nostril stinging bitter smell that disappeared almost instantly but no matter how hard he tried to remember the details the whole thing was gone. All he remembers is that the dream was bad and the dread and fear he felt in the aftermath took some time to disappear.

This dream was slightly different though, there was a woman in this one and she was screaming, a blood curdling scream that chilled him to the bone It sounded familiar, it sounded like his mother, and he could smell boot polish!

Danny at thirty-one years old was a career criminal, now working almost exclusively for his two uncles the notorious south London gangsters, Harry and Jimmy Parkhurst and had been for some years now.

He was on a job and this "bit of work" was for them and would be finished by the end of the week. Danny's speciality these days was "clean ups" literally translated, he was a hired killer whose penchant for this kind of work had grown his status amongst the serious criminal fraternity to legendary status At six foot one and a muscular fifteen stone, Danny would be a formidable opponent for anyone, his rugged good looks, well-groomed dark black hair and a beautiful mixture of green and hazel eyes made him instantly attractive to most women who came across him, however, when he was working, he never mixed business with pleasure, that sort of thing was for others, killing gave him his pleasure.

18 Truwin street is a four-apartment block of flats just off the main road of Clapham High Street in south west London where most of the old Victorian houses have been converted into flats and are perfect for the renting commuter due to the close proximity of the copious transport links into central London and the surrounding areas. A ground floor flat in the block where Danny was staying had been provided by his Uncle Jimmy, and was one of the "safe" houses that he had use of while waiting for the "bit of work" as his uncle called it to be done. Jimmy Parkhurst never used real names of people or things they were doing or planning to do, he had his own language for such things. Danny always understood, he and Uncle Jimmy had an uncanny way of knowing what the other was thinking, it wasn't the same with his Uncle Harry even though they were twins, Danny wasn't as close to him He always thought there was something strange going on in Harry's head that Danny could never quite put his finger on, he was strangely wary of him.

The added benefit of an area like this to Danny was with the high volume of people coming and going so regularly that you barely got time to know they were even there, affording him some form of anonymity. No one gave him a second glance when he arrived towards the end June, until now the most he's ever had is a nod on the street and the occasional how do you do from one of the neighbours. That suits him just fine as in his line of work, and with his previous form any contact with the authorities would not be beneficial or welcomed.

Delroy Chambers and his missus, Sandra, had moved in a few days after Danny and were living right above him on the first floor. Almost instantly they had made their presence known. The loud music, shouting and arguing and generally being a pair of fucking nuisances (Danny hated loud people). He had come across them both two days ago, while entering the building after returning from another meeting with his uncles. Although nothing was said, Danny knew just by their demeanour that confronting them about the recent noise would not end well so he decided to leave it, he couldn't afford any issues as the job was imminent and he had to stay focussed.

Slowly coming to consciousness from his dream Danny realised that the screams were real and coming from the woman upstairs, it was also very clear that it had got physical.

As much as he hated interfering in domestic shit like this, he had seen the fear in Sandra's eyes during their brief encounter a couple of days ago and despite the voice that was screaming in his head to leave it alone he couldn't. His instant dislike of Delroy Chambers even though he knew nothing about him or indeed had ever spoken to him took over any reasoning or self-control he may have had. He hated bullies with a passion especially ones that attacked women, he had more reason than most.

He got dressed quickly, put on his gloves, and ascended the stairs to the next floor. When Danny reached the flat, the door was slightly ajar with a luggage bag jamming the entrance. It looked like a bag of clothes, probably Delroy's meagre belongings, he thought. The noise that was coming through to the hallway was louder than ever. Sandra was crying and screaming for Delroy to leave her alone, that he was hurting her and to get out, but he was having none of it as he continued his assault.

There were only two flats on the landing and Danny could see movement behind the other one through shadows flashing across the peep hole but no one came out. Typical he thought but understandable. Delroy was a big guy six foot at least and powerfully built, scary to most but not to Danny. He had come across many like him before, especially in his line of work, but would definitely not underestimate him. Delroy would be a formidable opponent just going by his size alone, Danny was no lightweight either at six foot one and a well-built fifteen stone he would give anyone a run for their money and had, however, he was no fool either, he had seen bigger and much more powerful men put away by sheer arrogance and would not be making that mistake with Delroy.

Pushing the door slightly more open and moving the bag to one side Danny could see that directly in front of him was the kitchen. Immediately to the left was the front room that was where the noise was coming from. A quick glance right down the hallway, he could see the bathroom and other rooms, these had to be the bedrooms, he quickly assessed the situation, and was confident there was no one else in the flat.

He took a deep breath and walked into the hallway, he slowly pushed open the front room door all the while expecting to be confronted, and he was ready. The sight that met him produced a rage in Danny that had been suppressed for years. The last time that he had lost it properly was over ten years ago now and had cost him a five stretch in Maidstone Jail, He thought he had learned his lesson, but he was too far gone now, and he swore he could smell boot polish!

The still screaming Sandra was face down on the floor with Chambers kneeling on her back while pulling her hair spitefully back towards him, she was clearly struggling to get away and crying uncontrollably while Delroy continued his assault, shouting obscenities while doing so, in his blind rage, he was oblivious to Danny moving in behind him.

Danny didn't hesitate, he aimed his size ten boot straight in to the side of Delroy's head with real venom, This would normally have done the trick but Delroy was no snowflake, although stunned he managed to roll to the side, and was up on his feet very quickly. Danny was taken a little by surprise at this, but kept his momentum going by stepping forward and letting loose a couple of quick punches to his head, Danny had been a decent amateur boxer back in the day, and knew how to throw a punch, however, these only stunned Delroy and didn't put him down, this guy was resilient if nothing else and left Danny with no choice but to aim his right boot straight into Delroy's groin. This time he went down doubled up in agony, Danny moved in and finished the job.

Sandra was screaming again, not in fear or panic this time but directly at Danny pushing him off her stricken boyfriend and calling him a fucking bastard and who the hell did he think he was barging in here like that and attacking her man for no reason?! Delroy was on his back out cold with blood oozing from his mouth and nose, there was a large pool of blood on the carpet right beside his head, and was getting bigger by the second, Danny's gloved hands were covered in blood. "Leave him alone, and get out of my flat you fucking arsehole, go on before I call the police on you," she screamed while kneeling beside the stricken Delroy.

Danny eventually stopped, his rage was palpable and Sandra was frightened, she thought Delroy was dead, Danny simply left without looking back.

"Damn it. Damn it. Damn it, why the fuck did I get involved, domestics never end well, and you know it," thought Danny moving down the stairs to his apartment, "not my brightest move" but there was something about that Chambers guy that got my back up from the start and attacking that woman like that he got what he deserved he thought. Fuck it what's done is done there is no going back now, time to leave; he would need to find another place to hide out for a few days.

Back in his flat, Danny immediately went to the bathroom, removed his gloves, washed his hands then gathered up his things, there was not much anyway as he was only using the flat for a lay down. A temporary bolt hole as it were, with just two bags which were always packed and ready to move. His "special" phone was already in the car boot under the spare wheel, his usual phone was on the front room table and he scooped it up, placed it in his jeans, and left the building. He knew he had a little time as any response by the police would be around ten minutes at least, but he was still done in less than five.

His car was parked about three hundred yards from the flat in a side street, he never parked too close to where he was staying, that way no one could confirm if he had a car or not and therefore couldn't give a description. Most crooks get lifted making their get-away, Danny knew that and always arrived at the flat on foot, hopefully that is what any witnesses would confirm, and this isn't his first rodeo.

He heard the sirens before he saw the police car and very deliberately bent down to tie his shoelaces while waiting for the car to arrive. The nosey but silent neighbour must have called them he thought, and they were quick! They must have been local when they picked up the call he thought, just as well he didn't hang about then.

The police car whizzed past, and screeched to a halt outside his old apartment building, where several burly officers decanted, and ran towards the entrance. Danny got up and casually walked in the opposite direction towards his car a few streets down, in minutes he was out of Clapham and driving towards Wandsworth, he wouldn't head for his secret apartment in Putney south London just in case The flat in question was located in a private little cul-de-sac just off Sutherland Grove and he had taken possession of it several years ago, no one knew he had it, or so he hoped, but you never know, he thought, best to stay away from known places until I can clear my head.

As far as his uncles and a few selected close friends knew he had an apartment just off the Old Kent Road in South East London, where he would occasionally meet them. The flat was owned by them but under a different name through an agent, in fact, not even Danny's name was on the books, he was known to his neighbours as Peter Smith, and he never made small talk with anyone he didn't know, not even to people he knew for that matter, no one really knew him, he was a bit of a loner in fact.

Danny headed to Wandsworth a few miles away, the job was still on and no matter what, it had to be done.

The Making of Danny Mason

Chapter 2 1964-1973

Daniel John Mason was born in poverty at the Chelsea and Westminster hospital Fulham southwest London on the 25th of February 1964 to Mr Ronald and Mrs Elizabeth Mason, nee Lane, and weighed a bouncing 7lb 6ozs, a normal and unremarkable birth.

Elizabeth was kept in for a time following the birth to allow her to recover, the norm back then was around four to five days, however the nurses had taken pity on her after Lizzie had told them about her situation, "I'm homeless" she told them, "my husband is in prison, and I have nowhere to go when you let me out." The nurses took pity on her and had found "complications" to keep her under observation but couldn't continue this pretence for long as the ward matron was becoming increasingly suspicious, and after seven days she was discharged, clutching her precious bundle, onto the cold streets of Chelsea and into homelessness. She tried her mother of course, but all she did was send her down to social services with a letter stating that she couldn't stay at her place; she had never been a loving mother anyway. Social services referred her to the local borough council, in this case Wandsworth, they informed her that they had no mother and baby places available at this time and that she would have to find private lodgings and that they would, of course, assist her with that so gave her a list of known boarding houses in the area. She moved into a local lodging house with her new baby shortly after.

The house on Alfarthing lane in Wandsworth was a large Victorian house set over three floors and was owned and run by a man called Billy Saunders. Billy was a well-known nasty piece of work who she didn't like, neither did her family, as his reputation had proceeded him and they had stayed well clear of him and his family, up till now.

The house was only a few streets down from her mother's house where she was brought up and knew the Saunders family well, "Tinkers" the lot of them her mother used to say, however, as he was the only one that would take her and the baby in at short notice, Lizzie's mother, Nellie, didn't want to know. "You made your own bed with that man now, my girl, so you can lie in it!" she proclaimed referring to Lizzie's husband, Ronald, when she was informed her of her new grandchild. It seemed, she had no choice what with her husband in jail and the council not really helping, Billy had taken her social security book on arrival. He was the local money lender amongst other things who used to confiscate women's family allowance books when they borrowed money from him until they could pay what they owed, he was well known to march them down the post office on "payday" to collect his money.

Chapter 3

Danny's father, Ronald Charles Mason was a thief, a liar, and an out and out "wrong-un". Although his profession on the birth certificate, registered on his release from prison in April the same year, stated that he was an artist, some may have found that funny as the only thing Ronnie ever painted was his own intricate web of lies and deceit. Danny's mother, Elizabeth Marjory Mason, was quite simply a "housewife" on the certificate, commonly used at that time, but not necessarily accepted as a "profession" more of a duty according to most men of that era, that was Ronnie's view anyway.

Ronald Charles Mason, Ronnie to his friends came from a well to do background, and was privately educated. His father, Albert Mason, was a retired army captain who was stationed in India from 1932-1946, his mother, Elsie Shaw, a nurse, was also stationed at the same barracks where they met and married in 1935.They repatriated back to England in 1946 with their two boys Ronald, ten, and his brother, Ralph, seven, following the end of hostilities with Germany and Japan. They settled back to normal life in the quiet suburb of Crawley, a sleepy little town in West Sussex. Ronald was the eldest of the two boys by three years, and was trouble from the start, indeed just after the news came in that Hitler had surrendered, and while everyone was celebrating out on the parade ground, he was caught in the officers' mess, aged nine, stealing from the canteen takings. His parents and peers alike were mortified that an officer's son could do such a thing, The commanding officer of the regiment demanded immediate action from the horrified Captain Mason, he duly obliged and despite his wife's protestations, Ronald was brutally thrashed on the parade ground by his father with an audience of the entire barracks who came out to witness the punishment that Albert had seen fit to administer. It never worked; Ronald just rebelled and hated his father even more. His father was a stern and somewhat brutal man whose one and only form of discipline involved violence, the beatings were a regular occurrence for the two boys but especially Ronald who seemed to take great pleasure in getting his father angry. Psychologists would surmise that this behaviour was a cry for acceptance and attention and this was the only way to get any form of interaction with his father who was distant and inadequate in expressing any kind of feelings to his sons, "They need to be men," he would often tell his wife, "spare the rod spoil the child," was one of his favourite idioms, that clearly didn't work, and Ronnie continued his petty crimes and bad behaviour throughout his adolescence, which he would go on to take this into adulthood. His parents didn't understand and sent him away to boarding school at the earliest opportunity, this seemed to work for a while and he excelled academically, however, there was always some underlying issues, including petty theft, fighting and just being a damn nuisance according to his housemaster. Most of his misdemeanours were brushed under carpet of course and just recorded as an adolescent boy misbehaving. However, in the summer of 1953 when Ronald was only seventeen, he was arrested for burglary. An unusual crime of this era and especially coming from a boy of such upbringing in the quiet suburbs of middle class England, he was subsequently given twelve months in a young offenders prison, Inevitably this behaviour continued until his father finally broke and turned him out of the family home following an "unfortunate" incident that involved burglarising another close neighbour, and friend on their quiet street in Crawley, talk about on your own doorstep! He was given a further eighteen months in prison, and on his release one year later in 1961 his father turned him out, declaring that he should, "Never darken these doors again." His mother, Elsie, was distraught but Albert's mind was made up, Ronnie ended up moving down to London and stayed at an old crook's house he had met in prison by the name of Norman Pelluet who lived in Balham south west London and was the local "fence". He met Elizabeth, Lizzie to her friends, a few months later the same year, she was seventeen years old.

Elizabeth Lane was from a large but poor family who had moved to south London at the start of World War II before Elizabeth was born. According to the family, it was to escape the bombings in the East End but mostly it was so that old man Parkhurst could avoid the call-up, he too was a thief and criminal who had been dodging the authorities for some time, He was eventually caught in 1940, and sent to jail for six months, on release he was drafted into the army to serve his country, unfortunately for him and his family back home their fears were realised, and soon after he was killed in action in 1941.

This unfortunate event left the widow Parkhurst, Nellie as she was known, husbandless with four children, no money, and no prospects and close to homelessness.

Nellie wasn't a particularly bright woman by all accounts, but was quite attractive and canny, and she used this to her benefit by working the local streets and bars as a prostitute. There was no real support from the government at the time and she had mouths to feed, this continued throughout most of the war until early 1943 when she met and married Johnny Lane the local back street bookie. She used to do some "running" for him around the streets of Wandsworth taking penny bets from young and old housewives alike and anyone who just wanted a little excitement in their lives, it was illegal of course but rarely enforced by local policemen as most just saw it as harmless fun which it was until someone didn't pay up, then it could get nasty, the punters nearly always paid for bets in cash but some bookies would give credit and that's where the trouble started. However, very few tried to "Knock" Johnny Lane, Nellie would do her rounds and if they wouldn't or couldn't pay, Johnny would pay them a visit, he always got his money.

During the evening when she wasn't working her job in the streets and pubs of south London collecting bets, she continued with prostitution and obviously without Johnny's knowledge. He paid her a pittance and with four children to support she had little choice, there was to be no state support to talk about until much later, so she did what she had to do. She gave birth to Elizabeth in 1944 at the hospital for women in Clapham South; it was a difficult birth and caused the poor unfortunate Nellie a great deal of pain and substantial long-term damage, not only physically but mentally too. Nellie never forgave her husband who incidentally wasn't at the birth, but more disturbingly blamed Lizzie for her trauma.

Johnny was spending more and more time away and wasn't around much anymore, and took very little interest in the young child. These days he preferred to gallivant around the racecourses and dog tracks across the country and stay with "his whores" when he wasn't drinking with his gangster mates of course. Nellie dreaded those days, Johnny would get pissed across the road in the Old Sergeant pub, then either come home and beat her, and the kids or take what he wanted from her! Mind you, he always had a few quid in his pockets, and when he fell into a drunken sleep Nellie would "wash" his trousers, always profitable!

His untimely death following a knife fight in 1952 at the Old Sergeant pub on Garrett Lane Wandsworth was the culmination of a rumour that had spread like wild fire.

Someone had recognised Nellie from her old working days, and a local drunk was talking about it to his equally drunken friends in the main bar, unbeknownst to the mouthpiece, Johnny was in the snug out of sight and heard almost every word as did most of the pub. Confrontation was inevitable and although Johnny held his own in the fight, the drunk's younger brother pulled a knife and that was that, the young man was hung in Wandsworth jail just under a year later.

The unfortunate Nellie was a widow again, this time with five children, including an eight year old Lizzie, she never remarried.

Ronnie and Lizzie met some years later in 1961 at "Cipriani's" the local café on Northcote Road in Clapham, it was the local hangout for all sorts of waifs, strays and local villains where they sat, drank tea and talked about their next scheme for "making" a few quid. Lizzie was having difficulties at home; her mother, not a caring or stable woman following years of abuse and destitution had made her bitter, and for the most part blamed the children, especially the totally innocent Elizabeth. This made no sense to Lizzie and she was always puzzled as to what she had done. Lizzie spent more and more time just roaming the streets to keep out of Nellie's hair. Her older half-brothers Harry, Jimmy and her sisters had left the family home if you could call it that some years ago and made new lives for themselves in various locations around London. They were never close to Lizzie anyway and they never visited, this of course left Lizzie isolated and to bear the brunt of her mother's anger and abuse.

Nellie would think nothing of dishing out a vicious beating to her for the slightest indiscretion or perceived slight, as a consequence the young and impressionable Lizzie found solace amongst the other unfortunates of the area and soon got involved with petty crime leading to her meeting with the recently arrived Ronnie Mason in the café.

Her abusive and disjointed home life made her vulnerable and susceptible to anyone especially for a man like Ronnie who was educated and well-dressed. He seemed a million miles away from what she was used to, however, and as we all know looks can be deceiving. He knew very quickly that he could mould her in any way he chose, although uneducated and a little simple-minded she was young and pretty, a useful distraction while Ronnie robbed or burgled, and very soon she had moved out of Nellie's house and "taken up" with Ronnie.

Staying in various friends' houses and when times were good the odd guest house, unfortunately times were rarely good, and the couple struggled with finding appropriate accommodation where they could stay for any prolonged period of time and often spent time homeless. They would spend weeks sleeping in old buildings or church refuges, the latter providing the hapless Ronnie further opportunity for stealing and therefore rendering that particular outlet unattainable for future use.

Ronnie's crimes were numerous and Lizzie accompanied him almost everywhere, he often used her as a decoy and with his new found pretty young girl, he soon found his favourite means of hiding and transporting stolen goods was using an old silver cross pram that was stolen from a nursery in Fulham and went with them everywhere. On one occasion Ronnie had burgled the local church and stashed the goods in the pram, Lizzie just strolled down the road like any other young mother and pushed it to Norman's house while Ronnie casually walked away just in case the police were passing and met up with her later, Ronnie didn't give it a second thought that Lizzie could get caught and take the blame. Only one day she did get caught and spent a six week sentence at Holloway prison in north London for aiding and abetting a theft, she too now had a criminal record. She never once mentioned Ronnie while being interviewed or during her stay at the notorious jail, she knew better than that, her Ronnie had a temper and any form of disrespect was met with violence, so no, she kept her mouth shut and just got on with it. On release she simply went back to Ronnie in south London and resumed her disjointed lifestyle, she loved him.

Norman Pelluett's house was in Balham where Ronnie briefly stayed when he first arrived in London. He was the local "fence" and would buy anything, usually paying peanuts "to take it off your hands" but he was the only fence Ronnie knew at the time in south London and had to get rid of any stuff he had stolen and quickly before the police came calling. Norman asked no questions.

Ronnie and Lizzie were staying with Norman for a short time in early sixty-one but he had turned them out a few months later following a discovery that someone had tried to get into his safe one day when he was out, they had failed but Norman knew it was Ronnie despite his protestations and a ludicrous suggestion that it could have been a burglar who got disturbed when they had come back and had fled the scene. Lizzie was distraught as they had nowhere else to go and it was freezing outside, they had no choice but to use the old run down and empty derelict houses that littered the area, the regeneration of London after the war was slow and there were plenty of these houses just waiting to be used.

Elizabeth was homeless, scared and pregnant by late summer of sixty-one, she hadn't told Ronnie as yet because she feared his reaction, as it turned out didn't matter anyway, and she had miscarried just before the end of the year following a vicious beating from Ronnie after she made the stupid mistake of questioning something he had said. The assault was reported to the police by a concerned passer-by and he was arrested a short time later. Lizzie refused to make a statement and he was released later that day without charge, however while he was in the police station she had moved back home to Delia street in Wandsworth to her mother's place, when she was released from the hospital in the hope that she would take pity on her and the situation she was in. However, there were no open arms or comfort to be had here. Their relationship was a difficult one even before Elizabeth had met Ronnie and moved out, absence definitely did not make Nellie's heart grow fonder, and her mother hadn't changed and was still a spiteful and bitter old woman who seemed to hate the world and everyone in it including her own children, especially Lizzie. Needless to say it didn't last long; she was soon back in the clutches of Ronnie and living day to day in one derelict house or another, despite his promises that things would be different.

In the spring of sixty-three Lizzie and Ronnie were married, the young Lizzie was pregnant again, this time she had told him and Ronnie decided he didn't want to "bring a bastard into the world". They had a civil ceremony at Chelsea Registry office on the Kings Road with one of Ronnie's friends and a passing labourer as witnesses. No one from Lizzie's side were informed or invited, not that they would have come anyway, shortly after the wedding Ronnie was arrested and sent to jail again for theft.

Ronnie was released early in the April of sixty-four and promptly robbed the halfway house where Lizzie and Danny were living, Billy Saunders was away on business that day, but ultimately caused her to lose the lodgings, she didn't mind that much as the landlord had raped her twice during her stay when she couldn't pay the rent.

Finding a place to stay for Ronnie and Lizzie was always a problem but having a baby in tow was making things very difficult for them. None of his so-called friends wanted to know, probably because he had either stolen from them or owed them money, but the main reason was that he had Billy Saunders after him and no one wanted to be mixed up with him.

They managed to find a few sympathetic "friends" now and then but it never lasted long for one reason or another, usually because some little thing had gone missing or the gas meter had mysteriously been cleaned out or something of that nature, ultimately, they ended up on the streets and back in derelict houses. Billy hadn't caught up with them yet but the noose was tightening, Ronnie wished he was back inside, he would be safe there, be careful what you wish for Ronnie thought Lizzie while praying for this to happen, she'd had enough of Ronnie he was never going to change, and she desperately wanted a different life for her and little Danny, the thought of him getting sick terrified her, but more so she was thinking about this lifestyle: what chance would he have in life if this continued, she wanted him to be educated and away from people like his father and his associates.

She knew from first-hand experience that it never ended well, recently she had heard of local councils housing and supporting people, she wanted that stability for herself and her tiny son, that's what she wanted. "Please, God help me!" Even though she didn't have a religious bone in her body she used to pray most nights.

Ronnie got his wish in December 1966, this time it was for a more serious crime. It was still the same old MO for Ronnie burglarising houses and the like but this time the elderly gentleman who owned the beautiful and antique-laden house in Chelsea came home and disturbed him. Ronnie gave him a few "whacks" while trying to escape and hurt the old fella quite badly, however the neighbours had quickly come to his rescue and Ronnie was captured almost immediately.

Sentencing him at Kingston Crown Court, Judge Henry Dawson called him a "career criminal who was callous and vicious in his actions that day," and commented that it was only a matter of time before he killed someone while undertaking this kind of crime. "Mr Fotheringhill, the victim is an old man who was no match for a man of your age and size. You used a level of violence that was disproportionate to the situation, the old man in question may never fully recover from his ordeal and on that basis, you will go to prison for ten years, take him down."

Judge Dawson wasn't wrong about the likelihood of him killing someone, but no one could ever have predicted it would be under the circumstances that would follow his release from prison in 1972.

Social services were now involved with Lizzie and the baby and had arranged a "short stay" in a mother and baby unit on a temporary basis until they could find her and the baby a more suitable setting and Elizabeth was eventually housed in 1967 by Wandsworth council to a halfway house complex on the York Road in Battersea, used as a "temporary" stop-gap for single mothers, the place was called Durham Buildings and was a shit hole. It was like something out of Dickens, a filthy hole consisting of six buildings each having four flats over two levels set around a courtyard with parking.

All were in appalling condition, broken windows with Sellotape holding the glass together, rubbish and old furniture strewn around the courtyard as standard, rats were also a part of the furniture.

No one cared; to them it was a stop-gap until the council got them into something more permanent or so they thought! For most they would be there for years, they were the forgotten unfortunates, but to Lizzie this was a new start and to her it was a palace after her previous living arrangements. She and little Danny were safe at last, for now.

All of the tiny flats were occupied by women in a similar position with small children or babies, but somehow Lizzie felt at home here, this was the first time in quite a while that she felt a little more secure, a roof over her head, social security paying the bills, and the prospect of a proper home for her and little Danny on the horizon, she knew the area pretty well and soon began planning her and Danny's future, she was excited.

A bonus to this was her next-door neighbour, Silvia Armstrong, who had extended the hand of friendship from day one.

She too had a small child, a mixed-race boy of two called Corey whose father Winston was also in prison, she never told Lizzie for what.

Silvia had confided in Lizzie that her family had thrown her out due to the colour of the boy's father, Lizzie understood, she came from a family of bigots and had a husband who seriously disliked black people, to her it made no sense, the black people she knew seemed to be suffering just as much as she was, she thought he was afraid of them but kept her thoughts to herself, Ronnie would have beaten her black and blue if she so much had suggested such a thing.

They became good friends over the following months and shared stories of their past, within limits of course, and discussed their dreams for themselves and the boys. They helped each other out when money got a little tight, they even found some cleaning work that paid cash with no questions asked at the local candle factory right next door to the flats, peanuts of course, but "it kept the wolf from the door". They shared the childcare for the boys and had them down for the local nursery and schools. They also looked after each other's boys while they visited their fellas in various prisons up and down the country. During the last visit to Albany jail on the Isle of White, was over a 200-mile round trip and was a full day outing for Lizzie, during this visit Ronnie had promised her that this was the last time he would be in prison. He was going to get a job and be the best dad ever to little Danny, "Just hang in there, my girl, stay faithful and the time will fly," he said, She didn't believe a word of it of course but she was too frightened to leave him, plus he would need a place to stay when he got out and Danny needed a father didn't he? Silvia had nothing to say when she told her, she was going through a similar tale of redemption, she didn't believe it either.

Things were going well for Lizzie, she had a roof over her head, she was working cash in hand while still claiming the dole, Danny and Corey were in primary school and her friendship with Silvia had gone from strength to strength. The only real friendship she ever had. In November 1971, the council had written to her about a new 2-bedroom house in Wandsworth that she was on the list for, they would be completed around the summer of 1972, she was ecstatic and couldn't wait to tell Silvia, in return she also had some news but it wasn't good news.

Winston was released just before the Christmas of 1971, Lizzie was happy for Silvia at first, but things changed rather quickly, Winston wasn't one for letting his woman stray too far, not even next door not when he was around. He seemed to take an instant dislike to Lizzie, but she suspected that he would have acted the same way whoever it was, Silvia did as she was told.

Ronnie had been writing to Elizabeth consistently over the past few years, declaring his love and that he had changed, the usual bullshit, Lizzie had dutifully written back to him declaring the same and how she couldn't wait for him to come home and start their new life in the two-bed house promised by the council, she had told him during one of her many visits about the council letter.

She didn't mean a word of it of course and couldn't care less if Ronnie never came back, in fact, she secretly wished he wouldn't, she had found some confidence and self-belief and things were looking up. Danny was happy at school and things were looking rosy, she was even contemplating sending a "Dear John" letter to Ronnie but she just couldn't do it, even Silvia going off the boil following Winston's return hadn't fazed her that much. She was enjoying spending some time with just her and Danny, he was a good boy, quiet, thoughtful and through his mother's eyes very handsome.

Ronnie's second parole hearing, he didn't get the first two years ago, was due in March 1972, he had written to Lizzie with confidence on this one, he had been a model prisoner for the past two years and would have served just over six years of his sentence, two thirds of a sentence or thereabouts is the norm for prisoners to be released for those that have spent some reasonable time behaving and conforming. They also need to show some regret and convince the parole board that they have reformed, he was very good at lying and could be charming when needed, the parole board were convinced and in April 1972 Ronnie was released to a parole hostel near Wanstead in Essex. The terms of his parole were quite clear, he had to report in the first instance to a Mr Lavery on the first day at the hostel to register his arrival by no later than four pm, he had been given a one way train ticket to Wanstead park with five pounds and sixty pence accumulated during his time in prison alongside a further five pounds release fund, this was the first time he had handled "new" money. Decimalisation had occurred while he was locked up, he had heard about it of course but it was still strange to him, he also had one pound, three shillings and sixpence in old money that were stored in his belongings on his arrival at the prison back in 1966, and was assured that the bank would exchange this money for new upon presenting it. He also had to report every night to the hostel manager no later than 6pm as part of the parole conditions and he was also to report for work on the next morning at the Mackenzie brothers joinery shop in a commercial complex just down the road in forest gate and ask for Arnold Richards the Mackenzie brothers factory foreman, Mr Lavery would give him directions to get there.

Mackenzie's brothers were a small to medium sized joinery shop on the complex that produced all kinds of timber products to local builders, tradesmen and the public. Ronnie had spent some time in the prison woodworking shop as part of his rehabilitation and had convinced the parole board that this would suit him down

39

to the ground; he hated it from day one, hard work and people telling him what to do never sat well with him.

The workshop consisted of six other manual operatives alongside Arnold Richards, Arnie as he was known to everyone on the shop floor took an instant dislike to Ronnie knowing where he came from, and why he was here, old man Mackenzie was always trying to do the right and decent thing and had signed up to help the rehabilitation of offenders who were recently paroled, "It is my civic duty" declared Mackenzie, "we can't just release them onto society with no means to look after themselves can we"? "They would just carry on in their old life and society will suffer" he concluded, Arnie just nodded in agreement, but he knew leopards couldn't change their spots, in his experience these people never change but said nothing, after all he was just the foreman, and it wasn't his money.

This was a precursor to the actual rehabilitation of offenders act of 1974 introduced two years later as a way of enabling offenders a chance to "rehabilitate" as the term would suggest, and give them the chance to make a fresh start, however, it never really worked out did it mused Arnold, "we've had his kind here before" he used to say, "they never last" he had told anyone who wanted to listen, this Ronnie bloke was no different and just didn't feel right, how right he had been thought Arnold following his discovery a couple of days later.

Two days into his new life Ronnie had broken into the workshop late one evening on a Saturday night and had stolen everything he could carry and was off back to south London in a stolen car the same evening, he never was one for manual labour or being ordered about by the likes of Richards anyway, but mostly he wanted to see why his Lizzie had objected to him going to stay with her when he was released, apparently when the parole board officer had visited Lizzie and asked about him living with her at Durham buildings she had said no, he was told in no uncertain terms by the parole board that under no circumstances should he make contact with his wife until such time as they could liaise with the probation officer and social services for visitation rights in regard to his son, to Ronnie this was the ultimate betrayal, she must have another fella it's the only obvious answer, well we will see about that won't we he thought angrily.

The first thing Ronnie did was visit Norman Pelluet in Balham, he had met Norman during one of his many incarcerations back in the early sixties and had done "business" with him before, Norman had let him and Lizzie stay at the house back in the day but had turned them out when he accused him of trying to rob him, still that was then and this is now thought Ronnie, water under the bridge and all that, he would convince him that he had changed, plus he needed a place to stay and had a few things to sell, who better than good old Norman to rip him off, better the devil you know as they say, also Norman had his ear to the ground and might have some info on Lizzies new fella, he was convinced this was the reason for her betrayal nothing else made sense.

Norman hadn't seen Lizzie for years he tells him, but there is this black fella called Winston whom I do a bit of business with now and then who sees a bird on the estate where your Lizzie lives. He's never mentioned your Lizzie though, what I do know is that Winston has a kid with this bird who lives next door to your old woman, he's a man who likes the ladies so I've heard and is always getting kicked out by all accounts, only recently I heard that she caught him with one of the neighbours and all hell broke loose, the police were called where he was arrested and sent back to prison , that's all I know.

"You can stay here tonight Ronnie" he added, but no longer, Billy Saunders has a long memory and if he found you here, I would be in trouble,, that wasn't his only reason of course, he didn't trust Ronnie following the last time and wanted him gone. Norman always thought that Ronnie would rob his own grandmother given the chance, he wasn't far wrong really.

That's all I need to know thought Ronnie, the fucking bitch, not only is she cheating on me but she has betrayed me with a black man, her neighbours fella to boot, the humiliation, what will my friends think, not that he had that many but the rage was in him now, it was time to pay her a visit before he got his collar felt again, no doubt old "Arnie" has reported the theft, and it won't be long before Lavery also reports him absent from the Hostel, with only a few pounds in his pocket and nowhere to live Ronnie doesn't really have any prospects or options and he knows it, if it wasn't for that dirty cheating whore he wouldn't be in this position, where he got this thought from only Ronnie's twisted brain could tell you, but he believed it, she has to pay, oh and thanks a lot Norman.

Silvia and Lizzies relationship had picked up again in the weeks since Winston's latest incarceration, Lizzie hadn't seen Silvia for quite a while prior to this latest bust up, Silvia had caught him with the tart across the courtyard and had confronted Winston, a fight ensued and the police were called, with Winston still being out on licence he had been dragged back to prison. In the weeks that followed, the girls went back to their old ways, sharing childcare, shopping and quite simply rekindling their relationship, however, something had changed in Silvia, she seemed happier but a little distant, Lizzie thought that Silvia was embarrassed by cutting her off like that, she needn't have been, she understood, in fact she told Silvia one morning "I've refused to let Ronnie come here, the parole board contacted me a little while ago and said they were considering his release" "I don't want him anywhere near me or Danny anymore. I want to start fresh in our new house and I don't need the aggravation or the bloody beatings that go with him" " I want my Danny to get educated and live a different life" "you understand don't you love"?, Silvia did and had some news of her own, this time there's no going back she tells Lizzie, "I've found a new fella, he treats me like a goddess and he's great with Corey in fact he's popping round later if you want to meet him."

"Oh I'm so happy for you sweetheart that would be lovely," said Lizzie, I'll bring some wine and nibbles if that's ok?"

"Of course," said Silvia, "I've told him all about you."

"Great, shall we say six o'clock?

"Fine, six it is," says Silvia smiling.

Ronnie had made his way late the following afternoon to the sprawling public gardens just off the York road in Battersea; he had a birds eye view of Durham buildings from there and could clearly see the flats and the courtyard from where he was. The trees gave him great cover, Lizzies flat was on the ground floor number two and that other bitch whatever her name was would have to be number four, she had described her flat during a visit to one of the prisons he was stuck in, he can't remember which one, strange as he can't seem to remember even the smallest things lately! It was only the fact that he had the address on a piece of paper that he knew where to go. Lizzies flat was right on the corner facing the main York Road, the odd numbers were on the other side of the square, it was 4.00pm.

Lizzie had already been to Mr Singh the friendly "local robber", sorry the friendly "local shopkeeper" she laughed inwardly around 3.30pm just after picking little Danny up from school, the big store was a bus ride and for a few bits and pieces it just wasn't worth it, not only that, Mr Singh, although a little dearer had helped her out from

44

time to time, letting her have a bit of tick when she was short that sort of thing, it's only fair that I shop there sometimes she thought, She bought some wine, a nice little bottle of blue nun, a six pack of assorted crisps and a bag of peanuts, she headed back to the flat, Mr Singh gave Danny a small lolly, he's such a nice man thought Lizzie glad she came here now.

Dead on 6.00pm she gathered up her bottle of wine and nibbles and made the very short journey next door with Danny in tow, opening the door and leading Lizzie into the front room where a very good looking and muscular black man sat, sprawled, legs apart and looking like he owned the place! "This is my new fella Jerome" declared the flushed Silvia, the first thing Lizzie noticed was that he was sitting in Winston's chair, he would not like that she thought but cleared it from her mind, Winston isn't here is he she mused, "how do you do Jerome very nice to meet you" she says in her best and poshest voice, they all laughed.

"Hi Danny, why don't you go and see Corey" says Silvia, you know where his room is don't you, Danny does and scuttles off and almost immediately they can hear the two boys playing and laughing, no better sound in the world thought Lizzie, life is just so good right now.

"So what do you do for a living, Jerome," says Lizzie hoping that she is not being too pushy.

He leans back in Winston's chair, hand on his chin and says, "Well, I do a bit of building works but by trade

I'm a plumber, mostly house bashing you know but sometimes on the big sites, we just gone and done that new development in Wandsworth up the road mostly houses but a couple of blocks of flats as well he says, they were going to be finished soon."

"Oh my goodness, that's where I'm moving to in June, what a coincidence. The council have just confirmed it," she says excitedly.

"Wow man that's great," says Jerome, "they are really nice houses, we got nothing like that in Jamaica, not where I'm from anyhow, you're one lucky girl."

Yes I am thought lizzie.

Across the road Ronnie can see all the comings and goings from the flats, he sees the famous Winston pull up in his van around 5.45pm and go straight to number four, what the hell is he doing here? Norman told me he was banged up he's supposed to be in prison, lucky I waited though he looks like a bit of a handful, typical bloody woman he thought, took him straight back and there he is bold as brass walking around like he owns the place after messing with my wife, he lights a smoke and waits, he wonders what his next move should be, he certainly won't be confronting that fella he's at least six foot and well-built, not only that he appears to have at least ten years on him, if he goes to Lizzies and it kicks off, she will surely raise the alarm and he will come running, no I'll wait, she will get what's coming to her don't worry about that.

Stubbing out his cigarette he looked up and just catches Lizzie come out of her flat with his little Danny and going into next door, a second or so later and he would have missed it, how old is he now? He hasn't seen him for almost six years, Lizzie never took him on visits as she didn't want him to see his father in prison like that, he must be eight by now he thought feeling proud of his mathematical genius, she goes straight into number four, what the hell he thinks, surely they can't still be friends after what's happened, they must be sharing him or something, bloody women he had never understood them, he never really had any female role models or girlfriends so never learned about them, his Lizzie was only the second woman he had ever been with, his own mother had been loving and caring but somewhat aloof, she was completely under the control of his father, the beating in India came back to him clear as day in that short moment and the shame and humiliation that went with it, he didn't understand why this memory sprang to mind but all he could think about was his own mother. She had just stood by and let his father beat and humiliate him while never once stepping in to stop him, she condoned it by doing nothing. His own mother, she even stood there without a word while his father had thrown him out of the house and did nothing! They're all the same he thought in that moment, his deep hatred of women surprised even him, they had all let him down. Lizzie is no exception. She needs to pay for this latest humiliation! I'm not a boy anymore he thought clearing his mind, although his mind wasn't clear, he was in the first throws of a breakdown but couldn't recognise it, he only had one thought at that moment, pure revenge.

"Jerome," said Lizzie, "can I ask you something?"

"Sure baby, what you need to ask?" he said in his laid back Caribbean drawl.

"I'm due to move out of the flat in a few months and the council have written to me reminding me that I need to ensure that the place is exactly how I found it before I hand it back, not that it was in great condition before, you understand but I can't afford to be charged with anything I'm barely surviving as it is, would you be interested in taking a look at a few things being a builder and all, it's only minor stuff and mostly caused by Danny bouncing off the walls, I'll pay you for it, friends rates of course."

They all laughed again, "No worries, sister, let me take a look and I'll see what I can do," said Jerome in that lazy Caribbean style.

Lizzie realised in that moment what Silvia sees in him, "Is that ok? Silvia? I don't mean to steal your man but I'm desperate," says Lizzie.

They all laughed again, "That's fine, sweetheart, Jerome's an angel and a good tradesman if he wants to help, I haven't got a problem with it. His flat in Clapham junction is immaculate, all done by his own fair and capable hands," she said with a wink, they all laughed again. Lizzie was so happy for her and was really pleased that she had finally found someone who was, well, so damn cool.

Ronnie couldn't help thinking he had a little bit of admiration for old Winston or was it jealousy? He couldn't differentiate between the two at that moment and was confused, his mental health was deteriorating rapidly, nothing made any sense, and his thoughts and feelings were jumping from one emotion to another in quick rapidity, he couldn't think. he snapped out of it, NO, it's not admiration or jealousy thought Ronnie chiding himself, he's just a bloke, his kind will take anything that moves if it's given up freely, then why not, no its her fault, if she wasn't so easy this wouldn't be happening, his hatred of Lizzie and her stupid little friend who probably encouraged it were the ones who needed to pay, Lizzie didn't have the brains to cook this little scheme up by herself.

"Listen man," declared Jerome standing up out of the chair "I got to scoot, I got an early start in the morning, and I need my beauty sleep."

More laughter, "No you don't," said Silvia, "but you got to do what you got to do," she said mimicking his Jamaican accent, "see you later lover boy." They all laughed again.

"Hey Lizzie," said Jerome, "why don't you show me these bits and pieces that need doing in the flat before I hit the road, you're not exactly a million miles from here are you, it will give me something to think about on the long ride home." Even more laughter, his house was about a mile from Durham buildings.

Across the road, Ronnie couldn't believe his eyes, his wife and that bloody Winston were going into her flat without the boy, she's left Danny with her stupid mate while she goes off do whatever with this man, this can't be happening, these are sick people nothing but bloody animals he's barely been there an hour or so and now he's in my wife's flat while I'm forced to take it all in from across the road, the rage inside him was now burning with a ferocity that even he didn't understand, his natural instinct was only to use violence when needed, or if it was a woman he heard himself say, shut up you bastard this isn't about me it's about my cheating scummy wife, he realised that this was all in his head but couldn't for the life of him stop the voice inside of his head from talking, you're a wrong'un, shut up! You're only brave when it's you against a weakling or a woman, shut up! Shut up! Shut up.

Sometime later he found himself sitting with his back to the tree with his head in his hands, he wasn't sure how long he had been in this position, but it could only have been a few minutes, right? Wrong, it was dark now, how long had he been like this? He looked at his watch "Bloody hell! Its eight o'clock." He had heard and seen this type of thing before while in prison, the warders called it "an episode" where the prisoner in question would need to be taken to the infirmary kicking and screaming while having some sort of breakdown, this usually occurred shortly after getting a "Dear John" letter, most prisoners kept well away from these guys, a jilted man in prison was a dangerous man.

With Jerome long gone, the girls moved back to Lizzie's flat and set about finishing off the wine that was left while digging into the crisps and peanuts, the boys were top and tailed and fast asleep. Danny's bed was a little bigger than Corey's and made more sense to settle them here, just like the old days thought Lizzie, "So how did it go with Jerome?" asked Silvia.

"Oh pretty well he definitely knows his stuff and said he would do it for free because of you."

"You're one lucky lady, sweetheart, to find a man like that."

"I know" she said.

Across the road, Ronnie had finally got to his feet and was watching the lights flickering in Lizzie's flat, he felt strange but at the same time he felt a weird kind of elation. A fresh wind, it was almost like he had found himself somehow and now he knew what he had to do. He was strangely happy and had a purpose, he looked across at the flats. Winston's van had gone, he's had what he wanted thought Ronnie, but all he's left is misery for them two slags, he walked across the road smiling to Mr Singh's, he knew what he needed.

Mr Singh was just getting ready to close the shop, it had been a long day and he was satisfied with the takings and for the most part, was tucked safely in the safe towards the rear of the store. He always made a point of sporadically plugging the takings away throughout the day, and always closed around this time before the night stalkers came to life he chuckled to himself nervously. He had been robbed on more than one occasion and with one time putting him in hospital, the shop was closed for three days and he nearly gave up the ghost, but a very nice gentleman from the insurance company had put him in contact with a company that provided plastic screens to protect the shop keepers from attack. They also provided cameras, panic alarms and advice, cameras were for the big boys and cost hundreds, he bought a panic alarm and plastic screen for forty pounds, the advice was free.

With York Road slums and the infamous Winstanley Estate only a short walk through York Gardens, robbery and violence were normal; most of the shops that lined the road had been hit at one time or another, panic alarms were being snapped up throughout London as the scale of these robberies and violence had increased massively in recent years. Times were hard and desperate people take desperate measures mused Ranjit as his family knew him, he was no exception and had his one installed almost immediately following his release from hospital and his meeting with the guy from Banham.

Ronnie walked in and began looking along the cramped aisles, he was sweating profusely and muttering under his breath, he seemed to be looking for something in particular and had this strange grin on his face. He made Ranjit nervous, "Can I help you, sir?", No response, "Excuse me sir but I'm closing can I help you with anything?."

Just when Ranjit thought he wasn't going to get a response and with his hand hovering over the panic button the man let out a ,"Oh there it is," promptly picking it up and bringing it to the till, much to Ranjit's relief he paid and left.

"Strange man," Ranjit thought, "there was something rather scary about that fellow!" Ranjit thought he looked a little mad! He wished later that he had pressed the panic button.

"Who's that at the door this time of night?" said Silvia. Lizzie was in the loo and didn't hear the door, "No idea love," she shouted through the toilet door, "it may be the providence man, he sometimes comes this late in the day as he knows I'm likely to be in, his money's due, there's two pound in the kitchen drawer by the sink, be a love and let him have it will you".

No sooner had Silvia opened the front door when she found herself flat on her back, blows raining down on her, it was instant and she had no time to react, she desperately fought back screaming from the top of her voice for help but the maniac who she now knows as Ronnie Mason was too strong and was really letting her have it, she must have blacked out.

Lizzie came bursting out of the loo just in time to see Ronnie rushing down the hall towards her, she could just make out Silvia in the hallway behind Ronnie and it looked like he had killed her, the front door was wide open, it had only been a few seconds but such was the ferocity of the attack on her friend it was over in an instant, her first instinct was to run, but where to? There were only the bedrooms behind her where the boys were sleeping, and she definitely didn't want the boys to see what was inevitably going to happen. Ronnie had beaten her before so she knew what was coming, or so she thought.

Ronnie rushed toward the toilet and immediately grabbed her by the hair and started dragging her towards the front door all the while kicking and punching her, he slammed the front door shut and continued with the assault all the while screaming obscenities, something about a black man called Winston, women like you and things of that nature but she couldn't really make out exactly what he was saying with any certainty because she was frightened and screaming, and she wasn't the only one, Silvia had come round and was on her feet screaming and desperately trying to help her friend, Ronnie threw Lizzie to the ground, turned and punched Silvia straight in the face knocking her out cold instantly. Lizzie was now on her back in the defensive position hands up facing him and begging him to stop, he had real madness in his eyes, she was really scared, he put his foot into her chest to stop her moving, and then he did the strangest thing, he pulled a small tin from out of his pocket and began unscrewing the lid. He threw the lid down the hall then began taking great big fistfuls of whatever was in the tin and began smearing the contents all over her face, then he continued to beat her, this wasn't a beating to subdue someone or punish them for some perceived misdemeanour this was a beating that would cause serious damage if it continued, and continue it did, Lizzie wasn't moving and Ronnie stopped temporarily to pay some attention to the prone Silvia, she too needed to have the contents of the jar smeared on her face, they had brought it on themselves he thought, he was quite mad by now and had lost any form of self-control. It was like someone or something had taken over his mind and body, at least that's what he told his barrister during one of their subsequent meetings following his arrest, he had never been this violent or out of control, "I don't know what possessed me" he had told him.

He returned to Lizzie with the same ferocity as before, beating her brutally around the head, her face was now a mush of torn skin and blood, mixed with some sort of black substance, Lizzie Lane was clearly dead, but he continued for a little bit longer anyway just to make sure, she was twenty-eight.

Danny and Corey had been woken by the screams and a quick glance into the hallway revealed the horrors happening in the hallway, Corey had run back into the bedroom and hid under the bed, lying face down while covering his head and whimpering, Danny stood at the entrance of his bedroom, he never moved and watched the whole thing to the end, he was frozen to the spot and could only look on in terror. He only found out later that it was his dad, who seemed oblivious to his presence while beating his mother to death, he was eight years old and never forgave himself for not doing anything, could he have saved his mum? No, but he never tried, did he? Plus, he had wet himself, the nightmares that followed reminded him of this often in the years to come where quite often especially in the first few years he would wake up to find he had wet the bed and the smell of boot polish lingered in his waking moments

The tin contained black boot polish, extracts from Ronnie's trial at the old Bailey the following year revealed that during his initial interview while under arrest he was quoted as saying, "If they wanted a black man, they should have been black."

In January 1973 Ronald Charles Mason got life with a minimum of thirty years at the Old Bailey for the brutal murder of Lizzie and the brutal attack on Silvia, he tried to claim insanity, but the jury were having none of it, Mr Singh's testimony about the boot polish purchase on that fateful night had proved intent and Judge Dawson's remarks at Kingston Crown Court back in 1966 put the final nail in his coffin and put paid to that defence, the judge recommended he served a minimum of thirty years, Ronnie was thirty-six.

Lizzie's funeral at Lambeth crematorium, only a few weeks after the horrors of Durham buildings, was a large affair attended by lots of people all wailing and sobbing about how she was taken too soon, and how they wished they could have been there to save her, blah blah blah thought Danny. None of them cared about her or ever visited the flat. The chief mourner among them that day was her mother although Danny noticed that his grandma's eyes were dry.

Although only eight years old, he observed everything, he also noted that he hardly knew anyone there, he knew Auntie Silvia and Corey of course, but not anyone else except his Nan who he was staying with in Delia Street following his mother's murder, the wake was held back at the Old Sergeant pub in Wandsworth, where ironically his grandfather had been murdered back in 1952, no one gave that a mention or a second thought.

Sometime into the evening two great big men came up to Danny who at this time was adjusting to temporarily living with his grandmother in Wandsworth, he recognised them from photos in his nanas parlour. The sacred parlour where Danny was never allowed to enter, he had of course on a few occasions when his Nan was out or in the outside loo They were the twins, Harry and Jimmy Parkhurst, his mum's half-brothers, they both slipped him an envelope, said they were sorry and that they would come and see him soon, the envelopes contained cash, a hundred pounds, more than Danny had ever seen in his life, he liked the feeling of paper cash between his fingers, he had only ever handled small change before and was struck dumb, he never forgot their generosity, but even then he thought he owed them, he was wise beyond his years, Mum's sisters, Judith and Mary barely said a word to him, he didn't care, they were strangers to him anyway.

Danny only lasted four weeks at his Nan's, she wasn't the most maternal of women anyway and had a wicked temper, looking after an eight year old boy wasn't for her, at least one that was bad to the bone in her opinion and wet the bed almost every night, she made no allowances for the fact that he had witnessed his own mother's murder by his father only a few months ago, was eight years old and was probably still seriously traumatised. The beatings were frequent and would be triggered by the slightest indiscretion, locking her in the outside loo for a prank and running off to play with his mates one afternoon wasn't his best move.

She didn't have a sense of humour and boy did she show it!, The beating he received on his return to the house in Delia Street later that afternoon was vicious, she had been locked in the outside loo for four hours!, The beating was so bad that it had prompted a call to the police by a concerned neighbour and Danny was taken into local authority care shortly after.

He ended up at a children's home in Blackshaw Road, Tooting, only a few miles from Wandsworth shortly after being released from hospital, his arm had been broken in the beating and two of his teeth had been knocked out, it may as well have been the other side of the world for Danny, though, as he had no one to turn to, his so called family hardly knew him and never visited anyway. He was there for nearly five years before he killed his first man.

Danny's uncles, Harry and Jimmy Parkhurst had moved away from Wandsworth before he was born, he had never met them until the funeral, however they would go on to play an integral part in the shaping of his life, but that was much later, they never came to see him "soon" though, it was close to thirteen years in 1986 before he had any further contact.

The Parkhurst Twins

The twin brothers had left the family home in Wandsworth back in 1951 aged fifteen. Their two older sisters had left the previous year before their stepfather, Johnny Lane, had been murdered. They had no love for him, the beatings he had dished out to them had in fact made them hate him, and he was a bully. They had also witnessed him beating their mother since he moved in after their father had died and seriously wanted to hurt him, however, they were not quite ready to take that task on. Johnny was a big fella with a fearsome reputation and the boys were just teenagers, they were just watching and waiting for their chance, that opportunity never came however, as someone else had done the job for them in the Old Sergeant pub the following year, by that time they had already moved on to stay with their auntie, Mum's sister, Rene, was married to the notorious gangster Bertie Reynolds, and lived in south east London. Bertie and Rene couldn't have children of their own and were more than happy to take the twins in. Bertie Reynolds was a well-known criminal and gangster with connections all over London, his biggest earners were whore houses, pubs, clubs and money lending, one of the brothels along the Old Kent Road was his own building and was his first foray into this type of earning, he soon owned several others across south east London and took a percentage of the takings from the "madam" of the houses and never interfered unless they asked. He wasn't a pimp but provided the accommodation and security, at a cost of course! Most men that used these "services" were drunks from the local pubs and bars and were easily dealt with when they got stroppy, his main enforcer was a man named Arnold Kozlowski, a polish refugee who had landed in the area during the Second World War, and everyone knew him as "Arnie" and was a man to be respected. Bertie had taken him under his wing after watching him take out three soldiers on leave who had thought he was a German spy! Arnie took great exception to this and summarily beat the living shit out of them all, Bertie was watching all this unfold from the end of the bar and was seriously impressed, he offered him a job and a place to stay immediately. He looked after Bertie's interests with extreme violence and prejudice, when needed and was fiercely loyal to his boss. The only problem was the secret affair he was having with Rene, loyalty wouldn't count for shit if Bertie found out, and he would be part of a new flyover by the next day! He would have to be extremely careful.

Harry and Jimmy Parkhurst thrived away from the hostile environment of Wandsworth and were soon to become a formidable force in south east London, mostly due to their uncles' reputation and guidance but mostly because they were fearless and would take anyone on. Uncle Bertie had insisted on the boys taking up boxing and they soon became local champions, not quite good enough for the professional ranks, but good crowd pleasers nonetheless mostly at dinner shows and local working men's clubs where Uncle Bertie held court. He and Rene had never had children of their own due to a bout of mumps rendering him infertile and treated the boys like celebrities inside and outside of the house. The boys wanted for nothing and were almost constantly with Bertie and his friends in the local bars and clubs that he had an interest in. They had nothing but genuine affection for and extreme loyalty to Bertie and Rene, and would do anything for them. Bertie knew this of course, and was slowly grooming them to take on a bigger role within his organisation, after all they were family and Arnie was not, besides, Bertie had noticed a change in the big pole these last few years and couldn't put his finger on it, he just put it down to familiarity.

He started the boys on the door of his biggest club named after his wife, "Rene's", on the Old Kent Road when they were just twenty-one and were under the wing of his right-hand man, Arnie. He needn't have worried, the boys soon built a reputation that they were not to be messed with, and he realised quite quickly that they didn't need a "minder" and left the boys to run the place, much to Arnie's annoyance, he hadn't taken to the boys from the outset and could see where this was heading, they had already eaten in to his "takings" and were looking for more. He knew their type and would usually have dealt

62

with them by now, but they were Bertie's "boys" and untouchable to a point, however, there was always a way wasn't there? I'll get my opportunity one day and God help them he often thought.

Jimmy was the leading influence in the twins' "partnership" and the most violent of the pair, he was usually the one who lost his rag first and steamed in regardless of the consequences, whereas Harry was more reserved, he was just as committed and spiteful when provoked but he always considered the options first, preferring to plan or talk his way out of any situation, but God help you if you cornered him. It was Harry, who saw the potential in everything and was always coming up with new ways to make a pound or two, he was the first to see the potential in buying up property along the Old Kent Road and surrounding areas, the place was a shit hole post war and there were numerous derelict and bombed out properties for the taking at stupid prices, the huge influx of refugees and people just wanting a better life for themselves and their families meant they needed housing, who better than them and their uncle to provide them? Plus, "it was legit" Harry had told his uncle, Bertie was impressed but reserved, his whole empire had been built on pubs, clubs, prostitution and the violence that went with that world, but times were changing, weren't they? It was 1959 and the boys were twenty-three, pubs and clubs were subject to all sorts of regulations, licensing and rules where finding an experienced bar manager who didn't have a criminal record and could handle himself was always a problem, they brought in good money but weren't huge earners. Sometimes the reputation of a particular pub or club was more hassle than it was worth, brothels were illegal of course and not a week went by where one of them wasn't raided, quite often getting closed down in the process and having to relocate to another premises at huge expense. Sometimes the girls would disappear to other establishments and finding new girls was getting harder and harder, during the war it was easier, their men were overseas and they needed money, simple as that really.

Bertie was old school and never really took to change, he was comfortable and really not that ambitious anymore, he had his beautiful house where the boys had spent the last eight years, they had their own place now, he had his beautiful and ever loving wife and his hunger for "taking over the world" had diminished somewhat before the boys had come along. They had reinvigorated him of course, he had found a new purpose and very much wanted the boys to succeed, after some reflection he eventually put up the money (ten thousand pounds) a huge amount at the time and to the twins it was at the very least a start, the average house price in south east London in 1963 was around two thousand pounds and this would mean they could buy at least three or four to start with, they hit the ground running and bought four properties, Spending a grand total of just under seven thousand pounds, mostly due to some "renegotiations" with some of the sellers. They also had a huge pool of resources from the recently arrived refugees and the huge influx from the Caribbean, they all needed work and a place to stay. It was a perfect storm, the brothers very quickly became serious players in the property markets of south London and by the late sixties had acquired over two hundred properties, including commercial interests in factories and shops, they still controlled their brothels and pubs of course but had also taken on a more sinister undertaking for other gangster families across London, mostly violent beatings to teach someone a lesson but also every now and again, murder.

Very soon the brothers were running most of their uncles' interests and Arnie was growing more and more resentful of them, unbeknownst to him they had discovered his dirty little secret and were weighing up what to do about it. Telling their uncle would mean certain death for the man and possibly Aunt Rene, they adored her and were devastated when they found out about her and that filthy Pole, they definitely didn't want her hurt but just as importantly they were unsure as to how their uncle would take the news coming from them. The messenger sometimes gets hurt or worse, killed just for letting the injured party know, the humiliation could make Uncle Bertie act out of character and do something stupid. No, they decided that they would have to deal with it themselves somehow. Jimmy just wanted to blow his brains out in public to send a message and to hell with the consequences, Harry reeled him in and used one of his many sayings, "There's more than one way to skin a cat or in this case a dog," he told Jimmy, "No, if we've learned anything from Uncle Bertie it's to play the patient game, don't get me wrong, son, I want him just as dead as you do, but we have to be smart! Uncle Bertie won't take kindly to us getting rid of his right hand man without a reason and it can't be for screwing his wife, our dear old auntie. Don't worry I'll think of something," he finished.

They soon got their chance when one evening the brothers got a call from the madam of the brothel in the Old Kent Road, Jock McTavish, a violent man they both knew from the bars and clubs of south London had caused some trouble in the house, and was refusing to leave He was a well-known hard man from Glasgow and had worked for the boys and their uncle on the door of Rene's and other establishments on a few occasions and his reputation of being a pain in the arse wasn't without merit.

According to Maureen who ran the house he had got a bit rough with one of the girls and was refusing to pay up. He was probably pissed thought the boys but nonetheless he was the real deal so they went armed. When they got there Arnie and a couple of his thugs were already there and had already beaten the outnumbered Scotsman unconscious. Arnie was standing over him in the reception area, and had a gun pointed at his head, it seemed he was considering a more serious and permanent punishment for this man, Harry stepped in just in time, Jock was awake now and was staring up at the scene surrounding him, two men were holding him down and Arnie was pointing a gun straight at his temple, "There's no need for that," Harry said stepping forward. "He's just a drunk who's gone a bit over the top that's all, shooting the man will only cause us more issues, let me and my brother take it from here."

Arnie was furious, he felt undermined yet again by these fucking upstarts! He cocked the gun as if to fire it, "I wouldn't do that if I were you," said Jimmy standing just inside the doorway, he was pointing his gun directly at the midriff of Arnie and the look in his eyes told Arnie that he meant business, the two men holding Jock looked terrified and were looking at their boss for reassurance.

He lowered the gun and took a step back, "Do what the fuck you want, it's your uncles' place, but let me tell you something, boys," he said with a sarcastic tone in his voice that the brothers definitely didn't like, "this man beat one of my guys so badly last week that he's still in hospital, he needs to be taught a lesson!"

"You let us worry about that Arnie", said Harry, "go on we will take it from here"

Arnie had no choice really as he knew Jimmy meant it, he didn't fancy dying over this fucking Scotsman! He nodded at the two men who were holding down Jock and they released the badly beaten Scotsman, walking off Arnie gave the boys a cold and contemptuous stare, and left into the rainy street beyond. It was pissing down outside. He walked to his car; his two men had gone back to the bar just up the road for a well needed drink. He hated those boys now with a vengeance, they had made him look weak in front of his men and something would have to be done about them he thought, "Fucking upstarts, I'm the man in this firm but since they've been here Bertie has given me less and less." He was muttering under his breath, the money he used to bring in had almost halved since their arrival and now it seemed they were going to take a little more from the brothel, plus he knew about the "building projects" he wasn't part of that and when he asked Bertie why he had merely shrugged and said "They're our nephews Arnie, we are just giving them a leg up, son." He was feeling the pinch and had never felt more distant from Bertie. He had to do something and quickly before they took fucking everything, the only problem was Bertie and his wife Rene. They could never know he was involved with anything happening to them, he would need outside help, but who could he trust? The answer, in reality, was no one really, he would have to separate them somehow, and that was not going to be easy as they were usually inseparable and went everywhere together. He started the car and drove off into the pouring rain towards his flat just off the Woolworth Road and the waiting Rene.

It was late when Arnie got back to the flat, he had stopped for a "livener" at a bar they owned locally and had almost forgotten that she was waiting for him. It was a dangerous game he was playing and he knew it, if Bertie found out he would be toast, he shuddered at the thought. Maybe it was time to put a stop to this he thought , the consequences were too great plus he was getting a little bored with her now, but he had to be careful, she was just as ruthless as her husband and hell hath no fury he mused as he turned the key and entered the apartment.

Rene was waiting patiently in the lounge, she was sitting provocatively on the couch and beckoned him to come sit with her, and he did so but hesitantly, she noticed this immediately of course and asked him what was wrong. "Nothing, sweetheart, I've just had a tough day that's all and I'm tired."

"Don't worry, lover boy, Bertie is away up north and won't be home until tomorrow evening, he thinks I'm sitting in the parlour knitting or something." She laughed, Arnie laughed along and relaxed a little bit but inside his head he was nervous and already plotting a way out of this, what if someone saw them or worse the boys found out, Jesus! They would love that wouldn't they? Not only would they take great pleasure in killing him they would take over the whole thing, no, I have to get out of this he thought, he already had suspicions that they were planning something, tonight's events had all but confirmed that to him, his brain was working overtime and it was only Rene tugging on his arm that snapped him out of it. They went to bed where the love making was mediocre and left the disappointed Rene also contemplating where this was going.

She too had thought about the consequences if this ever got out, she didn't think Bertie would kill her, she couldn't be sure of course as he had his reputation to think about but she knew at the very least she would be left with nothing! Maybe it's time to put an end to this she thought to herself.

Several girls were now peering out of the doorways along the landing, Maureen was rooted behind the counter of the reception and by the look on her face, she was relieved, "Nothing to see here girls," she finally said. "Go on, get back in your rooms, I will let you know when it's clear, my darlings!"

Meanwhile, the brothers were getting Jock to his feet, the smell of alcohol coming from the man was overpowering and Jock was having trouble staying upright. "Get some coffee Maureen," said Harry. "We need to get him livened up before we let him loose on the world!" He laughed.

Maureen wasn't laughing, she had almost witnessed a killing and was starting to wonder if all this was worth it, Harry could see this written all over her face and simply said, "Don't worry sweetheart it never happened, did it?"

"Yes but if it wasn't for you two, I think Arnie would have done him right here in my reception, with me and half the house as witnesses, where would that have left me?"

She was visibly trembling now and close to tears, Harry put an arm around her and said, "Don't worry, love. He won't be back, me and my brother will make sure of that won't we, Jimmy"? Jimmy nodded, "Now go and get that coffee, there's a good girl".

Eventually, they got Jock to some kind of normality and sat him down on one of the reception comfy chairs where visiting punters waited for their "turn". Luckily it was quiet tonight, it must be the rain thought Jimmy, "Listen

Maureen love, get rid of the girls and close up for the night." He drew a wad of money from his pocket and handed her a stash of folded notes, "Here, share this out with you and the girls and get yourself off, Harry and I will lock up."

The relief on her face was obvious and she very quickly marched up the hallway banging on the doors while saying, "Come on girls, we are finished for the night." Several frightened looking girls peered out from their doorways and cautiously started walking down the hallway; thankfully they had no punters which made things a lot easier. They all left into the dark rainy street and made their way home, none of them looked back.

It was just Jimmy, Harry and the Scotsman now, Jock was coming round quickly and was eyeing up the boys with suspicion while sipping on his coffee. He knew they were armed and couldn't work out why they had saved him, after all, he knew that Arnie and the boys worked for the same man and that they both had an interest in the brothel. He was also extremely nervous that they had gotten rid of the girls. Leave no witnesses a part of his brain was telling him, he thought about making a run for it but something else in the back of his brain had told him to see it out. Besides he knew he wouldn't get far, he was badly beaten and still felt a little groggy, no they would hunt him down in seconds, plus he knew the boys and didn't think they would kill him, not here and not now anyway, there were still witnesses who knew he was there and they weren't that stupid, but what did they want?

They told him, Jock was flabbergasted and somewhat suspicious.

"You want me to kill him?"

"That's right," said Harry. "We have our reasons and that's none of your business. All you need to know is that he has to go and you need to make it look like it wasn't planned. We hear that's quite easy for a man of your talents Jock. He won't have his goons with him. If we play it right and you get a thousand pounds cash, he's off your back and we get what we want, don't forget he was going to blow your brains out half an hour ago and we stopped him! You now owe us, Jock, and we want paying, plus you get to work for us at Rene's place and we will put other "work" your way. Think about it? A regular income, protection from the firm, all the birds you can handle, you won't have to pay, and more importantly no more looking over your shoulder waiting for Arnie to finish what he started."

Jock was starting to think it made sense, he knew the boys were ruthless and with Lenny out of the way they stood to take over the whole operation, maybe this was the opportunity for him to become someone. Up until now he was drinking heavily and drifting. He had very nearly got himself killed this time! The twins had clout and numerous interests and he could earn some serious money at last! A thousand pounds for one killing would set him up rather nicely! He had indeed killed before up in Glasgow and had no problem with that, in fact to get paid that much money for killing someone was a first! The most he had ever "earned" was fifty pounds back home in Glasgow when he had stabbed a man to death in a staged bar fight for one of the local gangsters. He had hardly thought about it since, he had no remorse, "I'm in," he finally blurted out, "when do you want it done?"

The twins smiled and Harry merely said, "As soon as possible, Jock, preferably before the week's out, we don't want to hang about, mostly because he won't and don't underestimate him. He's canny and probably planning your demise as we speak and maybe ours as well! We can't give him the chance to get something going, Don't forget it needs to look random and don't use a gun that's too obvious as a hit and makes the Old Bill try a little harder, they won't investigate too long or too hard if it looks like a dispute gone wrong. They know all about Arnie and will just put it down to his lifestyle, me and Jimmy will find a way to make sure he's alone. He and his boys still take orders from us, we will let you know what time and where he is. You just make sure you're ready, you're only going to get one chance at him! Once it's done you go to Sullivan's yard straight away and wait! There's always a key to the gate under the grating at the front, let yourself in and just stay out of sight in the back office and just sit it out. Jimmy and I will meet you there and get you paid up, following that I reckon you should disappear for a few weeks until the heat dies down, maybe a trip up home would suit"?

Jock nodded his agreement, he knew Sullivan's yard, a scrap metal place just off the Peckham High Street, he also knew it was a front for money laundering as it was all cash transactions and the boys had an interest in it. He also knew Jimmy Sullivan, they had done business before, Jock got on well with Jimmy and trusted him, plus he hadn't seen his old Mum for a while and it would be nice to get up to Glasgow and spend a bit of time with her.

"Good," said Harry, "now get yourself home, stay there and wait for my phone call and for fucks sake stay off the booze until this is over, we need you ready to move instantly when we make the call".

Arnie had dropped Rene off on Tottenham Court Road the following morning. She wanted to do a bit of shopping and in all honesty he was glad to be rid of her. The spark had gone and he wanted out of the situation. Driving back towards south London, he was thinking about the twins and that fucking Scotsman! He needed to do something about them all but would have to be seriously clever. Jock was no lightweight and the boys, well they were just the boys weren't they? They had an uncanny way of knowing when something was going on and their sixth sense was extraordinary. He would have to be very cautious as to how he went about it, getting rid of Jock shouldn't be a serious issue. He was a drunk and just couldn't help himself when he was in that condition. He nearly always wanted a fight and wouldn't be hard to provoke into a situation. I'll get a couple of my boys to pay him a visit in one of the bars he frequents he thought, a nice bar brawl ending in a stabbing was not unusual in most of the bars he frequents, no, he would be easy to take out, it was the boys that caused him more concern. I'll deal with the Scotsman first he mused the boys can wait but not for long!. He put the word out to his men, locate Jock and put him out of his misery.

The following evening Arnie was just out of the bath when he got a call.

"We need your help Arnie!"

It was one of the twins, Jimmy, "What's happened and what can I do" he said cautiously.

"We have a problem with a few fellas down at Rene's. There's a group of "out of area boys" who are causing a stink," said Jimmy, "Tommy the manager has called and told us these boys are scaring the customers and there's only one man on the door, Jack, he's a handful but seriously outnumbered he tells us and needs back up. Me and Harry are about an hour or so away and are leaving now, in the meantime we need you to get yourself and the boys down there sharpish and sort it out! If it's too much just wait till we get there, and we will give you a hand".

Jimmy knew that comment would get Arnie riled up, he was right!

"Cheeky fuckers!" he thought, "If it's too much!" Arnie simply said "leave it to me, Jimmy, I don't need your help, me and the doorman Jack who's a top bloke can sort out a few drunks, you and Harry stay where you are son, I'm leaving now"

Arnie dropped the phone back into its cradle, and immediately tried to call his own back-up, no answer. Unbeknownst to him the twins had arranged for his two "soldiers" to be elsewhere. They knew that despite his bravado he would call his men!

"Fuck it!!" shouted Arnie to himself. He would have to go it alone and rely on the bouncer. I can't lose face to those two pricks, he thought. He quickly got dressed and took his favoured truncheon out of the top drawer of the cabinet in the hall and left. The bar was only a few minutes' drive.

An hour before the call to Arnie, Jimmy had called Jock.

"Listen carefully, sunshine," said Jimmy, "it's on, Lenny will be at Rene's in about an hour, we've created a diversion in the pub and the two boys that usually work with him are working for us elsewhere. Don't forget he never parks right out the front when there's trouble; he always comes in through the rear door for the element of surprise. His man, Jack, who is on the door will know this and will be covering the front so you shouldn't have to worry about him .you've only got one chance at this and you need to be ready!".

Jock was ready all right, in fact, he was looking forward to it, and the boys had been right about that prick Arnie! Several people had told him that his goons were looking for him in all the bars around the manor. He had been wise to listen and take refuge until now, Arnie would get what's coming to him tonight, and too right he would!

Arnie drove past the front of the building where Jack, the only bouncer on duty this night, was looking around nervously for support. He knew that the landlord had made a call and was relieved to see Arnie's car drifting by and turning into the car park. Jack gave him a nod turned and walked into the bar, the group of men who were making the lives of the patrons and bar staff pretty uncomfortable for most of the evening almost immediately quietened down and started to drift away, Jack didn't understand, it was almost like someone or something had turned off a switch in them, they began to drift away towards the exit. Jack approached the bar manager and said, "What the fuck was that all about, one minute they're shooting their mouths off and now they've just left without so much as a kiss my arse!"

"No idea, Jack, but I'm glad to see them gone," said Tommy. "Still it's strange," he continued, "by the way where's your backup, you know I called the boys, right?"

"Don't worry, Tommy, the governor has just pulled into the car park, the boys must have called him," said Jack. "I'll go get him in a minute; he will probably stay for a while just in case they come back".

Out in the car park Arnie had parked the car as he usually does in these situations with the nose facing out to the street, "You never know when you need a quick getaway," he once told his boys after a rather nasty encounter with another mob from over the water that ended very messily. "You don't want to be trying to reverse out of a situation when you're in a hurry!"

This time was no different, the car was carefully reversed towards the rear wall of the car park, he could see into the bar and the main road from his position and all seemed quiet with just the usual revellers milling about in the road beyond, getting out, he tucked the truncheon into his belt, buttoned up his coat and started walking towards the door.

Jock was waiting in the dark and gloom just beyond the rear door, it was nearly closing time and he could hear some revellers in the distance singing their way home. Hidden by the pub's bin shed, he had the perfect cover and could see everything going on in the car park. It was pitch black towards the rear but through the gloom, he could just make out the model of car that Arnie drove, it was definitely him. He watched him carefully and deliberately reversed into a spot at the far end of the car park and watched him get out of the car. He also saw him tuck something into his trousers but couldn't see what it was, it didn't matter to Jock, by the time he could react it would be too late! This man can't be taken lightly though, thought Jock who had seen him in action and knew how dangerous he could be. "I'd better make sure first time when I get the chance," he thought to himself. It was cold but he undid his jacket nonetheless, Arnie was walking towards him.

Walking through the car park towards the pub, his eyes were fixed on the bar door which had a clear view into the pub. It was usually locked and never used for patrons to exit or enter the pub, the side door in the alleyway was the way out to the car park, and Arnie however had his own key. The problem was focussing on the job in hand had caused him to neglect everything else around him, Lenny had just reached the pub door, key in hand when he sensed something was wrong but it was too late, before he knew what was happening and before he could draw his weapon he felt a stinging pain in his right side, turning to face what was happening he found himself looking straight into the eyes of the big Scotsman who was grinning but silent. Before he could react he felt another pain in his stomach, in that moment he realised that Jock had stabbed him, but there was nothing he could do about it! He had been rendered useless as the first stab in the back had gone straight through his kidney and penetrated his lung, while the second stab had gone straight into the top of his solar plexus and continued into his heart. It was a "Kukri" blade, the well-known side weapon of the Ghurkha soldier. Jock had "acquired" it from an old soldier who owed him money and had given it to him as part payment, these blades were lethal in the right hands, they are around ten inches long or more and curved, if used right they nearly always caused fatal damage to crucial and vital bodily organs, Arnie was dead before he hit the ground.

Jock casually wiped the blade on Arnie's jacket and tucked the blade into his trousers, zipped up his jacket and walked out of the car park, joining the ever-growing crowds of people making their way home from the pub. No one paid him a second glance, Arnie's lifeless body was slumped behind the bin shed and in the gloom no one entering or leaving the car park would even know he was there. He made his way to the car he had left in the adjoining street got in and made the relatively short drive to Peckham and the scrap yard to meet the twins, traffic was light he was there in fifteen minutes.

Jack came out of the rear door a few minutes later and promptly threw up his dinner at the sight of his boss lying there with half of his insides hanging out on the floor. Tommy had followed him while the rest of his staff were clearing out the pub, he very nearly threw up himself when he saw the stricken enforcer on the ground and the conditions surrounding him, however, he was old school and had seen it all before. He knew what had happened here and very quickly took the younger man to one side, "Listen very carefully, son," he said seriously, "you saw nothing you know nothing, got it?"

The younger man was in shock and didn't seem to understand, Tommy had him by the shoulders now and was shaking him while shouting into his face

"For Christ's sake Jack pull yourself together, do you understand me, son? You saw nothing and you know nothing!"

Jack was slowly coming round; he was looking directly into Tommy's eyes and said, "Yes, I understand."

"Just mind that you remember that, son, or it might be you lying there next time, these people don't fuck around, do you understand"?,

"I do," said Jack. They both walked back into the nearly empty pub and locked the rear door as if nothing had happened, the bin men found the body the next morning.

Pulling up beside the gates to Sullivan's yard, Jock was surprised to see that they were open and there were lights on in the cabin beyond. Jimmy stepped out through the gates and beckoned Jock to drive the car inside; Jock did as he was asked.

Parking further up the drive Jock turned off the lights and cut the engine, Harry was waiting at the door of the cabin while Jimmy was walking up the path, "I suddenly thought earlier," said Harry as Jock got out of the car, "that you would drive here, stupid of me to not think of it before, we can't have you loitering outside for everyone to see can we, son?"

I suppose not thought the big Scotsman and didn't give it a second thought, he got out of the car and made his way to the door, Jimmy had caught up and was now walking into the cabin, Jock had been here many times before and felt comfortable. He was looking forward to getting his money and visiting his old mum up in Glasgow. The twins sat down behind the desk and produced a bottle of whisky, "Let's have a little celebratory snifter or two," said the smiling Harry sitting back in Jimmy Sullivan's well-worn chair. He poured three glasses, passing one to his brother and the other to the big Scotsman, Jock was gasping and gulped his one down without taking a breath; boy did he need a drink after that! The twins took a brief sip of theirs while Harry poured Jock another, and Jock had settled, it was Jimmy who wanted to know all the details. The big Scotsman obliged and told him every little detail. The boys just watched and listened to him talk, both of them had a strange look on their faces and for a moment Jock was a little unnerved, there was madness in their eyes and Jock could see it! These two are bloody mental, he thought and was feeling a little bit worried, he reached down through his jacket and felt the reassuring touch of the Kukri handle, he held it there for comfort just in case and was ready to use it if needed, the twins noticed this of course but didn't let on, they knew the big fella was armed and extremely dangerous, "a cornered animal is a dangerous animal" Harry was thinking, he also knew the Scot was not a fool despite his drinking habits and would be on full alert until he had his money and was back in his car.

Suddenly, and out of nowhere, Jimmy pulled a large envelope out of his jacket and threw it on the desk, he had read the situation and thought the best way to calm the big Scotsman down would be to produce the money, "There you go big lad," he said, "we are men of our word, it's all there count it if you want."

Jock had no intention of counting it there and then he was just relieved to see it, and relaxed back into his chair, perhaps he had misunderstood that look in their eyes, it's just that they seemed to revel in the gory details almost to the point of salivating! "No need for me to count it fellas," he finally said. "I'm just a little on edge that's all; it's been an eventful evening!" They all laughed.

With that, Jock drank the remainder of his drink and stood, picked up his envelope and declared, "I'll be off now lads, I'm going to get on the road while it's quiet, if I'm lucky I'll be in Glasgow by the morning."

"No worries," said Harry walking to the door with him, "you've done an excellent job for us and we both look forward to working with you when you get back, don't we Jimmy?"

"Damn right!" said Jimmy walking out into the darkness with them both and patting the big Scotsman firmly on the back, "You've really impressed me and my brother tonight, son, there will be plenty more waiting for you when you get back, not too soon mind, we need the heat to die down and I'm going to state the obvious, Jock, this stays with us, you can't tell anyone what happened tonight",

"Leave it out, Jimmy," said Jock angrily," I'm not very well going to go around bragging about it am I?" Jimmy nodded as if to say of course not.

Jock went to the car a lot more relaxed than he had been five minutes ago, took off his coat, pulled the blade from his trousers and dumped the lot into the boot, Harry had opened the driver's door and walked to the other side of the car, Jock got in and was wondering why Harry had moved to the other side of the car, he was looking at him with a strange grin on his face that unnerved the usually staunch Scotsman, he was just about to start the engine when he suddenly realised that he hadn't seen Jimmy for a few moments, he was concentrating so hard on Harry's demeanour and trying to piece together that look on his face that he was distracted, suddenly but unfortunately for him he had realised just that split second too late what was going on. He glanced in the near side mirror and there was Jimmy holding a sawn off shotgun point directly at him, he tried to react but it was far too late, Jimmy almost in the same moment that Jock had spotted him, shot Jock in the back of the head, the big Scotsman's head almost exploded but Jimmy discharged the second barrel into his lifeless body anyway, the big Scotsman's brains and blood were splattered all over the steering wheel and windscreen, at that range there was little left of his head, even his own mother wouldn't have recognised him.

Jimmy was grinning, Harry was too and said "I thought for a minute that he was going to pull that fucking knife son, you pulling that bit of money out definitely calmed him down." Jimmy said nothing, he just stood there grinning at his twin brother.

The twins returned to the cabin, picked up their things and left, Jimmy Sullivan would clear things up in the morning, the thousand pounds in Jock's pocket would be a nice drink for the scrap man, plus he would dispose of the car, Jimmy Sullivan was a good friend and could be relied upon to be discreet, it wasn't his first time.

The following day the twins went to see their uncle at his angry insistence.

Bertie was raging, a vein was popping out of his neck and his face was red with anger, "What do you mean there are no witnesses? Someone must know something! You don't just get stabbed to death at one of my pubs and no one knows or saw anything!! Bring that fucking landlord and the doorman round to me here now!, I'll talk to them myself. That man was like a son to me and I want the person responsible brought before me, do you understand boys"? They understood all right, Uncle Bertie was on the warpath and he wanted blood! The twins left, and twenty minutes later Tommy the landlord was standing in Bertie's kitchen.

Rene had been sent out with a few quid, "Go get yourself something pretty," she was told and don't come back till this afternoon, she took one look at the twins standing there stern faced and didn't argue, she knew when Bertie got like this there would be trouble, plus she wanted to get out anyway, when she had heard the news about Arnie she was devastated and really wanted to have some time to herself, she was upset and wanted to have a good cry, even though she had thought it was coming to an end she still loved him in some way and it hurt deeply to think of how he had died, stabbed to death by a bin shed, he was a war hero, what a way to end up she thought while leaving the house and holding back the tears.

"Where's that fucking doorman Tommy? He was there last night, and I want him here!" said Bertie angrily, "I don't know where Jack is" said Tommy, honest I don't he's on the missing list!"

"We went round his place uncle but it appears he's done a runner," said Harry.

"Do you think he's got something to do with this Tommy?" said Bertie, "and don't fucking lie to me, I'll know, we go back a long way son and I don't want to hurt you".

All the blood had drained from Tommy's face and it was all he could do but to blurt out, "There's rumours Bertie, that's all I know, but I can definitely tell you that Jack had nothing to do with it, he was on the front door of the place all night and never left his post only to go and have a piss or get a drink from me"

"Hang on a minute!" said Bertie, "what's that got to do with Jack, fucking rumours."

"I don't really want to say Bertie, it's a bit sensitive, pub talk that's all and I don't believe a word of it!" He was seriously regretting opening his mouth now, the twins were staring at him, it was like they could read his mind, he was seriously frightened but it was too late, me and my big mouth he thought.

"Just spit it out Tommy I promise I won't shoot the messenger" said Bertie unconvincingly.

When Tommy had finished telling Bertie about the vicious rumours that were circulating around the pub Bertie was slumped in his chair looking like a man defeated, the room was deadly quiet, and no one wanted to be the first to speak.

Eventually Bertie stood up, scooped his hair back into place and declared, "My Rene and Arnie?" and burst out laughing.

"You've got to be fucking joking with me, my old woman wouldn't go for a man like that, she's as loyal as they come and besides Arnie wouldn't have dared!, No! Not a chance I would have known, the boys would have known," he said looking directly at the twin brothers stood stock still in the middle of the kitchen,

"Isn't that right boys?"

"Not a chance," said Harry seriously, "Arnie was loyal to a fault, besides our dear Aunt Rene wouldn't dream of acting like that even if the opportunity arose, it's a filthy lie and a dirty rumour, Tommy, and you need to play your part in putting a stop to it! If me or my brother hear one person talking about it on our travels they will regret it, do you understand Tommy?"

"Listen lads," said Tommy terrified, "like I said, I don't believe a word of it either, in fact anyone that even suggests it in my presence has been given short shrift I only told you about it because of what's happened and thought it might be important."

Bertie walked over to Tommy, put his arm around him said, "You've been loyal to me for years now, Tommy, I know you had nothing to do with Arnie's death and I know you won't let anyone bad mouth me or my family behind our backs, now, get yourself back to the pub and keep your ear to the ground, I'll pop in for a beer or two when this dies down and we can have a proper catch up, you OK walking back? Its only ten minutes or so as I need to speak with my nephews"

"No problem!" said Tommy he was just relieved to be getting out of there, he had known Bertie long before the boys had come along and knew how volatile he could be, messengers were not usually let off Scott free and Tommy would now have some thinking of his own to do, these were dangerous men and if there is any truth in the rumours they might want him to stay permanently silent! He walked back to his pub and was just happy to be alive and breathing fresh air.

When Tommy had gone, Bertie had sat the boys down with him at the kitchen table, he had a serious look on his face and it was clear he had something important to say, the boys were dreading it as they both thought they knew what was coming, sure enough Bertie spat it out,

"It's true boys," he declared, "I've known for a while but I didn't want Tommy knowing that I know if you understand?"

They understood the Tommy aspect all right but were itching to know why he hadn't done anything about Arnie? Surely he would have dealt with it by now. Bertie was astute and could read his nephews' faces like a book, so he told them.

"I found out about a year ago, one of the girls from the brothel had seen her with him in Oxford Street one afternoon acting all lovey dovey and told me all about it one evening while I was banging her at Maureen's place." The boys were genuinely shocked, they never thought for a minute that Uncle Bertie would cheat on their auntie and with a prostitute and all, they were disgusted, but kept silent,

"I know what you think," he continued, "how could I and all that, but the truth is me and your aunt haven't been "active" in that area for some time now, we all have needs you know, including your auntie."

The boys were disgusted just thinking about it but kept their own counsel, "My opinion was that it's better with someone I know and at least she's happy, the change in her has been huge, we've never got on so well and that's the truth, don't get me wrong, I was furious at first and wanted to kill him but the more I considered it the more it made sense, don't you agree lads?"

They didn't but it was Harry that said, "Each to their own, Uncle, I can't say I'm happy about it but it will stay with us forever, we would never say a word that could cause you or our dear aunt any embarrassment."

"You're good boys," he said, getting to his feet, "now let's get back to the matter in hand, I still want to know who done this to Arnie, we can't let this go unpunished, everyone will think I've gone soft, make all the enquiries you can and I'll make mine, I want this wrapped up by the end of the week, make it a priority to find that doorman, Jack, he must know something and him disappearing like that is causing me some concern." The boys took this as their dismissal and left.

"He's got to go you know," said Jimmy getting into the car, "he's weak and will bring the whole thing crashing down if we don't step in, that prostitute has been running her mouth, I mean she told us didn't she and I wonder who else she told? Bertie has already played his hand by not taking credit for Arnie, that's what I would have done as it sends a message to everyone out there that he's ruthless and would not think twice about killing someone so close to him."

"I know," said Harry, "he's not thinking straight, we done what had to be done on his behalf and he should have seen that, he has dropped the ball here, maybe it is time for a new start!"

They both chuckled, they knew this day was coming, Bertie had taken his eye off the ball over the past few years and the "Arnie" thing proved that, not only that times were changing and Bertie wasn't keeping up with it all, the big money was in property, extortion and controlled violence. The twins wanted to build their own little empire based on legitimate income whereas Bertie was simply happy with his clubs, brothels and money lending, they all brought in enough money to live comfortably of course, but Harry and Jimmy wanted more, besides all those activities brought unwanted attention and the possibility of arrest and incarceration almost daily, other serious players around London had moved their operations away from these high risk activities and were moving into more lucrative markets, they still had high risks of course as nearly all of them involved criminality but the new way was to get someone else to take the fall while keeping themselves in the background.

The twins enjoyed mixing with these big players, they were building friendships and a reputation in those circles, the Kray twins from east London for instance were leading the way, where the Richardson's from the south were fast catching up, while in the north a new breed of criminal was evolving, they wanted their place amongst that and their next move should cement their place, they were ready for the next step.

Bertie had made his own enquiries of course and soon found out about the incident in Maureen's brothel a few nights before Arnie's murder, she had told him everything including the boys arrival and the tension between them and Berties enforcer. "I have no doubt the twins would have killed him if he hadn't done what they asked," she told Bertie, "you could see there was no love lost between them and to be honest it was terrifying," she continued, "I've known Arnie for years and have never seen him back down to anyone before, he wasn't exactly scared, but you could see from his demeanour that he knew they meant it and done the only sensible thing he could do in that situation and backed off."

Bertie was confused, why would the boys and his trusted lieutenant have bad blood? I mean fair enough I have given the boys a few extra "earners" these past couple of years but I've always looked after Arnie, the only thing that made sense was jealousy, a very powerful emotion mused Bertie,

"Was Jack one of Lenny's boys that night?" he asked her.

"No," she said, "it was big Gary Simmons and Ronnie Baker, Jack wasn't there, although I've just remembered something," she said looking skyward.

"And what's that?" replied Bertie,

91

"Well Lenny was saying that Jock had given one of his boys a good hiding a few nights before and had hospitalised him, maybe he was talking about Jack?" Bertie thought that made sense but still couldn't understand the animosity between his trusted men.

"Do you know where Jack is, sweetheart?" he finally said looking straight into her eyes.

"Unfortunately, yes I do, Bertie, but I really don't think he had anything to do with this. He's running scared because he was on the door that night and assures me that although it looks suspicious he had nothing to do with it. Tommy and he had come across his body when they went to look for him and kept quiet about it for fear of reprisals."

Funny what men will tell prostitutes thought Bertie and Tommy knew more than he's letting on?

"Don't worry, love. I just need to talk to him, I don't think he had anything to do with it either, now where is he?" she had no choice really and told him.

Bertie called the twins and told them where to find the elusive Jack, "Once you've got him, take him to somewhere secure and let me know. Keep him calm and relaxed just tell him I want to talk with him and that we just want to know and understand a few things, I don't want him shitting his pants, I need to talk to him personally and need him "compos mentis" no rough stuff, and by the way, Tommy knows more than he's saying but let's keep them separated for now."

The boys already knew where Jack was, indeed, they had advised him where to go and to keep his head down, "Bertie will want to speak with you, son," they had told him, "We know you had nothing to do with this Jack but Bertie will know you were at the bar that night and will want to hear it from your own mouth, there's nothing to worry about, when the time's right we will personally take you to him, just sit tight for now and don't talk to anyone."

When the doorbell rang Jack very nearly hit the ceiling, he was seriously on edge as Tommy's words were ringing in his ears, "It might be you next time," he didn't understand what was happening, he and Tommy had come out and found Arnie stabbed to death, that's all he knew, what more could he possibly tell the twins or Bertie, he wanted to run but had nowhere to go, plus he hadn't done anything wrong had he!

Opening the front door Jack was greeted by Jimmy, "Get your coat on son, Bertie wants to see you now," said Jimmy,

Jack looked terrified, Harry was standing directly behind him and was merely smiling, "Don't worry, son," said Harry, "we know you're innocent in all this but like we said before, Bertie just wants to have a word and get as much information as possible, you'll be back here in an hour, I promise."

Jack didn't believe a word of it, he had little or no choice but still tried to talk his way out of leaving the house, "I don't know any more than I've already told you, Harry, I swear on my mother's life!"

"Listen, Jack," said Jimmy rather menacingly, "if Bertie wants us to bring you to him, that's what's happening, there's an easy way or a hard way, son, your choice."

Harry stepped in, "If you've got nothing to hide, Jack then it's all good but Bertie won't take no for an answer, surely you understand that?"

Jack sighed and said, "Fair enough, just let me turn the telly off, Mum's out and will go mental if she comes back and finds it on and I'm not in."

The twins knew what was going to happen next but let it ride out anyway, sure enough Jack bolted for the back door, but the boys were quicker and on top of him in seconds, he never even got the door open. Jack was screaming and squirming, he was fairly strong but no match for the twins, he just kept repeating, "I've done nothing wrong fellas, please let me go, I don't know anything, I've done nothing wrong."

The boys were trying to keep him still all the while reassuring him that there wasn't a problem, "Bertie just needs to talk to you, don't make us have to knock you out son," said Jimmy, "I don't fancy carrying your fat arse out to the car, I promise, we will have you back here in an hour, now calm down."

Jack was beaten and he knew it, the best he could hope for now was a few slaps from Bertie for not telling him what he knew, when he knew it and hiding away from him, one thing that went through his mind in that instant was that the twins had told him to hide, that didn't make a lot of sense but as with most things in this world he had chosen, it wasn't that strange he supposed, they must have had their reasons, he was helped to his feet and the three of them walked to the car, each brother with a grip on the now subdued Jack's elbow, they drove to one of the boys' potential new building projects just off the Walworth Road that they knew about but hadn't made formal enquiries on and went inside the quiet and empty building.

Ten minutes later, Harry walked down the road to the nearest phone box and made a call, "We've got him Uncle Bertie," and told him where they were.

"Excellent, I'll be there within the hour, is he calm? I need him calm Harry," said Bertie,

"Yes, he's calm and relaxed, Bertie, he's having a cup of tea and a bacon sandwich as we speak, don't worry he knows how things are and is more than willing to talk to you, we will pick up Tommy from the boozer later and get his version as well, it won't take long to get to the bottom of all this, Uncle."

Bertie was satisfied and put the phone down with a grunt, he went into the hall put his shoes on, picked up his car keys from the half desk in the hall and left, Rene was taking all this in from the parlour and had heard almost every word, she was worried but not for Bertie, she was worried about where all this was leading, she too had heard the rumours and wondered if Bertie knew.

The boys were watching the road from the first floor of the building, sure enough and less than ten minutes later they saw their uncle's car headed towards them, they both went downstairs where Jimmy disappeared into the rear room of the house and waited just inside the door. Harry went to the front door and was waiting for his uncle to get out of the car. Bertie was on his own of course, he would never have normally travelled to a rendezvous like this without his trusted Arnie in tow, but that wasn't an option now was it he thought rather sadly, it was strange that he would never see him again, still I have the boys he thought and cheered up immediately, seeing his young nephew standing there in the doorway just made him think of himself when he was their age, full of style, vigour and bravado, he sighed and whispered under his breath, "The young are there to replace the old," and rightly so he thought, "maybe it's about time I retired and moved down to the coast and let the youngsters get on with it, I've made my money and to be honest I'm bored with all this shit."

Harry took his uncle by the hand with a huge smile and beckoned him inside, "Jack's in the rear room with Jimmy, Bertie, it's the only room that's got all its floorboards," he said laughing. Bertie laughed along with him and walked towards the room, Harry was a few steps behind and had his hands behind his back, Bertie opened the door and the sight that greeted him made him take a step back.

"What the hell is going on here?" he exclaimed. "I told you to keep him calm, not trussed up like a rag doll." Jack was tied and gagged to a chair in the middle of the room, his eyes were bulging and pleading with Bertie to help him, blood was oozing out of his left ear and his eyebrow had a deep cut and the bone beneath was on show for all to see, it was clear at first sight that he had been beaten quite severely,

Bertie was furious now and started walking towards the stricken man with the intention of releasing him from his bondage, all the while shouting

"This is not what I wanted boys! I wanted to fucking speak with him not kill him! Help me untie him!"

For a few seconds Bertie thought the boys hadn't heard him,

"Come on," he continued, "help me get him straightened out, I want him conscious and fucking calm like I told you!"

All the while he was attempting to loosen the bonds holding Jack to the chair,

"We can't do that, Uncle Bertie," said Harry quietly behind him.

Bertie stopped what he was doing and turned around, the sight that met him was one of complete and total horror, the boys, his boys were standing less than six feet from him and both had guns pointed at him.

"What the fuck do you think you're doing?" he screamed at them, he knew of course but he couldn't believe it, no he didn't want to believe it, outraged, he

97

finally said, "I took you in, gave you refuge, fed you, nurtured you and this is how you repay me?" he spat the last words out in his anger, if he was going to die and it looked likely, he was going down as a man, "You pair of fucking inbred bastards, I knew when your aunt told me about your fucking lives with that worthless piece of shit, Johnny Lane, that you would be trouble but I wanted her to be happy, she said you were only children and you needed help before that animal killed you both, by God I wish I had listened to my instincts, go on get it over with you pair of fucking psychopaths I'm ready to meet my maker!" he said standing as tall as he could get and pumping his chest out.

"Just promise me one thing," he said pleadingly to the twins, "don't hurt my Rene, promise me that much and I'll die a happier man."

"Why would we?" said Harry, "she's blood!" and then they simultaneously fired their weapons into their helpless uncle and continued until they had emptied their eight-round "Luger" pistols completely into the now very dead Uncle Bertie.

The terrified and watching Jack had urinated where he sat and was desperately trying to wriggle out of his shackles but he only managed to tip the chair over, such was the tightness of his bonds and ended up just lying on the floor sideways, strapped to the chair and looking up at the twins who by now had snapped out of their maniacal reality and were descending on him, the twins had spent their ammunition so a quick and a humane bullet to the head was out of the question. Harry was sorry for that but Jimmy simply pulled his knife and proceeded to stab the badly beaten and helpless Jack to death.

Harry just stepped back and watched. The Parkhurst brothers had evolved, it was 1963 and were still only twenty-seven years old, the empire was theirs now to do with it as they pleased, they already had plans.

Their half-sister, Johnny Lane's daughter, Lizzie was pregnant with their nephew, Danny Mason; he was born the following year.

(1995)

Danny got to the car, a very discreet and unassuming blue Ford Fiesta, he wanted to get out of the area, get to a safe place and clear his head, what just happened in Truwin Street was completely against everything he had been taught, never ever get involved in domestics he reminded himself, he could hear his uncle Jimmy's voice in his head clear as day, he's really fucked up here but he has to make the call, after all, he's being paid for his time.

He made the relatively short drive from Clapham to Wandsworth, there was a Premier Inn there that he had used before, it seemed like as good a place as any right now, he drove into the relatively quiet car park and sat there contemplating his next move, after a few minutes he got himself together and got out of the car, he had a mobile phone under the spare tyre in the boot that was strictly for this job and took it out along with his two bags and entered the lobby, it was only 10.30am and the hotel was quiet, breakfast was almost over, and the last remaining diners were drifting back to their rooms.

Danny approached the desk where a rather pretty young girl greeted him with that all teeth and fake smile, "all fur coat and no knickers" his mum used to call them, you see that in almost every hotel and restaurant around the world, he mused, he didn't care he wasn't here to make friends or engage in small talk, he needed to clear his head and make a few calls, "May I help you sir?" she said.

Danny returned the smile and responded, "Do you have a room for tonight, please?"

Judging by the almost empty car park and being in the middle of the week, Danny knew the answer, the young girl began checking the computer as if she wasn't sure, this was the little game they always played to soften the blow when they gave you the cost.

"Well, we are a little busy at the moment due to the half term holidays but I'll see what I can do."

Sure enough there were rooms.

"We have a king room on the third floor or a standard room on six, the king is thirty pounds or the standard is twenty two pounds which would you prefer?" she said.

"The standard will be fine," said Danny.

"Would you like me to include breakfast with that?" she said.

"No, thank you. I'm good," said Danny, he didn't think he would still be here for breakfast anyway, not only that even if he was he didn't want to mix with other guests, you never know who you're talking with, he could hear his Uncle Jimmy in his ear and was engrained in Danny's brain. Small talk with strangers was not something he engaged in, he would make his own arrangements when he was hungry.

"Excellent, may I take your name and a card, please?"

After all the formalities were done, Danny headed to the lift.

"We hope you enjoy your stay, Mr Parker," the girl behind the counter said.

Danny didn't look back or acknowledge her, she was nice enough, but he didn't want her remembering him just in case the police caught his trail.

Danny had used aliases in the past, but John Parker was new, he was however pretty confident it would not be flagged, Uncle Jimmy was to be relied on.

Once in the room, Danny took out the phone, took a deep breath and dialled.

"Is everything all right, son?"

His Uncle Jimmy was already on full alert, Danny never called him in the middle of a job unless it was arranged. Danny wasn't due to call until this evening something was wrong. Danny told him the full story.

Jimmy was angry, "Are you fucking mental, Danny? How many times have I told you, never ever get involved with domestics! It never ends well! There are too many witnesses and their loyalties usually mean they stick together no matter what! Please tell me this Chambers guy isn't dead?!"

"He was breathing when I left," said Danny "so I don't think so".

"What do you mean you don't think so? I don't pay you to 'don't think so!'" spat Jimmy.

"Why on earth did you get involved? We have bigger fish to fry and this fuck up could put a serious spanner in the works! You know who is off to his little villa in Spain on Friday, the money and goods go with him if we don't deal with this beforehand, I don't have time to arrange anything else should you get your collar felt."

"Don't worry, Uncle Jimmy, I will still get the job done." Danny always reverted to calling Jimmy "Uncle" when he was in trouble, it always seemed to calm him down.

"Nothing's changed except I've lost the safe house," said Danny, sorry about that."

Jimmy hadn't calmed down, "Sorry! Fucking sorry! That flat belongs to a good friend of ours and now the police are going to be all over it, and don't Uncle fucking Jimmy me! I know that game sunshine!"

"It wasn't in my name," said Danny. "They don't know who I am."

"That's not the point, Danny. We don't have safe houses coming out of our fucking arses you know, and you have probably left your fucking prints all over it!"

No, I haven't thought Danny but kept quiet while his uncle ranted on. "That flat has served us well for years and now it's fucked if the police go crawling all over it! My mate isn't going to be happy! That place was a nice little earner for him, now I'm going to have to pay him off if its compromised, its coming out of your money son, no ifs or buts! Out of your money, Danny!"

Danny said nothing he just let him blow, Uncle Jimmy always blew up like this when things weren't to his liking, and he always calmed down eventually.

"OK," said Jimmy. "Let's all calm down and think about this logically."

Danny was calm but didn't say a word.

"Get yourself out of that hotel immediately and get over to a bird's place called Bridie in Mitcham. Her old man's doing a five stretch on the island and her two boys have just been remanded into custody on charges of GBH, they may well be away for a while, she could do with the money. I'll call her and let her know you're coming. I'll text you the address in a minute. Get there and stay there until I call you, I'm going to make some enquiries about this Chambers guy. If he's dead, Danny, the job's off. The police will get a handle on you from the witnesses, and it won't take long before they know who you are and pick you up. If that happens you're on your own!"

What's new? Danny thought..

"Oh and the cost of a few days at Bridies is also coming out of your end, son," Jimmy continued. "Murder enquiries especially ones involving "civilians" get as much resource as the police need, if he's only injured we may still have a chance, especially if he has form, it's one thing doing a well-known villain or scumbag but it's an entirely different thing when you take out a civilian. The authorities take serious exception to that, are you with me Danny? Our resources are huge but murder squads are hard to crack and if it gets messy I will have to back off!"

Danny was "with him".

" "Don't worry, Uncle Jimmy, I'm leaving now I'll be at Bridies in half an hour, I'll wait there for your call".

"Oh, one more thing," said Jimmy, "ditch the credit card you just used, do not check out! Just leave."

He, then promptly hung up, the text came through almost immediately and Danny was on the way to Mitcham two minutes later.

Tommy Spillane

Tommy Spillane had rather stupidly been caught in possession of class A drugs and was now on remand in Maidstone Jail. What a fucking joke, he thought as the door slammed shut to his cell that first afternoon. This wasn't his first time in jail of course but it was certainly his most frustrating and definitely his most stupid.

Tommy was a well-known and respected criminal on the streets north of the River Thames, especially around the Angel/Islington area where he grew up. Everyone that was someone in the criminal underworld had huge respect for him and to some extent an element of fear. He was known to be a man of principal if there is such a thing amongst men of his nature, but didn't suffer fools gladly. Retribution, for any perceived slight or misdemeanour was swift and often brutal; such was the way of the world he lived in.

He was also a man of his word and a family man. His wife, Peggy, and their two daughters were the light of his life and he spent every waking hour making sure they were provided for and protected.

Tommy, although only five foot ten, was broad-shouldered with fearsome blue eyes and a head of hair that most men envied, a little greyer now but nothing that a little splash of hair dye and a generous dollop of Brylcream wouldn't sort out! He was always well-groomed and smartly dressed; you would never see him in jeans or tracksuits like some of the other gangsters that he knew.

Born in 1948 to the doting George and Rita Spillane, a proud working-class family from North London. George was a bricklayer and his wife, Rita, was a seamstress who worked mostly from home, following Tommy's arrival, but got a little part time work at the local tailors now and again. This was her "pin" money and allowed her and Tommy a few extra luxuries.

From as far back as Tommy could remember he was taught the proper way to dress and behave. It was always, yes sir and no sir! He always addressed the older members of his community with Mr or Mrs so and so, never their first names, "Mind your Ps and Qs especially around women," his father had always said, his mother was no different, a real north London girl from a good family, she was always immaculately turned out, always polite, courteous and generous to a fault, she insisted that her only child acted the same way, Tommy complied, he was a good boy.

Rita was fearsomely protective when it came to her family, no one could say a bad word or even imply any wrongdoing, especially about her husband or Tommy. She could fight like an alley cat, and had a mouth to go with it, "You can take the girl out of north London," they used to say, "But you can't take north London out of the girl!" George used to chime in, she was respected, and Tommy noticed that.

George was a little different, not a big man by any means. He was quiet, well-spoken and very rarely lost his temper. It took a lot to get him riled but like most men he would fight if pressed especially when it involved his beloved family.

One Sunday afternoon a local thug had sworn and made lewd comments to Rita while she was strolling down the street with her Tommy on the way to the local park to meet George, who as usual had a little "private" job close by. George had witnessed this from his vantage point at the park gate, as far as he was concerned there was a line you never crossed with women and children, and casually strolled over to confront this man. The beating George gave this thug was controlled but vicious and over in seconds, the fella never got a look in, this was the first and the only time that Tommy would see his dad do something like that, he never forgot it, Tommy was eleven and learned something that day.

George just wanted to work and provide for his family, he had no real ambition. He could be described as steady and a family man, he worked mostly on building sites but would often be seen in the neighbourhood working on someone or another's house, work was his life and brought in the money to provide for his family. They were his everything, if you asked anyone who knew George most people would merely say he was a hardworking and amiable family man that has a way about him that commanded respect.

George died in 1962 after he and another man had fallen through the corrugated roof of an old factory while pointing a leaking chimney in Stoke Newington north London. The factory boss was prosecuted by the authorities sometime later in 1963 and found guilty of criminal negligence for the "unnecessary and avoidable deaths of two family men just going about their day to day work". The remarks from the judge caused the watching Rita to break down in the courtroom; she was led out sobbing by the bailiff with the fifteen-year-old Tommy by her side. The man got a twelve month suspended prison sentence and an £800 fine, Rita got nothing! The factory boss was skint by all accounts and according to his lawyer while submitting his mitigating circumstances before sentence was imposed said, "My client is a broken man who has lost everything, his business and his reputation are close to ruin, with his means for making a future living doubtful and although the business is still running he is barely surviving, he is for the most part supporting his family on meagre savings prudently put by for a rainy day, therefore, I respectfully submit that this man has suffered enough and would ask for a suspended sentence to be handed down by the honourable judge in this matter".

The judge concurred and Giles Anderson walked free that very day, smiling and shaking his lawyer's hand while coming out of the building. He was laughing at them thought Tommy as he watched from the street. His mother was inconsolable and sobbing beside him. A man in a grey suit was telling her that this is the way it goes sometimes and to keep her chin up.

Tommy took a good look at "Mr Anderson", hands clenched into fists as the man got into a taxi and disappeared down the road, he hoped that one day he would be able to meet him again and make him pay.

Things spiralled out of control quite quickly following his dad's death and the court case. Bills were piling up, the rent hadn't been paid in weeks and Rita had started drinking!

Tommy aged just fifteen went and got a job, he dropped out of school and went off to work with one of dad's old pals on a building site where his mate, Albie Spires, was working. The money was rubbish and he soon began to "subsidise" his earnings with petty crime, starting out with thefts from building sites and warehouses around north London.

Albie was a couple of years older and knew how to drive, he also knew where to sell stolen tools and equipment. He was very useful and could be counted on if trouble arose; he also knew how to keep his mouth shut and was fearless. Inevitably their criminalities escalated and by the late sixties had learned their craft and were proficient armed robbers with a reputation for extreme violence where necessary. The criminal fraternity they mixed with had huge respect for both men, but there was something about Tommy that stood him head and shoulders above most men of his kind. Everyone that worked with or for him knew that he was a man of trust and loyalty.

His mother was for the most part too far gone to notice or even care what Tommy was up to or where the money came from. Her drinking had gotten seriously out of control and had descended into a spiral of drunken self-destruction. She died from liver disease in 1968, Tommy was twenty.

As armed robbers by "trade", Tommy and Albie had moved into fencing stolen jewellery and to a certain extent money laundering by the early eighties. This was mostly due to cameras and alarms that were everywhere and had improved massively, alongside better-protected security guards, plate glass windows in banks and stronger security vans. "Traditional" armed robberies were almost impossible now, in addition to this the police and especially the flying squad had a book on him as long as your arm.

"You can't fart anymore without the filth knowing about it!," he once expressed to his doting wife, Peggy, "and don't get me started about the fucking grasses. I need to do something else plus I'm far too old to do any more lengthy prison sentences!" he proclaimed. She just sighed and rolled her immaculately pencilled eyes up to the sky. She had been with Tommy since they were kids. He was her first and only love.

"Whatever you say, sweetheart," she said sarcastically. Tommy ignored her.

The drug scene came roaring like a tornado in the eighties and anyone who had the balls and money could invest and make huge profits. Tommy and Albie were no different this was an "earner" and they wanted in; it was boom town.

Tommy got up at his usual time around 7.00am one Saturday morning in 1985, put the kettle on, and lit one of his Benson and Hedges Gold cigarettes, One of his few remaining pleasures, he made his usual coffee and took it out to the patio of his luxurious house in Islington, that was to be his last home-made coffee for a while.

"Who's that calling this time of the bloody morning?" he said, looking at his newly acquired "Motorola brick" mobile phone. These things were a blessing and a curse he thought, he pulled the aerial up and pressed answer,

"Tommy, It's Darren. I'm in Norfolk."

"Well, that's nice for you, Darren," said Tommy. "Nice part of the world but I fail to see what that's got to do with me? I'm sitting here trying to have a nice relaxing cup of coffee and you're calling me like Judith fucking Chalmers about your holiday," said Tommy rather sarcastically!

"Yeah sorry about that mate," Darren replied," but I've just had a call from you know who over in south London. The parcel that was supposed to be dropped last night never arrived, I've done some checking and found out our courier, "little Alfie", got himself lifted yesterday on an unrelated charge and is currently in a police station somewhere in north London."

"Well? What do you want me to do about it, Darren?

Get someone else to pick it up and drop it to our friend."

"That's the problem, Tommy," said Darren, "Our friend south of the river is the nervous sort and telling him that Alfie who he's dealt with before got lifted won't go down well, you know how he is? Plus, our lock up is pretty secure; do we really want someone else to know about it"?

"All right all right" said Tommy getting to his feet, "Don't get your knickers in a twist! I've given my word that he will get his goods and get them he will. I'll pick it up myself and drop it south of the river". "Is that a good idea, Tommy"? Darren sounded worried.

"Don't sweat it, son," said Tommy, "I've got a set of keys to where the goods are. I'll get them myself, drop it off and be back at home in a few of hours, give silly bollocks a call and let him know it's going to be me dropping off his parcel, besides I could do with a little jaunt over the river it's been some time since I was last over the water. The fresh air will do me good and as a bonus, I get to see old misery guts!" They both laughed.

Tommy wasn't laughing a couple of hours later.

The sudden appearance of several police cars, lights flashing and screeching tyres less than an hour into his journey across the river surprised even the usually steadfast Tommy. He knew immediately what was happening of course but nonetheless, he couldn't believe it! He was experienced and not stupid enough to try and make a break for it, the only choice he had was to pull over.

In the van that had arrived to take him away to Wandsworth police station Tommy was reflecting on the past hour or so and trying to remember from the time he picked up the goods from his lock-up in Kings Cross until being lifted only a few minutes ago. The police cars came from everywhere just after he had crossed Chelsea Bridge, and was making his way to Wandsworth, it seemed like they were expecting him! Also when the coppers first put their filthy hands on me they didn't ask me my name, they had just pulled him out of his brand new and distinctive red Jaguar, cuffed him and put him in the back of a stinking cop car until the transport van arrived a few minutes later. A tow truck was also there within minutes to take the car away. Something doesn't add up here, thought Tommy. In fact, something stinks and it wasn't just the van, I've been set up like a kipper he thought.

There were only three people that knew where the goods were being stored. Me, Darren and that little shit, Alfie, had he squealed like a stuck pig when under the cosh during his interrogation by the police last night? Darren never said what he was lifted for did he? Even if he had buckled under pressure from the cops how would he have known I would go and get the goods? He wouldn't, and even more unlikely the time that I would make that trip? It was highly unlikely that the police had him under surveillance, they would have lifted him almost straight away once he had picked up the parcel and not waited nearly an hour to lift him in another manor, none of this makes any sense, Tommy's old school radar was working overtime in his brain, something was all wrong about this and he was going to get to the bottom of it one way or another.

The only other person who knew about the journey over the water was Billy Saunders down south; no it can't have anything to do with him. Billy had nothing to gain from grassing on me, he was old school and wouldn't be a grass would he? Tommy pondered this for a while and, to be honest, he couldn't rule him out, but it didn't make sense, who would benefit from this? Whoever it was had dropped a ricket thought Tommy. There were only three candidates including Billy and the way the Old Bill had been prepared it was obvious that one of them had been involved, but which one? He would need to make extensive enquiries, and he knew just the people. Harry and Jimmy Parkhurst, they had connections in the metropolitan police, bent and greedy coppers "who had mistresses and a gambling habits to feed" he remembered those words uttered by Jimmy after a chance meeting with them nearly ten years ago, he reminisced.

He had met Jimmy and Harry Parkhurst one afternoon when he was "out and about" in 1978, he was looking for someone in particular with his good friend, Albie Spires, they hadn't found him that day, but he wasn't so lucky a few days later.

After he had exhausted the local bars where his quarry was known to hang out, he headed to a local "Spieler" he frequented from time to time in Soho. Those were the days when pubs closed at 3pm unless you got a "lock in", they didn't open again until 5.30pm. Spielers were the infill if you wanted to carry on drinking outside of permitted hours and were illegal. They were usually run by ex-landlords with connections. Mostly landlords that had lost their licences and were "sponsored" by people like Tommy. This was one of those places and Tommy knew the owner.

Tommy wasn't a big drinker, especially when there was work to be done but once he realised that they were not going to find their quarry today, he relaxed and ordered himself and Albie a large gin and tonic each. They went and sat at a nearby table minding their own business. Tommy took everything in around him as usual and noticed a pair of well-dressed gentlemen tucked away over in the corner. They looked like twins and, something else Tommy noticed. They both looked like serious men, not in the professional civilian sense you understand, they had an aura about them that Tommy had seen before Albie had seen it too, it was a certain look that only men of this kind had, they were spot on.

Two tables down a crowd of fellas were getting rowdy, pushing each other around, shouting and spilling their drinks. They were making a general nuisance of themselves, they were clearly pissed and there were six of them.

Tommy and Albie kept one eye on them, of course, but just wanted to enjoy their drink. It wasn't often that they got to have a drink together and have a good time. He had known Albie since his school days and trusted him with his life.

"Fancy another one?" said Albie.

Yeah why not, mate? replied Tommy

Albie got up and went to the bar where he ordered another round of gin and tonics for them both, while he was paying for the drinks one of the louts from the crowd of drunken idiots two tables down pushed his way to the bar, and was trying to order more drinks for him and his drunken mates. The barman very politely told the young fella that he and his mates had had enough and he wasn't going to serve them anymore. With this, the young fella tried to grab the startled barman and drag him over the bar. Albie moved in and tried to calm him down, the drunken idiot then made his first mistake, he threw a punch at him. Now, Albie was and still is a handful, his fighting craft came from the same cobbles as Tommy's and he was spiteful when provoked.

117

Albie decked him with one punch, and then all hell broke loose. The other members of his entourage were up and at it in seconds before Tommy could react and had descended on Albie like a pack of hyenas knocking him to the floor and raining kicks and blows on the stricken man. Tommy was up like a flash and steamed in to help his mate but he too was overwhelmed. A bottle crashed into the side of his head temporarily knocking him to the ground, he could feel wetness around his ear. He knew he'd been glassed, when suddenly and out of nowhere the two fellas who were quietly drinking over in the far corner were also in amongst the ruck In a matter of seconds the tide had turned, Tommy and Albie were back on their feet and finished off the remaining boys with clinical efficiency, some would go on to say too efficiently.

There was claret everywhere and not the drinking kind. Harry and Jimmy had to drag the two gangsters off the men who by now were a spent force. They very carefully got hold of Tommy and Albie and gently whispered to them both, "I think they've had enough fellas, time to go."

Tommy had a gash above his left eye from the bottle that was pouring with blood, his eyes were bulging with rage and he wanted to inflict the same on the bastard who did it, he asked the two fellas "Which one bottled me? Did you see who it was?

They had and pointed him out albeit reluctantly. Tommy picked up a large glass ashtray from the bar and smashed it into the face of the fella still stricken on the floor several times in quick succession, causing a huge gash to appear above his right eye, his nose was destroyed and several teeth also disappeared.

Spiteful but fair, thought Jimmy, The annoying prick deserved it, he liked Tommy immediately.

The barman although grateful to the men, very respectfully reminded them that the police were probably on route. A lot of patrons had escaped during the ensuing melee down the back stairs. Some with their girlfriends who were screaming, that was bound to bring some attention he added. The men agreed and all left by the same route. A few minutes later the bar was raided but Tommy, Albie and the Parkhurst brothers were long gone. The bar looked like a battlefield of the Somme remarked one of the coppers.

Outside, Harry Parkhurst was holding Tommy up. He was concussed and disorientated with blood oozing from above his eye.

"This is a bad one, son. We better get you looked at," remarked Harry, Albie and Jimmy agreed, Tommy didn't look well.

"Listen mate, my car is just around the corner we can get you to a doctor we know."

Through the haze, Tommy looked at Harry and thought why would they not want to take me to a hospital? Then he passed out.

He woke up sometime later laid out on a strange bed. His head was banging, and he felt like shit, sitting in the corner of the room was Albie,.

"Welcome back to the world, Sunshine! Fuck me. You had me worried there, Tommy lad! Albie proclaimed.

You've lost a lot of blood mate!"

"Where the fuck are we Albie?" said Tommy, "I don't recognise this place."

"Well, after you passed out, we got you in Harry's car and he drove us all here."

"Who the fuck is Harry?" said Tommy, Albie explained.

A little while later when Tommy was feeling a little better, the two brothers, Jimmy and Harry, accompanied by a very serious-looking man all entered the room.

"Dr Reese is just going to check you over before he leaves Tommy," said Harry, "The doctor here tells me you're a lucky boy. A little bit lower and you would have lost an eye!"

You've lost a lot of blood and were obviously concussed. Anyway you're all patched up now. Seven stitches and a tetanus shot that should sort you out!" Dr Reese said matter of factly. "In a few days you'll be right as rain," he continued while leaning over him and checking his temperature with the flat of his hand.

"Blimey!" thought Tommy he stinks of booze, but kept his mouth shut.

"He's all good lads," said the doctor, "he just needs a little rest and plenty of fluids."

Harry clapped him on the back while leading him out of the room, stuffed a few notes into his hand and thanked him, the doctor walked away without looking back.

"So where do I start?" said Tommy. "I clearly owe you one but please tell me who you are?" he said, looking directly at the two brothers.

They duly told him, adding that they were from south of the water and couldn't stand idly by when the odds were that stacked against you.

"Well I'm seriously grateful and indebted to you both," said Tommy while looking over at Albie, "but tell me one thing, why didn't you take me to the hospital, don't get me wrong lads and I definitely don't want to sound ungrateful but that's not the act of a couple of good old boys having a quiet drink is it?"

"I can answer that one!" piped up Jimmy," I recognised you straight away when you walked into the bar and I told Harry. I know who you are, Tommy. In fact I know some of your family; I was over in Islington some time back in a restaurant called Luigi's when Reggie Pullman was released. Your family had thrown him a coming out party and I was invited by your Uncle Terry on your dear old mum's side. Terry and I go back a ways and still do the occasional bit of work together. We never spoke that day as you seemed tied up in the proceedings and Terry didn't want to interfere, but I remembered you this afternoon straight away, you now know the reason why we didn't get you to hospital".

Tommy knew only too well what a hospital visit could have brought, and suspected the reason why the brothers hadn't taken him, following what Harry had just told him. Now it all made sense, one of the first places the police descend on after a bloodbath like that is the local hospitals, someone may have identified him and gave a description and he could have been in serious trouble, especially after hitting that bloke with the ashtray before they left. He looked in a bad way after that and was probably in the hospital right now. Tommy was smiling thinking about it,

"I'm extremely grateful fellas," he finally blurted out and offered to pay for the doctor's time.

"Not a chance, pal," Jimmy chimed in, "this one's on us."

A friendship was born that day and would stand the test of time.

Danny 1973-1984

Danny's time at Blackshaw Road Children's Home was pretty uncomfortable for the first few years. Bullying was part of a normal day and Danny was subject to quite a bit of it, especially once the boys found out why he was there. He had no choice but to accept it. He wasn't particularly big at that age or a fighter, he was also one of the youngest there, most of the other boys were older and bigger than him and they picked on him without mercy. Nothing too bad just punches, kicks and slaps that sort of thing, he was never really hurt except the one time a boy called Clinton had stabbed him in the arm with a craft knife. He needed a few stitches and never forgot Clinton, sometime later he would bump into him in a bar over in Fulham, and the outcome was slightly different at that meeting.

Things changed quite dramatically once he went to secondary school, he was sent to Balham Boys, later known as Hydeburn in 1977, and became a mixed school. Danny missed that as by the time it changed Danny was doing his first time stretch as a young offender.

Shortly after starting at Balham boys and as was the norm for young children Danny made a few friends. He never really had any friends before except Corey who he had not seen since that awful night. He had moved away shortly after with his mum and her fella whose name he couldn't remember, he missed him.

His new friends were Tommy Reynolds, Peter Andrews and to a lesser extent, Darren Jacobs. Danny would go on to keep in touch with Tommy and Peter but Darren fell by the wayside once the boys found out his true colours, he turned out to be a "wrong'un" as two years into their friendship and having been captured by the police for stealing lead off an old school roof, Darren spilled his guts and put them all in it. Darren got away with a slap on the wrist while the other three had to go in front of the local magistrate at the Juvenile Court on Balham High Road. All three got suspended sentences for theft due to their age and released, but now they all had juvenile criminal records where Darren got nothing. Needless to say, Darren got what was coming to him a little while later in the school gymnasium and was promptly moved to another school never to be seen again, Danny didn't miss him.

You could say a turning point in Danny's life came when he had just turned thirteen. He had been invited to a pre-arranged fight in the playground at lunchtime with a boy one year up from Danny who had "called him out". He can't remember why and to refuse the fight would have been seen as cowardice. Danny was not a coward, but the boy was well known and bigger than him, he went armed.

You could also say that Danny was a fuse that just needed lighting and was destined for the life that awaited him, who knows, but what we do know is that the fight didn't end well for either of the boys.

At the police station later on in the day, a police officer had asked him, "Why did you stab him? It was just a playground fight, why did you do it?"

Danny just smiled and did not respond; the officer was shocked.

Remanding him into custody to be sent to Stamford House, a boys remand centre in Shepherds Bush, the magistrate at the same juvenile court in Balham that Danny was now familiar with stated,

"There you will be assessed and returned here for sentencing at a later date. You can expect a custodial sentence. This was a brutal assault on an unarmed boy and as a result of your actions he has now lost the use of one of his eyes where you thrust your weapon into him. Luckily for him and his family that this incident is not a murder charge, take him away."

Stamford House situated just off the Goldhawk Road in west London was a holding and remand centre for boys between ages 11-16 who had been convicted of criminality in one form or another or were waiting on remand for hearings due to the nature of their offences. In Danny's case he was convicted but was there for assessment and reports prior to being sentenced, as were some of the other boys.

Stamford house consisted of five "houses". Two of which were remand centres prior to trial, two were for holding convicted boys prior to sentencing, and one "house" that held up to twelve boys who were deemed too dangerous for general population or were extremely vulnerable until they could be found a suitable institution that could manage them.

Danny was held in Hastings's House on arrival. A general population remand centre for convicted prisoners that held around thirty boys of varying ages. He was allocated a shared room containing four beds (two bunk beds on either side of the room) .The single window looking out onto the courtyard was barred, it opened about six inches and looked out to the yard beyond, you could hear the boys below during their daily exercise. Danny looked out and immediately began planning his escape.

Two days into his incarceration Danny had a fight with one of the older boys who had taken a dislike to him. The boy had tried to take some of Danny's tuck shop sweets on the way back to his cell. Big mistake! Danny never gave the boy a chance and brutally attacked him without so much as a word. The wardens had to drag him off this boy before serious harm was done. Danny's rage was scary. Even the wardens rarely came across this level of violence and it took three of them to drag him away. He was put in a holding cell for two days to cool off. The incident went into their report of course, and would not help Danny when he was back in court for sentencing.

"Still, I kept my sweets," he thought to himself.

Less than two weeks into his time at Stamford House Danny escaped. To him it was simple. The courtyard was an open space where the perimeter was mostly guarded by a few old men and a couple of turncoats (do-goody prisoners who were trying to curry favour with the establishment). Danny simply ran, head down until he reached the perimeter wall. The spot he had chosen was lower here and with a little effort was up and over it in seconds. He had no idea where he was going and had no plan, but he felt exhilarated, excited and more importantly free although even then he knew it would only be for a short time. He was soon captured and returned to the holding cell. This time for three days, a totally pointless exercise by all accounts, but to Danny it was necessary, he was evolving.

Social services had been advised of all this as he was under their care and for the purposes of sentencing at the request of the magistrate.

Psychological and psychiatric reports were deemed necessary. They thought there may be a case here for treatment rather than punishment and the recommendation was that Danny underwent these assessments prior to his sentencing. Danny found this extremely amusing and played with them both. This was not his smartest move, as the reports came back that he was not mentally ill, but in fact a clever but manipulative boy. His rage was a by-product of his upbringing and could be controlled if he chose, therefore he should be sentenced as any sane and "normal" person would. Danny was far from normal and the psychologists knew it to some degree, so did the judge at sentencing but due to his age this wasn't put on record.

In the summer of 1977, aged just thirteen and a half, Danny was sentenced to a young offenders institute in North Wales called Bryanston.

"Where you will be assessed in a controlled environment under lock and key for the safety of others," The judge continued while summing up his sentence and went on to say, "Following this brutal knife attack on a fellow student leaving him blind in one eye, coupled with a further brutal attack on another prisoner while incarcerated, your escape attempt from justice and general contempt of your peers, I would have liked to impose a far greater sentence. If you were eighteen months older you would be off to three years in borstal, however, your age restricts me, and may God help us all! Take him down."

Less than two years later, in 1979, and following a rather nasty attack on another inmate of the reform school, Danny got his three years in borstal and enjoyed every minute of it.

For Danny it was structure, something that had been missing all his young life. He had no role models, no routine and no structure and he was spiralling out of control.

He had already killed a man in cold blood, no one knew about that of course but the rage in him was uncontrollable at times and borstal was the perfect remedy. His daily routine was physical exercise, school lessons, and work training in specialist workshops around the camp. Danny excelled in all three disciplines. The only downside to all this for Danny was the strict discipline for any infraction. This was dished out by the screws of course, who seemed to revel in it. However the overriding factor here was structure. The boys were graded according to their attitude and general compliance. There were three grades: The first grade typically lasting around four to six months was a period of preliminary observation and training. If you got through that without too many problems you went on to the second stage. This gave the young boys a chance to join activities outside of the Borstal, like joining a local cadet force or something of that nature. It also gave them the opportunity to work with local businesses. In Danny's case this involved making strawberry boxes for the local farmer where he was paid the princely sum of 2p per box!

Danny had no intentions of joining any cadet forces, although he had earned the extra privilege of being allowed to go into town and spend his hard earned money in the local sweet shop. Although not exactly complying with all the rules, Danny was smart enough to play the game and earned the right by the summer of 1980, aged sixteen, the much sought after prize of home leave. This followed a further appraisal at grade three. Danny didn't use it, he had nowhere to go he informed his house master.

Danny was released from Feltham young offenders Borstal in 1980 and transferred to Brixton prison to finish his sentence. Feltham couldn't keep him as he had turned sixteen. He was eventually released from Brixton prison in early 1982, it would have been earlier, but he had a few "altercations" while there which delayed his release, he had done the full three years, he was now aged eighteen.

Danny had been doing OK since his release, he had met a girl called Deborah Taylor who he simply called Dee. He was working as a labourer on a building site over in Surrey Docks and the probation service had found him a one-bedroom flat on the notorious Silwood estate in Bermondsey where Dee and her newly formed "bump" soon moved in. By the summer of 1983, she left him and took their newly arrived baby, Danny junior with her. Danny wasn't a good boyfriend, and he would probably be an even worse dad she had told him while getting in the cab outside the flat, he couldn't really argue with that could he?

He had been out drinking almost every night with his newfound work friends and was dreading bringing a baby into this shit world anyway. Indeed when the baby had arrived, he was struggling with money due to his nefarious activities, especially the drinking. The baby would be better off being brought up in Streatham where Dee came from. Her parents had money they would look after them both, he watched them leave and moved on, he would never see them again.

Deborah took her new and beautiful baby boy back to the family home in Streatham south London, where she married her brother's best friend, Charlie, the following year. He formally adopted the boy officially a few months later and changed Danny junior's surname to his, Saunders.

Following this new episode in Danny's life his drinking and violence got worse. Hardly a day went by where he wasn't fighting or arguing with someone. He soon lost his job on the building site, and the flat soon followed. He was now homeless and "sofa surfing" with people he had met in Bermondsey. This didn't sit well with him and his anger was building, he had also heard from his friend Tommy Smith back in south London that his father, Ronnie, had died from a heart attack while in prison.

Danny didn't know him, the last time he had seen him was when he was murdering his mother, he had no feelings about the man at all, not even hatred but in his quiet moments he had wished things had been different, who knows where he would be now if his mother was still alive?

It seemed to Danny that the whole world was against him and that his route through this shit life was already mapped out for him and although he hardly knew his father he didn't take this latest news well, and decided the best place for him was back inside. He went out a very angry young man and picked a fight with the loudest and biggest person in his local bar. Using a broken bottle he had caused his unsuspecting victim a lot of damage and was given five years at Southwark Crown Court three months later for GBH with intent, it was 1984 and Danny was twenty.

Billy Saunders

1933-1964

Billy Saunders family had owned the house in Alfarthing Lane, Wandsworth since the 1930s.His father, the late Mickey Saunders had purchased it for the grand sum of £450 in cash from a recently widowed and childless woman who was moving "down to the country" to be with her elderly sister. Not a huge amount of money back then as in reality the average yearly wage was around £160 per year, and a world away from the cost of a house compared to salaries today. Not that Mickey ever had the average wage or indeed a salary. He was a travelling man and earned his money when and where he could get it.

The house was a three-storey Victorian creation with all the standard features that go with this kind of property. Beautiful red bricks with corbels, a high pitched roof, ornate gables, bay windows and of course the traditional stained-glass window decorating the substantial front door and its side leaf. The pathway was in keeping with this period and had been laid with a Victorian diamond pattern using vitrified black and white tiles laid checkerboard style along the path. Very fancy for an ex travelling man commented many of his visiting friends and family. The only thing that spoiled it for their more prestigious neighbours was the great big tipper lorry sitting on the drive.

Mickey, originally from the travelling community of County Cork in Ireland had decided that the family needed to settle down and take root. His wife had just given birth to their youngest boy, Billy, in 1932 and the two older boys were six and nine.

Years of being driven from one place to another all the while trying to support his family had taken its toll on Mickey's health.. He was a bull of a man with black curly hair, piercing blue eyes and a well-grown moustache. He always wore a crumpled old neckerchief around his neck and a black leather waistcoat that was god knows how old finishing off the look. His bare-knuckle fighting days were over.

He was getting older and had mellowed somewhat in the past few years, time to settle down and make the family a legacy he thought. The house in Alfarthing Lane was as good a place as any, plus they had family close by in Battersea and Tooting, they were a very large family.

Mickey and his young family settled into their new house and soon made a reputation that they were not to be messed with. One poor unfortunate soul decided to confront Mickey one Saturday morning to complain about his boys who were making a nuisance of themselves as young boys often do, he never made that mistake again as

Mickey had beaten him to a pulp in the middle of the street while his boys and half the street watched, the message he sent out was clear, keep away.

Mickey had made his money from various "work" throughout the years but had "bought" a stake in a scrap metal yard just off Garrett Lane just before the end of World War II. In reality, he had muscled his way into the business by pure intimidation, violence and threats, following the death of the real owner. "His business partner, Tom Farrell" towards the end of the war in 1944.Tom's only son who had inherited his father's stake in the business just couldn't cut it with Mickey, by the end of 1945 the business was run and owned by the Saunders family exclusively. Little Billy who was thirteen when his father took over the business had spent most of his youth working at the yard. School was a mere distraction, he liked to earn money and Mickey encouraged him.

Mickey's wife, Ivy, had passed away shortly after her husband in the spring of 1960, One year to the day in fact, following Mickey's untimely death from cancer in 1959. The beautiful Victorian house was inherited by Billy and his two brothers, Billy was twenty-eight.

The three brothers Michael the eldest, Joseph and Billy the youngest were well known in south London and had a fearsome reputation. Their family was large, if you took one on you took them all on, simple as that. Most sensible people gave them a wide berth.

Shortly after their mother passed away in 1960, the eldest of the boys Michael got himself married and moved away with his new wife just up the road in Tooting. They had two boys and one daughter. Charlie, the eldest, born in 1963, Kenneth Thomas the middle boy two years later and Deborah Mary the only girl born to them in 1968.

Joseph was killed following a car crash in December 1962 while attempting to evade a pursuing police car. He was drunk as usual and had foolishly decided to drive from the Hammersmith Palais dance hall in west London back home to Wandsworth and smashed into at bollard near Putney Bridge while doing so. The family buried him just before Christmas at Lambeth cemetery on Blackshaw Road, Tooting. It was a raucous affair, attended by the travelling community from all over the country, including their Irish connections, the police stayed well clear that day.

Billy now had the house to himself and decided to convert some of the rooms into bed sits. He didn't really need the money as he had inherited a share of the house, the scrap yard, and substantial cash reserves left to the brothers by their doting parents. He also had the tipper truck which he used for collecting scrap metal and sometimes rubbish clearing at the right price of course. He made more than a decent living off all of these things, he was just greedy and had no intention of sharing, if he didn't have to.

By the time Lizzie had taken up lodgings there in 1964 with her newly born baby following Ronnie's recent incarceration, Billy had converted four of the rooms on the first and second floors into the bed sits and had kept the ground floor for himself. His living space was substantial and separated from the main entrance. Lodgers still had to enter through the front door, but Billy had constructed a small lobby with a separate door leading upstairs. He had his own internal door of course, so he could access the upstairs rooms and frequently used it to go up unannounced whenever he felt like it, Sometimes disturbing people in their most vulnerable moments. The lodgers hated this of course, but Billy was an intimidating man who always did what he liked without apology. One evening in 1964, the heavily inebriated Billy walked in on the unsuspecting Lizzie. He had a spare key to every room and just let himself in. Lizzie had just had her nightly bath after she had put little Danny down. Billy knew this as he heard her coming out of the newly installed bathroom on the landing. She was in a state of undress when he entered and only wrapped in a towel, startled she asked him, "What the hell he thought he was doing."

She was behind on the rent and he wanted his money he told her.

She didn't have it right now she said, "I'll get it for you tomorrow I promise now please let me get dressed."

She was a pretty little thing thought Billy. "Maybe you could pay in another way," he suggested while leering at her.

Lizzie was horrified, and declared, "I'm married and I don't mess around on my husband whatever the

137

circumstances, you'll have your money tomorrow, now get out please."

Her voice had risen a few octaves and Billy didn't like that, oh no not one bit, he moved forward and slapped her with the back of his hand around the face, knocking her to the ground where her towel fell open. Her lip was bleeding and she was sobbing. With his eyes firmly fixed on her groin, he loomed over her smiling while undoing his flies, knelt down beside her and covered her mouth with his huge and calloused hand. He took what he wanted; it was over in seconds, which was no comfort to the distressed Lizzie. Who had curled up into the foetal position on the floor and was sobbing uncontrollably

Billy was unfazed, he was standing now and doing up his trousers. "You keep your mouth shut about this," he whispered looming over her, "and 'I'll knock a couple of pound off the rent, don't bother reporting me either. Firstly, no one will believe you, it would be your word against mine. I'll tell them you came on to me because your old man's in prison, and secondly you'll be back on the streets with that little brat," he said, pointing to the crib in the corner, "You don't want that do you?"

She didn't reply, Billy simply left and closed the door. This wasn't the first time Billy had taken what he wanted, he liked it that way. Lizzie didn't tell a soul, she was frightened and vulnerable, besides he was right, wasn't he? No one would believe her, and she couldn't risk her and little Danny being out on the street again. She wished Ronnie were here, he would know what to do. Billy visited her again a few weeks later.

His own lodgings had a huge bay fronted living area, which he hardly used. Two further rooms along the hallway including his bedroom towards the rear of the property. The first room was the dining room which by now was never used, and of course his own bathroom. However, the one room he used most was the "parlour" at the back of the house. This had been his mother's favourite room and was an extension to the house added sometime after the house was bought at his mother's insistence in 1936, not much had changed in there since she had died.

Billy spent most of his time in here when he was at home, he had a new black and white TV set up in the corner by the French doors and his mother's favourite red leather Queen Anne wing chair situated directly opposite the telly looking out into the garden. This room led out through a pair of French doors into a large garden. There was a paved walkway surrounded by well-kept lawns that led to a gate at the bottom of the garden, this led onto a shared alleyway which in turn led out onto the side street about a hundred yards from the house, Treport Street.

1995

Danny had arrived at Bridie's place. A fair sized townhouse on an estate near Mitcham. She knew of Danny but had never met him. If Jimmy says he's good then that's good enough for me plus he's his nephew she thought, she really could do with the money so agreed without question. She didn't ask why, she knew better than that. Charlie, her husband of nearly thirty years, he had got another five stretch about a year ago and her two boys had just gone back in as well, she definitely knew the score.

"Come in Danny, I'll show you to your room," she said on the doorstep, "your uncle called me earlier and said you need a lay down for a few days, you can have Trevor's room, he's away for a while on business you know."

Yeah, right! thought Danny, Trevor's banged up with his brother in Wandsworth Prison, but he never let on he knew, I'll play the game Danny thought, he simply said thank you Bridie and walked into the house.

His room, a nice sized en-suite on the second floor, was already made up and smelled fresh. Danny suspected that this was her room and she wanted to impress him. Looking around the house later he confirmed this was the only en-suite bathroom in the house. The other was communal and in the middle of the landing on the first floor with two further bedrooms besides. Why would she not use the bedroom with all the en-suite facilities? He said nothing, he didn't want to embarrass her, and if she wanted to give her room up for him then he wasn't going to argue.

She was standing in the doorway of "Trevor's" room looking Danny up and down while he placed his bags at the foot of the bed. When Danny looked round, she was doing her best impression of Cindy Crawford while running her fingers through her hair and pouting! Danny found this quite amusing but kept himself from laughing. Two things sprang immediately to mind, firstly she was old enough to be his mother and definitely wasn't his type, secondly even if she had been younger and prettier you never ever messed with someone's wife who was doing time in prison. At least he didn't, he knew people who had of course and that got very messy when it came to light. The kind of people they mixed with would not accept their friends or associates doing that sort of thing and it was seriously frowned upon. He remembered one incident a few years back when one of his uncle's mates had found out his old woman had been "indiscreet" she now had an eight inch scar down her face from her forehead to her chin and lover boy was now in a wheelchair. No, thank you! Not for me, Danny mused and proceeded to empty one of his bags on the bed with his back to her.

She lingered for far too long and Danny was starting to feel a little bit uncomfortable. To diffuse the situation Danny asked if she could give him a bit of privacy as he needed a shower, and he had a few calls to make. She took the hint and left. Shame she thought, such a good-looking fella and oh that body! She hadn't had so much as a sniff since her Charlie was arrested and sent to prison.

Danny did need that shower, he still had residues of Delroy's blood on him and he knew better than anyone if he got lifted the filth would have a field day forensically. the clothes needed to go. He would dump them later and his trainers too. You would be surprised how many idiots still keep their clobber and things like their favourite trainers following a bit of work. This and mobile phones are like gold dust to the old bill and Danny wasn't about to take any chances, it was 1995 and the police now had huge resources due to this DNA thing that appeared from nowhere back in the mid-eighties. People were dropping like flies in the underworld because some smart arsed copper twenty or thirty years ago had kept evidence in a bag and stored it in the unsolved files department at Scotland Yard. Danny knew of several "faces" that had disappeared to secret little villas in Spain among the ex-pats to hide in complete paranoia, basically they were shitting their pants and who could blame them. Some of these guys had got away with some serious crimes and were now worried that they had left some form of evidence behind that the clever scientists would now be able to find and use against them. Indeed he had met a few of them during his time there.

Danny was no different but since his "enlightened" meeting with the uncles following his release from Maidstone prison in 1987, he was pretty sure he had not left anything anywhere, if he had it was too late now anyway. His mind drifted back to Anderson, his first paid job but he soon shrugged it off, if they had anything surely they would have come looking for him by now.

While taking his shower he pondered on this DNA thing, and it reminded him of 1977, just before his incarceration for stabbing that boy in school. He had bunked off school and gone down to an estate in Battersea called the Winstanley to steal something with his mate, Tommy Reynolds, he recalls. They didn't have a plan, all they knew was that the day would not be wasted, and they weren't going home empty handed.

They eventually broke into a few of the sheds that were under a tower block on the estate. It was quiet during the day and they went undisturbed but the only things worth stealing were a couple of bikes. They were in pretty good condition and were probably worth at least a fiver each, the boys rode off with the intention of selling them to an old fella who had a pawn shop on Lavender Hill, a short ride from the estate. Talk about on your own doorstep but of course they weren't thinking. The old fella told them to get lost and wanted nothing to do with them. They could not take them home. Danny was living in the children's home and Tommy wouldn't have dared to come up with a story to his parents. They would have smelled a rat and beat the shit out of him.

Danny and Tommy didn't want to ditch their bikes, so decided the only thing to do was hide them in an old derelict house very close to the place where they were stolen and wait for an opportunity to sell them and that's what they did.

Unbeknownst to both of the boys, a local tramp was using the house to get his head down and observed the boys unnoticed while they stashed the bikes in the back of the house. He was living on a mattress made of cardboard boxes in the front room, old newspapers were his stuffing and blankets.

The following day Danny went back to the house alone to check on his goods. Tommy hadn't showed and was probably grounded. He found the old tramp in the front room pissed on cider and the bikes were missing. It didn't take a genius to work out what had happened. He confronted the old man and wanted to know where his bikes were, but all he was met with was a torrent of abuse and yells of, "Well you should have been more careful then you little shit, I've sold them, they're gone," and started laughing.

Danny left but was furious, they were his goods and he wanted revenge, he knew just what to do.

The Winstanley estate was a maze of alleyways interlocked between rows of tower blocks, two storey flats and small houses. In the evening it was the perfect place to hide and wait. He needed to make that tramp pay and Danny knew just how he was going to do that.

Danny came back later that same evening and was observing the derelict house from across the square, lurking amongst the garages under a tower block, Danny had a bird's eye view of where that thieving tramp lived and waited. Sure enough just after 7pm the old man could be seen staggering back to his lodgings from Danny's vantage point, carrying what looked like a bag of booze bought with my money! Thought Danny and could feel the anger and hatred boiling up inside of him. The old man staggered inside and immediately slumped onto his bed of newspapers and cardboard where he soon fell into a drunken sleep.

Danny waited until it got pretty dark and from outside could see that there was no movement in the house, walked over and entered the hallway. The front door creaked and to Danny's horror made a sound that seemed like firecrackers! He didn't remember the door making this much noise on his first visit to the house, but then again it was during the middle of the day at night it was much quieter and every sound was enhanced, especially when you are trying to creep around, he thought, and stored that information into his brain bank for future use.

He almost bolted on hearing the noise and ran, instead he stood firm and still, controlled his breathing and listened. After a few seconds all he could hear was his own breathing and the old man snoring from the front room. He quickly checked behind him while still standing in the front door and gently and quietly pushed the door shut. This time it didn't seem to make as much noise, was his imagination just running away with him? It didn't matter, either way he was doing this and a little creaking door noise was not going to stop him. He steadied himself and carefully crept down the hall to where the old man was sleeping.

The door to the room where the old man was didn't seem as creaky but still made a noise that would wake most people. The old man started mumbling, Danny froze again, he was standing in the middle of the doorway with his head poking around the door. From this position Danny could see that the old tramp was curled up in a ball and snoring his head off while obviously dreaming about something, he seemed to be talking to someone and was telling them to leave him alone.

Danny thought he was talking to him for a moment and nearly bolted again, however, after a few seconds, he soon realised that it was just the old fella talking in his sleep. Danny recognised and understood this, as he also had vivid dreams.

Danny walked further into the gloomy but not completely darkened room, it was fully dark outside but there was a streetlamp just outside the house that illuminated parts of the room. The window was curtain less and if it wasn't so covered in grime and cobwebs would have lit the room up like a beacon. Danny was

146

cautious as anyone walking by would easily see him, he couldn't linger for long. He moved towards the old boy and stood over him for a few moments staring at him lying there snoring. Danny took the box of matches out of his pocket, pausing to take it all in and smiling he took one out, struck in onto the pad of the Swan Vesta box he had in his hand. It lit straight away and he quite simply dropped it onto the bed of newspapers and left.

From across the street, he watched as the place went up in smoke. The front room was the main area of the fire and was raging intensely, fuelled by the huge amount of paper and cardboard that was accumulated in the room. Danny watched as the fire brigade turned up five or so minutes later and started their work, quite a few other people had also now gathered to watch the spectacle, a bit like moths to the flame he thought while standing there in fascination. Watching the windows crack as the heat and flames took hold. He remembers one woman that night saying to the neighbour beside her, "I wonder if that old tramp, Bertie, I think that's his name was, is in there."

"Good riddance if he is," said the other woman, "he was known to interfere with kids, the dirty bastard!" Danny smiled as the flames started shooting out of the window; he knew he didn't like him.

They found the old man's charred remains whilst checking the smouldering embers about an hour later and put it down to drunkenness and probably a discarded cigarette.

147

Danny had killed his first person; it would not be his last, he never told a soul not even Tommy.

Danny had finished his shower in Bridie's en-suite and was now lying on the bed, deep in thought. He was still tired from the lack of sleep last night and the events that had taken place a little earlier. Dozily, he was trying to remember the circumstances that led to his complete loss of control with the noisy neighbours, something deep had stirred inside of him? He knew why of course, he was present and witness to those awful events in Durham buildings all those years ago, caused by his own father of all people, but those memories had been hidden so deep since then that they were almost unreal and made him question if they were actually real at all

They were of course, and he knew that, but time had clouded his memory, he still couldn't picture his mother's face no matter how hard he tried. Is that a defence mechanism? He thought lying there, probably.

The brutal moments of that night only really surfaced in his nightmares, details of which he could never remember anyway. Besides, Delroy was nothing like his father, was he? Sandra wasn't his mother, so why on earth did I interfere, I should have known better, Danny dozed off and slept dreamlessly.

He was woken a few hours later by his telephone ringing. It was on the bedside cabinet right beside him and Jimmy's number was flashing up on the screen,

"Hello, Jimmy," said Danny, "what's the news"?

"You my son are one lucky boy," said Jimmy." That Chambers guy is alive and well and has got form as long as your arm, he's well known to the filth as a nasty piece of work that dabbles in drugs, he's also done a bit of time in prison, couldn't have happened to a nicer bloke, my contact informs me, in addition to that his bird, Sandra, or whatever her name is, is not saying a word, she's currently consoling poor old Delroy in St George's Hospital, Tooting, and hasn't made a statement, our friend who owns the block has already spoken to the neighbours who live opposite them and "advised" them to play the three wise monkeys, he's sure they will, they owe him he tells me."

"Let this be a lesson to you, Danny, it seems we have got lucky this time but we can't afford any more mistakes like this one," Jimmy continued, "we've got off the hook this time or more importantly you have and we move on, but you have to understand how differently this could have turned out son. Look, I'm your uncle and I know why it happened but you can't let personal tragedy interfere with your life! Look how far you've come in a short space of time. You very nearly allowed a no-mark like Chambers ruin it for you! Control that temper, Danny, as I've taught you, we have bigger fish to fry."

"I know, Uncle Jimmy," said Danny, "let's put it down to a one-off moment and get back to the business in hand."

"Fair enough son, now about this fucker in Wandsworth?"

Back in north London, Tommy Spillane was waiting for a call from one of his most trusted lieutenants, Darren, to tell him a parcel had arrived and would be planning a delivery time and date with that fucking Pikey, Billy Saunders, across the water.

He never usually referred to people in a disparaging or racist way, but this time it was different, what he had found out following his release from prison in 1992 had changed everything and the wheels were now in motion to finally get some payback, no one grassed on Tommy and got away with it.

Tommy Spillane had got seven years back in 1987 for possession with intent to supply class A drugs and was released on parole five years later. He had been home and back to his beloved Peggy and the girls for nearly two years in 1994 when he got the phone call from his friend, Harry Parkhurst, who had some news that could only be discussed one to one and in complete privacy. They arranged to meet on their turf south of the river at the Thomas A Becket pub on the Old Kent Road, a well-known boozer in south east London the following day and

Tommy would be accompanied by his old friend, Albie, on agreement with the Parkhursts of course.

"No problem," said Harry. "My brother, Jimmy, will be there as well."

What Harry had to say for himself was mind-blowing and would change the dynamics of Tommy's life for ever.

They met up at the pre-arranged time and settled into a private booth towards the rear of the pub, ordered some drinks and got down to business. Harry got the conversation started by getting straight into the incredible story. Darren, he was saying, was on a pre-arranged drug run for you back in 1984, "He was delivering to your dear old Pikey friend across the water, but never made that drop, he got pulled by the police just coming into Wandsworth and arrested for drug possession with intent to supply due to the quantity, he had stashed under the passenger seat. He was also out of his head on crack and taken to Wandsworth police station where he was processed by a Detective Sergeant Peter Thomas and his then partner, Detective Constable Lenny Smith, I'll come back to them in a moment," Harry said,

"However and unbeknownst to Darren who was out of it anyway, he had been set up by none other than Billy Saunders."

"Now hold on a minute!" Tommy said interjecting, "That doesn't make any sense? What would Billy have to gain from getting Darren lifted? And more than that, I would have known if Darren had drug issues I saw him every other day and he was always compos mentis. I would have known if he wasn't! In addition to that he's never had his collar felt for drugs, and another thing," continued Tommy hardly taking a breath, "I always got my money from the runs and I would definitely remember if I hadn't!"

At that moment and as if a light had gone on in Tommy's head, he remembered that Darren had gone on the missing list, one particular day back in 1984 and didn't come over with the money until much later the following day in fact, citing some excuse or another. Tommy couldn't remember the nuances of the conversation at the time and it was unusual for Darren he recalled but had accepted it at the time and moved on.

The penny had suddenly and devastatingly dropped. This was starting to make sense, he thought without saying a word.

"All will become clear, Tommy," said Harry, "Let me finish the story but by the look on your face, I think you already know."

One of Tommy's main cocaine customers was one Billy Saunders, part of a large gypsy family in south London. Most travelling people of the time steered well clear of drugs as most thought they destroyed families and the prison sentences that went with this particular crime were disproportionately high. This changed dramatically in the nineties as everyone wanted a piece of the action but at this time Billy kept his involvement on the down low. He wasn't embarrassed or anything like that, he just didn't want the grief from his family for dealing with such things, besides it was a really good earner and Billy wasn't going to miss out. He too had his "mules" and a small network of distributors around the clubs and bars of south London, his trusted lieutenant was an Irishman called Karl Green who had arrived in London by the late seventies via Dublin. According to sketchy and unsubstantiated rumours, he had connections with the IRA and had to leave the Emerald Isle rather rapidly following the discovery that he was involved with dealing drugs in Dublin's fair city. The IRA frowned upon this kind of activity and was looking for him, causing Karl to get on the first available ferry and leave, he ended up in Tooting.

A few months later and at the recommendation of one of Billy's vast family members who had befriended him, he ended up staying in one of Billy's bed sits on Alfarthing lane where they also struck up a friendship.

Karl was a street man and Billy could put him to use he thought. The realities of the rumours surrounding Karl's "connections" were quite different to Karl's well-rehearsed story. In fact, he had no connections to the infamous paramilitary group whatsoever and was simply caught shagging a married woman whose fella was a small time player for the IRA who would have "knee-capped" Karl at the earliest opportunity had he caught up with him. He had in fact "dabbled" in the drug scene around the clubs and bars in Dublin but was such a minor player he went relatively unnoticed and was left alone.

Harry, with his brother, Jimmy, sitting next to him continued explaining the nuances of this story to the ever-incredulous Tommy who just sat there quiet now but listening intently.

"Darren was held in that station for nearly eight hours," he continued, "do you remember ever getting a call from Billy to say his parcel hadn't arrived"?

No, I didn't, thought Tommy but said nothing and simply shook his head, even though it was some time ago he would have remembered that, and knowing Billy like he did, if his parcel hadn't arrived on time he would have been on the blower ten minutes later. Tommy started to get agitated and angry but kept it hidden and kept his thoughts to himself he wanted to hear the rest of this story. Albie was squirming in his seat he knew that look on Tommy's face and knew this wasn't going to end well, "That's because Billy had set the whole thing up," continued Harry, "with those two bent coppers DS Thomas and DC Smith, those two and Billy go back years especially Thomas. The only reason I know about them is me and Jimmy had some trouble back in the 70s and Thomas, a basic plod back then was one of the officers involved. Although we never met him, he was training to join CID and was tagging on the back of "our" policeman, a certain detective chief inspector who has worked for me and Jimmy for a while and still does. He retires in a few months and is trying to get a little extra pension before he does. Thomas is now an inspector in CID and according to our man also wants to "bump" his pension by doing a little bit of work for us. We always pay well for useful information, don't we Jimmy? It pays to be in the know," he chuckled.

Tommy wasn't laughing; Harry cleared his throat and went back to the story.

"Well our bit of "trouble" disappeared as quickly as it came. We paid off our man who took a share for his "trainee" PC Thomas. I'm not going to name our man Tommy, I hope you understand."

Tommy did, he wasn't concerned about this fellow he just wanted to hear about the now Inspector Thomas and his involvement in his incarceration

"Anyway," says Harry, "Jimmy and I went to meet this delightful fellow Thomas last week. We had a few beers down by the coast in Brighton, and asked him what he could do for us. It wasn't a foregone conclusion that we would work with him you understand, even though we sort of had several years ago, so we were sounding him out. He started by saying that he knew who we were and that he was glad that our paths hadn't crossed while he was active in the CID," Jimmy and I nearly walked out there and then, he thought he was being clever.

"Why's that then? we asked him. "Do you think we don't know about your part in that bit of work back in the seventies? You got a nice little drink out of that didn't you son, even if you had "crossed our paths" you wouldn't have been able to do anything would you?"

"Probably not," Thomas had said clearing his throat "It's just that I moved away from that for a while when my career was moving forward."

"We thought that was bullshit, didn't we, Jimmy?" who nodded in agreement,

"Once a bent copper always a bent copper," and I told him so, he didn't like that much and I thought he was going to leave then and there but he didn't. He regained some of his composure and started talking. He told us he had some information about a certain fellow from south London and another fella from north London., We told him to stop playing games and if he had any information to just give it up," stated Harry.

"This information is huge," he said, "and I want to know that I'll get the proper money for it, I'm looking for twenty-five large."

"Twenty-five grand," I said, "fuck me for that kind of money it had better be good, give me the names of these men and we will consider it," we said, he then went on to name Darren, you and Billy Saunders but wouldn't say anymore until we agreed the financials, needless to say we put him on ice and told him we would come back to him in a few days. We worked the story out for ourselves and knowing you as we do, I'm sure you have it worked out too," said Harry.

Tommy sat there stone-faced in total disbelief; he had worked it out all right. All this time they were sitting under his nose, laughing at him, five years of his life taken away from him rotting in prison and missing some of the most important times in his girls' lives and for what just because that snake Darren can't do a bit of bird, I would have made sure he was OK, he knew that so, why? This is far too close to home and Tommy is still having trouble believing it. He's been in my house, slept in the spare room and partied with my family, all the while hiding this dirty little secret. He still does business with that other snake, Saunders, over the water but not for long, thought Tommy. Not for long, as for Darren, well he knows too much doesn't he, he's got to go.

"I need a few moments to think," Tommy finally said, "I need to go for a walk and get some fresh air. Come on, Albie, let's take a walk. we will be back in a while."

The brothers understood, got up, shook Tommy and Albies hands and said they would wait in the main bar until they returned.

Back in 1984 Darren Davis, was one of Tommy Spillane's trusted lieutenants but had developed a drug habit. He had started out in the usual way smoking pot and having the odd cheeky line now and then, but soon developed a flavour for something that was called free-base. Better known as crack on the streets, this drug had took a hold on tens of thousands across the water in America and had swept into British society like a tornado by the mid-80s.Use of this drug usually led to the even more debilitating heroin and the downward spiral that usually followed. Darren never got into heroin thankfully as that would have been the end of him. No, Darren was what you could call a functioning addict, he knew for the most part when he could and couldn't partake, he hid it very well.

Tommy had grown his empire in north London on good old-fashioned personal beliefs and values. He never took liberties; he paid a fair price for stolen goods and was loyal to his friends. It was never in his mindset that someone so close to him would do something like that.

"Where have we gone so wrong with Darren," he asked Albie, "I trusted him."

"You never know with some people," said Albie, "drugs have clearly clouded his mind but I'm just as shocked as you, I would have never had him down as a grass mate, he's got to go you know."

"I know," said Tommy, "and so has that other snake across the water but we have got to be smart on that one, his family are dangerous and any sniff that we were involved in any harm coming to him would bring about a war that we just can't win. Those Pikeys just keep coming and coming. We have to think about our families they have no respect for women and kids. Everyone is fair game to them! No, we have to make sure that our involvement is completely out of the picture."

A plan was already formulating in his mind. Albie had seen that look before and welcomed it, he knew how ruthless Tommy could be, especially in situations like this that were totally justified. He wanted those "fucking grasses" dealt with too.

"Let's get back to the pub son, I need to talk with the brothers, I've got a plan," said Tommy.

Back in the pub the four men sat down and continued their discussion.

"Set up another meeting with this Thomas fellow," said Tommy getting back to the matter in hand.

"Tell him that you are willing to pay him the twenty-five grand, but you want all the details. I don't want to tell you how to conduct your business but make sure you get him recorded and photographed at this meeting, and obviously don't tell him I'm involved, yet. I'll pay you ten grand each just for setting it up and a further ten each once in possession of the details. There's another twenty large for your contact but I need to know who it is, is that fair?"

Jimmy and Harry looked at each other for a few seconds, they had an uncanny knack of knowing each other's thoughts and nodded their agreement shortly afterwards.

"Good," said Tommy, "oh and by the way is Danny available?

The Parkhurst brothers had arranged their first "hit" for Tommy back in 1988.It wasn't their first work of this kind of course but their usual man, Archie Wiggins, was currently doing a double life sentence for killing his wife and her lover following the discovery of them both in the marital bed two years ago. He was obviously no longer an option and contrary to popular belief, hired and more importantly professional killers were not that common.

They had needed to find someone and quickly, work was piling up.

Danny was only out of jail a few months and under the wing of his notorious uncles. He was living in an apartment owned and provided by the brothers just off the Old Kent Road in southeast London, it was Archie's little bolthole when he was "working" but it was Danny's place now.

They knew Danny had a penchant for extreme violence. They had seen the wild animal and hungry look in his eyes during that first meeting back in 1986 but could he make the next step, could he be tamed? Jimmy thought so with the right people behind him and said as much to Harry who took some convincing and even commented, "He's just a thug who likes hurting people."

"That's my point," said Jimmy. "He's already halfway there and don't forget he's family. We just need to nurture his violent impulses while he grows."

Needless to say, Danny gravitated towards his Uncle Jimmy when he was released and kept Uncle Harry at arm's length. .Jimmy was the brains, thought Danny, he was wrong of course. Harry was the one with the schemes and was by far the better planner.

The first "opportunity" for this kind of work had come about following a call from their friend over the water in north London, Tommy Spillane. He had an old grudge to settle and would pay the boys handsomely for their expertise in these matters.

"I'll leave it to you of course who you use, but make sure it's clean and nothing comes back my way." Tommy had insisted.

"No problem!" they told him. "Let's set up the meet and discuss the finer details."

Meeting a few days later, Tommy explained the job to the brothers and the reasons behind it. Harry and Jimmy understood, they didn't really need to know the whys and wherefores they would have taken the job anyway. It's what they did. However they listened intently concurred that the man had to go and agreed a price. They knew just who was going to do this for them, but was he up to it?

Jimmy thought so but Harry, despite growing to like his young and inexperienced nephew, wasn't so sure, "Don't worry son, Danny will do us proud you'll see!" declared Jimmy.

He was right, of course.

Danny had been briefed on the job extensively by his uncles following a series of meetings at Danny's apartment.

At the last meeting Harry had said he would supply the gun and the rest was down to Danny. They had already told him that fellow in question was a retired gentleman living in Grinstead, East Sussex, who owned a metal works factory and had caused a dear friend of ours some hardship some time ago and now the time had come for him to get his payback for that.

His name is Giles Anderson, a married man with two sons, one of who still lives at the house.2

"You will have to pick your timing," Jimmy said as you don't want things to get messy by involving other members of the family. Multiple killings bring a whole lot of shit down on your head, do you understand Danny?"

He understood all right but wondered why a gun was necessary and said, "So this is an old, retired gentleman in his late sixties or seventies?" Harry nodded, "A shooter won't be necessary then, I'll deal with it in my own way if that's OK with you?"

His ice cold demeanour had surprised the brothers and they were caught slightly off guard by this revelation. The kid has more to him than meets the eye thought Harry; he was warming to him now.

The thought of ten grand in his back pocket wasn't Danny's overriding motivation although it helped. He had been making good money with his uncles anyway just doing "errands" and giving the odd idiot a slap now and then. He also had a place to stay provided by them, didn't really have any expenses and was relatively happy with his lot. No, His real motivation came from the act of planned violence. His forays in and out of borstals and jails had taught him one thing, unplanned violence nearly always led to a bit of "Porridge". He wanted to hurt bad people and make a living doing it while not spending his time in a stinking cell over some fucking idiot. He knew from that first meeting with his uncles two years ago in Maidstone prison that they could provide that opportunity. He was finally ready.

Danny had come across Tommy Spillane in prison while Tommy was doing time for some drug offences and Danny was nearing the end of his sentence. Tommy had mentioned his uncles and knew he was their nephew, so he knew who the man over the water was. It was just the in-built and time served way in which his uncles spoke. Loose talk costs lives they often said. Not that it mattered. He didn't need to know who the job was for as he didn't care. He knew Tommy was a serious player and a professional villain, he welcomed the opportunity, besides which, he liked Tommy

Maidstone prison

His first encounter with Tommy on "D" wing was just another ordinary day of routine and more routine.

Danny had decided that the best way to get some extra privileges was to work rather than doing "a lay down", a slang term used in prisons for doing absolutely nothing and subsequently got a job working on the hot plate where daily food was dished out in "rations" to the eighty or so prisoners on his wing.

Some prisoners frowned on this as their mentality was Fuck the System, and anyone working for the prison was in some way a traitor or a "Lackey".

Danny didn't give a shit. Working on serving food to the prisoners meant he could get a shower every day, and more importantly access to the gym, plus he was out of his cell far more than most of the prisoners were and could make some extra money passing messages under the cell doors and distributing contraband to those prisoners who were "banged up" and not allowed out of their cells for food or recreation.

Danny wasn't interested in their contents as long as they didn't contain drugs and made this very clear. He just took his reward, usually some cigarettes or a bar of chocolate and asked no questions. However drugs were becoming more and more available and prevalent as currency within prisons up and down the country, and Maidstone was trying hard to keep up!

Danny wanted nothing to do with them. They were bad news and caused some of the most violent attacks between the prisoners who "needed" their "fix". Danny wasn't frightened to be involved with violence but saw the devastation caused by their use and decided to keep away from it. One time he had witnessed a young mother with her baby on a visit to her drug addled partner called Jack, pull something from under her skirt and pass it on to him. The screws had witnessed this small interaction and as a consequence had arrested the woman and thrown Jack straight into the "block" as punishment for three days with total lack of privileges., Alongside all of this, social services were called who took the baby into care immediately while the mother was on remand and awaiting trial. A short time later the mother got six months for passing contraband and sent to the infamous women's jail, Holloway, in north London, Jack hung himself shortly afterwards.

On another occasion, one prisoner who had not "honoured" his drug debt was attacked in his cell during exercise when the cell doors were left open for an hour or so. Some prisoners didn't want to take up the right of this privilege as was their prerogative and stayed behind to play backgammon or cards with other prisoners. This was one such time and a couple of chaps who hadn't been paid decided to teach the young fella playing cards in his cell, a lesson. Using a makeshift "shank" they had "opened him up like a can of beans," according to the prisoner who witnessed this assault leaving the unfortunate man with life changing injuries. The doctors had to remove his spleen the following day.

Danny's routine consisted of being let out of his cell an hour before the other prisoners and escorted to the prison's kitchens, where he and his fellow workers would collect the mornings breakfast on wheeled trolleys called hot plates and wheel them back to their prospective wings. In Danny's case, this was D wing. Along with a huge urn of tea prepared by the screws and trusted prisoners.

Maidstone jail, like every other prison, had a " "Nonce's" wing that were on E wing. Nonce's were mostly made up of child molesters and rapists and these urns were sometimes contaminated with urine and other disgusting substances if possible, to make the lives of "E wing" prisoners as uncomfortable as they possibly could. Subsequently the making of these urns were out of bounds to general population prisoners like Danny and his "colleagues. However, if Danny and his mates got the chance they would "contribute" such was the hatred toward this particular group. No one likes sex offenders.

Another method of injuring sex offenders, especially child molesters was a burning jug of hot water or tea mixed with sugar. Anyone getting this "treatment" would be left with horrific scarring and sometimes blindness, some would say they deserved it, Danny was very definitely in that camp.

Danny had finished his morning chores on the hot plate and was delivering newspapers to several of the prisoners who could afford them. Another perk for Danny was that it gave him the opportunity to deliver other things as well. The wing consisted of five levels ground to fourth and were all interconnected by a central staircase and a further interconnecting staircase at either end of the landings all painted in battleship grey as was most of the 19th century prison with its dour external façade and completely unwelcoming appearance. It was originally a prison from the 1740s and was rebuilt in the early 1800s under the architect John Witchcord Snr who incidentally had also designed the Kent county lunatic asylum in the 1830s.Some of the inmates who cared to look into the history of their place of incarceration were not surprised by this information and wondered if he had taken inspiration from the initial intake of this prison! The locals hated it but there it was.

All the landings looked over a central core covered in "fall" netting. Essentially this was to prevent someone from serious injury should they be thrown over the railings but mostly to stop suicide attempts. It was a long drop from top to bottom!, Danny was on the "4s" delivering his papers and messages when a fellow in one of the cells, called Lewis, a car thief from Kingston had asked Danny if he could deliver a message to another prisoner on the "2s," this was how the landings were identified just by the level numbers.

Danny said no problem of course and reminded him of his no drug policy. Lewis said he knew all about this policy and wouldn't dream of getting him involved with that sort of thing. They agreed a price and Danny said he would do it. Lewis handed Danny a small package and Danny left to deliver it. Suddenly and without warning the screw on level two came rushing down the landing all the while blowing his whistle. This was to notify other screws that there was a problem and he needed assistance.

Danny was caught off guard and within seconds was face down on the landing with several large screws kneeling on his back and screaming at him to behave. He was but the screws mentality was to go all in anyway just to make sure. Danny knew better than to struggle and just let it happen. Another set of screws were also attempting to get Lewis under control but were struggling in the confines of his cell, all the while he was watching Danny just lying there and not fighting., Fucking Wanker he decided. Not fighting the screws was a coward's way, a stupid assumption by Lewis, a very stupid assumption indeed.

Danny and Lewis were taken down to the holding cells in another part of the prison. All the while with Lewis screaming obscenities, outraged by his treatment and making threatening remarks which the screws just ignored. They had heard it all before and would only take so much before they used extreme force. Danny knew this and just went along with it quietly. He knew how these things played out having spent most of his life in one institution or another and understood that fighting or making threats made no difference whatsoever to the inevitable outcome. Indeed, it usually ended up with some substantial injuries to the prisoner that were caused by the prisoner "falling down the stairs" or "running into a wall" while trying to escape. Lewis was a novice thought Danny and would or could not understand the situation he was in. He will learn the hard way and sooner than he realises if he continues to carry on like that! Danny was right. Lewis ended up in the prison infirmary that afternoon after tripping over his own feet while trying to escape and subsequently smashing his face into an open door, removing two teeth in the process!.

Meanwhile Danny was thrown in a holding cell and told he would go in front of the prison governor tomorrow morning.

"May I ask on what charge?" said Danny, the screw who knew all about Danny's illustrious past and penchant for violence merely closed the cell door with the comment.

"You know what for mate; we don't tolerate drugs in our prison."

Once locked away the screw opened the door hatch and said, "I'm surprised with you Danny. I never thought drugs were your thing".

Danny said nothing.

The following day, Danny and Lewis were marched, handcuffed and flanked by four huge screws, before the governor of Maidstone prison, a certain Mr Cecil Creighton OBE.A stern and imposing man who also sat on the local judiciary as a magistrate. His power was immense as was befitting for a man in his position and his harshness was legendary. Everyone in the prison system knew about and feared him

As was the way of these things, this meeting was to determine whether there are charges to be brought before a court or if they could be dealt with internally.

Danny had spent the previous evening going through the events of earlier in the day. He wasn't stupid and knew that the probability of drugs being involved were high. The package he had in his possession when overcome by the screws was confiscated almost immediately and he hadn't seen it since. He also knew that Lewis wouldn't have deliberately set him up. His reaction to the "arrest" that afternoon would have earned him an Oscar. No! He must have been under surveillance and Danny entering his cell had prompted the screws response. The more Danny thought about it the more he was convinced that they were waiting to raid the Lewis cell and Danny was just in the wrong place at the wrong time and he was for the most part collateral damage. Still, Lewis had given him a package knowing that it contained drugs despite Danny letting him know the rules and that would have to be dealt with later he thought .

The governor's office was an entirely different and almost alien environment for most prisoners. Danny and Lewis were no exceptions. The walls were an institutional lime green and decorated with old paintings hanging off picture rails that filled almost the entire room. Directly above and behind the governor's desk was a magnificent portrait of Queen Elizabeth the Second, the reigning monarch and directly to the left of this portrait was a letter from her majesty to Mr Creighton awarding him the honour of an OBE for his outstanding public service. Immediately to the right was a photo of him with the queen proudly wearing his medal with the headline above proclaiming this medal the "Most excellent order of the British Empire. Towards the rear of the office was a solid oak desk with a red leather inlay that looked like it was a hundred years old and behind that sat the impressive Mr Creighton, stern faced and looking directly at the prisoners. Unflinching and definitely unbending, he had come across all sorts in his many years of service and this was just the usual riff raff who were destined to be regular visitors he mused judgementally.

There was a distinctive white line about six feet away from the desk that the prisoners were not to cross under any circumstances. This was introduced some time ago following an unfortunate incident when a rather violent prisoner although handcuffed and flanked by several large officers had lunged at Cecil across the table and managed to head butt him before being dragged off and severely beaten by his officers. Cecil would not let that happen again, his rule was strictly adhered too.

The screws that had marched Danny and Lewis to the room had advised them of this rule, and the consequences of not following it. They were left under no illusions of what was meant by that advice. Cecil knew why the men were there, he had been briefed earlier by his head warden but as protocol would have it his lead officer in this matter asked the question in front of the men regardless.

"These men were caught exchanging banned contraband sir, namely drugs," said the officer standing directly one pace in front of Danny, as was the screw directly next to Lewis, with two further screws directly behind, this was another protocol that Cecil had introduced to protect himself The governor then asked the officer in charge for the particulars which were duly advised to him.

"I see," said Cecil, "Prisoner Mason do you have anything to say about this matter and how would you plead."

"I have nothing to say," said Danny,

"What! Nothing? This is a serious matter, Mason! Drugs cannot, and will not be tolerated in my prison. Do you not realise that I am considering taking this matter to a higher authority, for trial perhaps? You can help yourself now by mitigating your involvement."

Danny knew better than to bandy words with this man and he wasn't a grass. He had also come across his kind before and knew that no matter what he said it was probably going to court anyway.

"I have nothing to say sir," he said.

"What about you Lewis? I assume you are in the same camp as Mason here?"

"I have nothing to say sir," he replied.

"Very well," said Cecil, "You leave me with only two choices in this matter. The first being to consider involving the local police force and have you both arrested for drug dealing within these prison walls or the alternative of issuing you both with a suitable punishment within this prison."

"Officer, take these men to solitary confinement, following that I wish to hear all the relevant evidence and particulars of their arrest before I consider the aforementioned choices."

Two days later the solitary confinement officer called them both out of their cells and onto the empty landing where the governor was standing flanked by four burly officers. Both men were brought before him, and stood at least six foot from him as was the protocol, where he boomed

"Mason and Lewis," boomed the imposing governor,

"I have come to the conclusion that due to the relatively small amount of drugs found upon your persons, I could impose a period of a further five days of solitary confinement as sufficient punishment in this matter, this would save the taxpayer's purse the huge expense of trying you degenerates in a court of your peers. You do, of course, have the opportunity of defending yourselves in a court of law should you feel that you have a case to defend. However, and looking at the evidence provided by my officers, I doubt you would win it," he added stuffily. "The choice is yours gentlemen."

Both men agreed to the former and were returned to their cells, it was a no brainer for Danny.

The days went relatively quickly for Danny. In fact he quite enjoyed the solitude of his confinement where he managed to gather his thoughts and contemplate his next move. He had to be careful as he was due for release in seven months' time and didn't want to spend any more days than were absolutely necessary in this shit hole. However, he couldn't let go of the Lewis issue. He had very nearly caused Danny to suffer another few months or even years in this place. Not only that he had cost him all

173

of his privileges, he only had one shower in the seven days he had been down here and when the screws had brought his belongings from his old cell all his tobacco and chocolate had been missing.

The gym was also a privilege he had lost; Lewis would have to pay the price.

Once back in "general population", Danny was allocated a shared cell on the "1s" with another prisoner called Tommy Spillane. An old school type criminal that Danny soon found out was in fact a major player in the criminal underworld of London, they got on straight away and through shared exchanges soon found out that they had a mutual connection with two brothers out of south London. These were of course Danny's blood uncles and good friends with Tommy. Small world they both commented.

Danny dealt with Lewis a few weeks after meeting Tommy, who had told him the best way to go about it and even though the screws would know who was responsible they wouldn't be able to prove anything.

"Use your head for once," Tommy had advised. Danny would have normally just smashed his head in and got another five years, instead he listened to Tommy.

Tommy liked Danny and had told his darling wife, Peggy, during one visit to let the south London boys know who he was sharing a cell with. He knew that Danny hadn't seen his uncles since the burial of his mother, but he also knew that blood was thicker than water and their nephew had potential. They needed to know he was in here. Peggy came back two weeks later and informed Tommy that they were grateful of the information and were planning to visit Danny soon. She had also told Tommy that one of the brothers, Harry, had been closely watching Danny over the years, but had no control over his violent ways and although he was a blood relative to take great care when dealing with him. Hearing this, Tommy was a little disappointed with Harry as it was clear that he didn't really know the boy, indeed they may have been watching him from afar but they hadn't helped him had they?

It seemed to Tommy that they had the resources and power to help but had chosen not to.

"I need to talk with the brothers," he had told Peggy, "I want to know why they hadn't helped him before."

Peggy said that Tommy should mind his own business, "The twins must have their reasons," she added. However, Tommy was puzzled by their attitude.

Lewis was by now "living" on the "2s" and he and Danny hadn't spoken since both being released from solitary. In fact Danny had deliberately avoided him on the advice of Tommy.

"Don't let the screws know you hold a grudge," he had said.

"They know your history and they also know the circumstances of your recent solitary spell. They will be waiting and expecting a reaction from you, don't give them the satisfaction, Danny."

Lewis had taken this as cowardice, he thought Danny was a fake, "All fucking street reputation based on beating up drunks and old men," Lewis had commented to his new cellmate!

This comment had spread around the prison like wild fire and made the situation even more difficult for Danny who just wanted to smash the living daylights out of him, "Bite your tongue for a little while longer son," Tommy had said, "It will all die down in a few days and someone or something else will take the attention of the screws, then you can move on him but not before!"

Danny wasn't happy but something about this Tommy fella had made him listen. He had a calmness and way about him that he respected and wanted to emulate. Tommy wasn't a particularly big fella and definitely not a big mouth Danny thought but no one ever messed with him on the wing and Danny noticed that.

He noticed everything, he was evolving again, but this time to a place of calm and thoughtfulness. He had found himself considering the implications of his actions, and the consequences that this could bring. This was new territory for him and adopting this way of thinking, it was surprising but he welcomed it none the less, Danny was a very quick learner. He wanted to be like Tommy and would do whatever it took to get to that point.

His chance to pay back Lewis came a few weeks later when the doors were opened for recreation.

Danny had been secretly watching Lewis's cell during these times and quite often he didn't come out for the legislated but individual choice of daily exercise. He had told Tommy about Lewis's unusual behaviour a few days previously.

"That is your chance, son," he had said and went on to tell Danny how and why.

The bell had gone for the routine one-hour exercise out in the courtyard. Danny had stayed in his cell, he had pushed the door almost closed and was waiting quietly on his bunk pretending to read a book, while Tommy had gone to the yard. Once the wing had emptied and was quiet Danny had very carefully moved towards the end of the landing where a metal staircase served all the landings, and waited out of sight. He had learned to control his breathing some time ago and had an almost instantaneous flashback of his time in a derelict house some years ago. He grinned and kept himself stock still. He couldn't be seen from his position as the only screw left on the wing was on the ground floor watching for prisoners that were coming and going from the yard. The other landing screws were out in the courtyard where the probability of violence or distribution of contraband was more likely to happen while the prisoners intermingled with each other, Danny waited.

Out in the yard, Tommy was just roaming around in a circle and metaphorically kicking his heels just waiting for an opportune moment. He had told Danny what to expect and stated, "Don't fuck about! You will only have a small window to get the job done once the balloon goes up."

However, and unbeknownst to Tommy, Danny had played it all out in his mind for most of the morning and was more than ready. He knew exactly how he was going to "get the job done".

Danny was patiently waiting under the stair canopy of the "2s" when the noise from the courtyard came rushing into the wing like a tornado. He watched the only screw left on the wing rush towards the exercise yard, took a deep breath and ran up the short flight to Lewis's cell. Lewis himself had also heard the kafuffle, no one would have missed the noise, and was just coming out of his cell when Danny arrived.

Danny had anticipated this, and knew he only he had a small window of opportunity to catch Lewis out before he got out to the landing. He did as he planned and launched himself into a lightning and brutal assault on the surprised and unprepared Lewis. Knocking him backwards into his cell, Danny overwhelmed him very quickly and Lewis was quickly unconscious.

"Don't do too much damage, Danny!" He could hear the words of caution from Tommy ringing in his ears. "If you do there will be an inquiry which you will find hard to get out of. Don't forget this man's a drug dealer in here and the screws know it. They won't give a fuck as long as it's just a good hiding and no weapons, Danny!"

Leaning over the hapless and prone form of Lewis, Danny's natural instinct was to destroy this man, and leave a permanent calling card but he also knew the consequence of that if he did. However, and despite the advice from his mentor and the voice in his own head saying don't do it son! He took the "shiv" from his belt, a knife made out of a toothbrush that had been sharpened like a razor and cut Lewis across the face leaving a four inch wound from under his left eye to the top of his upper lip. This was a well-known calling card for "nonce's" or " a wrong'un". At present Lewis was too out of it to notice but he certainly would when he woke up! He wouldn't be able to smile without pain for at least a month. Danny cleaned the handle of the makeshift knife and left it right there in the cell. Then, casually walked back down the stairs went to the latrine had a clean-up and went back to his cell., He was gone and back in less than three minutes.

Tommy was furious with Danny.

"You didn't have to cut him, that wasn't what we discussed son! Why on earth didn't you just give him a good hiding? I kicked it off in the yard with some totally random fella as discussed and gave you the opportunity."

Danny didn't answer; he just sat there and said nothing but in his mind was thinking he deserved it. He had nearly cost me a few more years in this shit hole and to top it all off going around telling everyone that I was a

179

coward who had made his reputation on drunks and old men. He's lucky I didn't kill him. Tommy wasn't as angry as he made out. He was looking straight at Danny while remonstrating with him and saw a little bit of himself in Danny's eyes when he was that age. He also saw something else, what was it? He couldn't quite put his finger on it, but much later he would know what it was!

He continued his admonishment while Danny just sat there and stared at him and for the briefest of moments Tommy also felt something else, something that he hadn't felt for quite some time, fear. He shrugged it off and continued.

"Listen, son! The good news is that he's kept his mouth shut and was shipped out to the local hospital. I doubt he will be coming back here; the authorities will want to keep him safe now and don't want the grief of explaining what happened to him here. He will probably end up on E wing at Wandsworth prison." Tommy didn't need to explain E wing to Danny, Every prison had one and he knew exactly what that was. A secure unit for vulnerable prisoners wronguns and paedophiles, Danny just smiled.

The screws knew who had done this. It didn't take a genius to work it out. They also knew that Tommy was the diversion but with no witnesses or statement from the stricken Lewis or anyone else for that matter there was nothing they could do. Indeed most were happy and more than a little relieved that the drug dealing and aggressive

Lewis had got his comeuppance. His violent resistance when they "shook him down" during their drug bust had done him no favours at all. Indeed, two of the screws had needed a visit to the infirmary for minor injuries and held no sympathy for him whatsoever.

Tommy and Danny were aware of this and for the most part expected no comeback. They were right, of course. Although, Tommy was worried when he heard about Danny slashing his face, and that it could have driven the governor to make more extensive inquiries. Thankfully, he didn't but that was more luck than good judgement thought Tommy. For Danny's part he couldn't have cared less, as far as he was concerned he got what he deserved and that was that.

As the months went by and Danny's release day was coming close, Tommy was contemplating the many conversations he and Danny have had following the by now regular visits from his uncles

They were close friends by this time and Danny had told him about "most" of their conversations and how he was going to work for the brothers while they coached him about the "business".

Tommy knew he had a hunger for the lifestyle that had been presented and promised by his uncles. He also knew what they wanted from him and feared for the boy but at the same time realised there was no turning back. The brothers were dangerous, undertook serious "work" and were not to be underestimated. They had a reputation for absolute confidentiality no matter what the contract and they were also known for complete ruthlessness, and you never went into any dealings with them lightly. They always delivered. Tommy had used them once before for a bit of work that ended up a little messy, however, they had cleaned it up very quickly and with their usual efficiency. No one came knocking at Tommy's door; I suppose he's in good hands if that's what he wants thought Tommy.

During their many conversations, Danny had shown a real hunger for learning the "trade" and confessed that he would do anything to please his uncles. Tommy felt a little sympathy for the boy as he also realised that he was just looking for acceptance and something to belong to. He knew about the boy's past and his tragic upbringing. This was something Tommy couldn't relate too, his parents were like a king and queen to him, even throughout his mother's decline into alcoholism and subsequent death.

Tommy often wondered how things would have turned out if his parents hadn't so tragically been taken from him,

"I would probably have been a bricklayer and taken after my dad," he often confided to his loyal wife in reflective moments.

Peggy just used to raise her eyes up to the sky and say, "Yes, dear, probably dear, why don't you go down the labour exchange I've heard the local building site in Clarence Street are looking for brickies." She wasn't being clever by saying those things to him, it was always to lighten the mood, and Tommy knew this of course and loved her all the more for it.

Tommy knew by now what it was he had seen in Danny following the Lewis incident. It was quite simply a pure and uncompromising penchant for violence that made him what he was. This appeared to be mixed with a tinge of madness that was for now at least undiagnosed but controlled to a degree. That was what he saw in that moment while giving Danny a dressing down. He shivered at the thought and remembered his own past and the violence he had himself witnessed and on more than one occasion dished out himself. He knew Danny had evolved from a common violent thug despite his lack of control with that Lewis fellow. In some ways Tommy envied him, he would have done Lewis like that back in the day but thought he had risen above that kind of over the top violence, it appeared he hasn't!

He actually admired the extra violence that to some would seem extreme but in Tommy's world was almost necessary to some extent, it certainly sent a message, and Tommy smiled.

Lewis was released four months later and disappeared from the "scene" in his hometown of Kingston. The scar that ran down his face was definitely not a badge of honour. Most people who lived that lifestyle knew, or thought they knew why he had it and shunned him. The more he protested his innocence the deeper the hole he dug, "no smoke without fire" most people would comment. He ended up addicted to his own supply in the nearby town of New Malden and went from one disaster to another with a regularity as was becoming of a heavy drug user. He overdosed on heroin less than two years after his release from prison.

GILES ANDERSON

Giles Anderson had moved out of London in the mid-sixties due to that unfortunate business at his factory where two men had died. He couldn't remember their names. He would never intentionally hurt anyone, he thought and the court case, and conviction that followed was harsh in his opinion.

Both men knew the risks, and how was I to know the roof was that far gone? It had never occurred to him to inspect it or get a specialist to make sure it was safe for the men to go up there. That costs money! He thought selfishly.

Nonetheless, the courts had decided he was negligent and had fined him £800 with a suspended prison sentence Still, my lawyer had saved me any further expense by claiming my situation was dire, and that I was living off meagre savings he remembered with a chuckle. In reality Giles had a tidy sum squirreled away in various safety deposit boxes around the country. Substantial cash reserves under his mattress and a large investment sitting with his wife. He could have easily handed those poor unfortunate women and their families a life line, but that would have meant declaring his hidden treasure and there was no way that was happening!

The nerve of them he thought. They never took into account all the employment he created in the area and the years of building the business to a profitable level, which in turn provided the chancellor much-needed taxation revenue. However, that part wasn't quite true though he chuckled. A large part of his income went undeclared. The books would show only a very small profit. Cash was king back then and old wily Giles Anderson had plenty put by for a rainy day, and by god did it pour down in the weeks and months that followed.

The factory was closed down within two years, but the shrewd and somewhat greedy man that he was, he had siphoned as much off the top as he possibly could during the final few months. He knew the writing was on the wall after the court case, work dried up, visits from the local authority had increased, bloody inspectors were ruining him with their demands for better and safer working conditions which cost money and to top it all his mistress had buggered off and left him when his moaning had gotten too much! Also, and more importantly the gifts, money and beautiful jewellery had also disappeared. "My wife is controlling the business now," he whined at his latest bit of skirt, "I'm on an allowance at the moment until all this business dies down, but things will get better sweetheart, I promise," he continued.

She wasn't really listening, all she knew was the past few months had been "dry" it was time to move on she decided and left him standing there to wallow in his own self-pity, with the parting shot of "I've given so much up for you Giles, you're never going to leave your wife, you're a pathetic excuse for a man and I wish I had never met you." Giles being the man he was, just shrugged and walked the other way. Of course, she was right, he would never leave his wife he thought with a smile. Still, plenty more fish in the sea, she was getting on a bit anyway.

Giles re-started his operation a few years later in 1970 following an unsuccessful attempt at working in the city as a stockbroker. He never lost his own money but was summarily dismissed after only a year for "underperforming". The reality was that he just couldn't hack it, the young bloods at the exchange took every new client and Giles just couldn't find a way into their niche and as clever as he felt he was, he didn't have the right kind of savvy.

His new factory down in sunny Uckfield, a small market style town about fifteen miles from Grinstead in East Sussex, was the perfect area for him and his family. It was a fresh start away from the hectic lifestyle of London. The boys were getting older, therefore his wife had taken on a more direct role in the business and they had employed a local chap to run the shop floor.

Giles wasn't the hands on type of guy anyway and didn't mix with the staff, most of whom didn't even know who he was. They simply knew that he and his wife Phillipa Anderson, nee Williams, owned the business.

The new name for this enterprise was "Williams Metal Works".

Giles didn't care as long as the business thrived and continued to bring in the cash. His wife had changed the previous name from his own to her maiden name when they bought the new factory. Giles was down on the books as the company secretary and drew a modest salary, certainly not enough to keep his new lover. He needed to make some extra cash.

He would visit the factory once or twice a week just to see how things were going.

He had his own set of keys and would often visit out of hours to meet a prospective buyer where he would usually broker some kind of deal that meant a small "envelope" stuffed with cash as a sweetener.

Phillipa knew about this of course as she kept a close eye on the accounts, but turned a blind eye. After all he was still bringing clients into the business through his extensive contacts and Giles was quite canny. The business still made a profit on his deals and that was the most important factor she mused. She also knew about his mistresses over the years but had long since cared. He physically repulsed her and she hadn't slept with him for years now. He was a good father and grandfather and their standing in this little community meant more than physical attention "Men will be men," she had once told him when she found out about one of his mistresses "Just keep her away from me and our family, and never bring her into this town! You can fuck her where her nest is," she said matter of factly, Giles got the message.

Giles was also a greedy man, the "lure" of the deal and a chance to increase his wealth and standing in the community would ultimately be the undoing of him.

The young fellow he had met only two days ago while enjoying his shepherd's pie and real ale or two had sparked his interest. There was a few bob to be made here and he wasn't going to miss out!

His factory on the Bell Lane industrial estate in Uckfield specialised in the "hot dip" of metals more commonly known as galvanization and as the term would suggest involved dipping raw steel into a very hot solution of molten zinc. The process of coating iron and steel with zinc, which alloys zinc with the surface of the base metal, usually iron when immersed in a bath of molten zinc at temperatures of around 450 degrees centigrade or 850 degrees Fahrenheit.

When zinc is heated to the required temperature and metal immersed into it, it produces a light blue flame which spit and dance above the bubbling solution like little blue elves!

Now retired, and sixty-six years old Giles spent every Tuesday afternoon in 1988 playing lawn bowls at the local green in Grinstead with members he had met as part of the local neighbourhood watch scheme.

This had come about following a spate of recent burglaries that had everyone in the community worried. Giles was an active member and often volunteered to chair various meetings in the local hall, he liked this role it made him feel important and part of the community in this rather sleepy town. He soon became well known and respected.

Every Thursday morning was spent at the golf club only a short drive from the house located in the nearby Ashdown Forest, this always led to a few drinks afterwards in a lovely little place called the Red Lion just off the A22 which was on the way home and served the best pub grub for miles. The homemade shepherd's pie was to die for and the always fresh and hand-pumped beer often led to him leaving the car there overnight and his dutiful wife or lover picking him up, depending on his mood. He liked the odd drink or two and why not he thought, I've earned it.

Danny had driven down to East Grinstead; he had arrived just before mid-day on the Monday and checked into one of the recently opened chain of hotels that were popping up all over the country. This one was a Trust House Forte version and was situated within walking distance of East Grinstead train station, not that Danny had taken the train; he nearly always drove where possible as he enjoyed the freedom of travelling at his own leisure. In this instance a car was vital as it involved a little travelling to other parts of West Sussex.

The car was a "ringer" essentially; it was cloned with another vehicle of the same make and model, that was legitimately being driven in another part of the country, usually up north where the likelihood of the two cars ever meeting was slim to nothing. In this case it was a blue Vauxhall Cavalier, nothing fancy there were thousands of them up and down the country. He was masquerading as a businessman called Robert Nash from Croydon, only about thirty miles or so from Grinstead. He had arrived on Monday afternoon and paid cash to the receptionist with no questions asked. He had some identification in the name he was using if asked but the girl had merely said welcome to our hotel and I hope you enjoy your stay, Danny just walked to the lift with a handful of the local papers he had picked up in reception and went to his room.

The well-known businessman and neighbourhood watch chairman in the area had recently been the subject of a local news item about rising crime in Grinstead and the surrounding areas where he had confidently declared that he and his fellow residents were going to "put an end" to the "horrendous" crime being perpetrated by gangs of thugs from London, with regular patrols, a campaign for more street lighting and lobbying the local MP for more policemen on the beat. In reality, Giles was using this platform as a tool to promote his own business and his aspirations for the local council.

"If it can happen here it could happen anywhere," was his catchphrase, "and I will promote and champion communities from here to Brighton and anywhere else that may need me to take up the responsibility of neighbourhood watch schemes to ensure that decent, honest and hardworking families can live in relative peace and harmony". He sounded more like a bloody politician thought Danny, in fairness he wasn't far wrong. Giles was setting the wheels in motion for just that by campaigning in the local elections for his good friend, Bernard Tubbs, the local council conservative representative. His motive was simple, get yourself out there, get yourself known, and when the time was right, get yourself in!

This costs money, of course and even though he was by now a millionaire on paper at least, "One could always do with more," he had proclaimed to his ever-loyal wife and his "secret" mistress.

Danny threw his overnight bag and suitcase on the bed, sat in the chair by the window, and began to read the papers. He already knew quite a bit about this fellow but was looking for something else he could use to give him inspiration. Ideally he would find something that would present an opportunity to get up close with this man, people like him always like to brag thought Danny, and sure enough there was a spread in one of the local rags about Anderson who was currently on the conservative campaign trail supporting a friend. Telling the reporter all about his candidate, and how he would make the best of his role should he be fortunate enough to win the upcoming seat on the majority conservative led council, how they liked to play golf when the time allowed but rarely missed their Thursday sessions and that the Red Lion pub served the best shepherd's pie and real ale in the county! He also added that he was hosting a community watch meeting at the local town hall this coming Tuesday evening, starting at 7.30pm where refreshments would be provided.

Perfect! thought Danny that's tomorrow! Danny was already formulating a plan; it was simple but needed a bit of luck and the reliance on Giles Anderson's greed to take the bait.

He immediately went down to the high street and found a telephone box, he called London.

Although Danny already knew about Anderson's metal works operation down in Uckfield, there was quite a large advert for "Williams Metal Works" directly beneath the article, which was proudly stating that they had been in operation since 1970 in the town and had served the county and surrounding areas proudly in providing, "All your metal work needs", including the supply of steel girders, railings and design elements etc, "We now also have our own in house galvanizing equipment for your special projects", the advert proudly stated, continuing with, "Saving you time and money by having this process undertaken here at the point of sale." "We also provide galvanizing to metal products provided by yourselves", it concluded and that you should call the following number 01248-009-808 for an instant quote or visit the factory at unit four on the Bell Lane industrial estate in Uckfield just off the A22.

Danny decided to make the relatively short trip to Uckfield. He jumped in his car and made his way to the industrial estate. Bell Lane was on the right hand side as you come off the A22 into Uckfield and had several entrances, either vehicular or pedestrian., Danny drove past the first one and came in via a roundabout just past the fire station located on the left. The main road to the estate was lined with all manner of factories, warehouses and workshops. Danny drove all the way to the end where unit four with a horseshoe shaped drive that was big enough to take an articulated lorry was located and was one of only two units at this point. The first, unit two was a scaffold yard and enormous. A little chuck wagon was parked just before the "horseshoe" drive and was still open; Danny wondered if they opened on Saturday mornings and if so what time? He needed to find out. The double gates of unit four were wide open and there was clear activity going on within the compound.

To the left was a pathway that appeared to lead straight into the factory, straight ahead was the factory roller shutter gates that were wide open. Danny could see all manner of activity going on beyond the shutters with steam and smoke filling the air. Men were walking about in dungarees and vests; it looks bloody hot in there! Thought Danny. To the right of the building was a further walkway.

This appeared to lead out of the estate and onto the main road, Danny took that, and sure enough it led to the main road he had just driven through. This path also branched off and led to the rear of the building where there was what looked like the staff entrance and offices. The windows were protected by inbuilt iron bars and the glass was obscure. He walked back to the main entrance, no one approached him or asked him what he was doing, indeed it appeared that no one had even given him a second thought, security was lax here he thought.

He continued on and went straight to the chuck wagon where a rather greasy but friendly fella asked him what he wanted, it was quiet and it looked like he was ready to pack up for the day.

"A bacon roll and a mug of tea please, mate."

The fella duly obliged and soon Danny was tucking into his roll A few minutes later the only other person standing at the wagon finished his tea and with a cheery, "See you tomorrow, Stan," left to go wherever he came from.

Danny saw him go off to the scaffold yard, it didn't take long for a conversation to strike up, the usual "how's business" responded by the usual "going to pot mate", followed by, "I barely make a living here anymore since the metal works boys over there built their own canteen, Their tight wad of an owner even lets the scaffold boys use it, for a price of course! It's nearly ruined me! According to his foreman it's so he can keep the boys' lunch breaks properly monitored!. I'm thinking of calling it a day to be honest as I only get the loyal ones and a few from the other units. He's stopped the Saturday working as well, he reckons he doesn't get the value from it and begrudges having to pay a full shift for half a day's work! What's the world coming to I ask you? These fat cats taking all the cream and begrudging the workers a small bunce on a Saturday."

Danny had switched off, this guy could talk for England he thought, I've heard all I need to know. He finished his tea, thanked Stan and left. He went straight back to Grinstead, he knew what he wanted to do, and how he was going to do it and it could be a Saturday, either way Giles would be dead by the weekend.

The following evening, Danny made his way to Grinstead town hall, more commonly known as the Meridian Hall. Elegantly set in parklands with a sweeping view of the Ashdown forest where Giles was giving a speech on the reasons to invest in the county, how to become a conservative member and the benefits this would bring to young entrepreneurs of the area. This group also included most of the affluent members of the county who were there primarily to drum up business for the ever growing town and surrounding areas. It seemed that the subject of neighbourhood watch was secondary to the self-important Giles and his cronies, the main hall was packed.

Danny sat pretty much to the back, and just watched, waited and listened. He wanted to get a feel for this man himself, assess his weight, watch him walk and talk but more importantly he wanted to know how he handled himself, with the end goal of getting a moment with him.

At the end of the speeches there was a small reception held in a large annex room just off the main hall where drinks and snacks were provided, amply funded by the local young conservative fraternity. Giles would never have dreamed of funding this himself!

Danny mingled with the crowd of eager old and young businessmen and some women it must be said that wanted to tout their wares to anyone who would listen, giving out business cards, swapping phone numbers and the like. When, quite suddenly the confident and formidable Giles Anderson was right up alongside Danny, and asking him what his business was, Slightly taken aback and unprepared for this scenario the young and apparently dumbstruck Danny was lost for words.

"Come now, young man," said the by now smiling Giles, "What's your business in this fine town? I've seen you looking at me quite intently this past hour or two, so come now, spit it out lad!" he boomed with his hand outstretched.

Danny had recovered somewhat and duly extended his hand in reciprocation.

"Now that's better, lad! Now tell me why you're here?"

The first thing Danny noticed was his accent, no one had told him he was a Yorkshireman. I suppose no one really knew, thought Danny, not that it really matters and got back to the topic in hand,

"You've caught me out," said Danny sheepishly. "You were right! I was sounding you out somewhat as you and I are in the same business."

"And what may I ask, can I help you with young man and please don't say investment, those days are over for me and if you want money I suggest you go to the bank," he said dismissively,

"Oh no I'm not looking for money sir!" said Danny "My metal workshop is in Dagenham, Essex and is a viable and profitable business!" Danny had found a metal works the previous week that fitted the bill but Giles never asked about it.

Danny continued, "However and although I produce and manufacture similar products to you, there is one exception."

"And what is that exception?" said Giles now looking disinterested and scanning the room for someone to rescue him.

Danny instantly recognised the old man's demeanour and quickly said, "Galvanization capability. The equipment needed is currently not at my disposal and out of my means at the moment, I'm looking for a partner to undertake this for me," he added rather rushed.

Giles interest piqued a little on this news but said, "Unless it's a substantial amount, young man, you would be better off getting a smaller company to do this for you! If you've done your research, you would know that my factory is one of the largest in the south of England."

With that, a rather posh man who turned out to be Bernard Tubbs the conservative candidate that Giles spoke so highly of in his address interjected.

"Having trouble, Giles?" he jokingly chimed in, "This young buck giving you a hard time?" he continued while chuckling.

"No not at all," said Giles, we have just concluded our business, haven't we son?"

Danny, a little out of his league amongst these kinds of people, could only nod, say thank you for his time and took off back to his hotel.

Danny was furious with himself, he thought it would be a piece of cake delivering a "pitch" to this man but clearly, he had been in business for far too long to be bored to death by a young upstart like him. He would need to rethink his approach. He thought about the news article regarding the Red Lion pub and decided that would be his next meeting with the smug bastard, Mr Anderson. Next time would be different he hoped, and it was.

Danny had made his way to the golf course the following day and enquired about playing a round of golf with his friends on the following day, Thursday morning at 9.30am,

"Even if you were a member, son, you wouldn't have a chance, councillor Tubbs and his party tee off at 9.00am, closely followed by another foursome from the same group at 9.15am, following that it's members only from 9.30 I'm afraid, I can fit you in early afternoon say around 2.00pm, or if you can let me know which member will vouch for and sign you and your group in?" asked the somewhat officious club secretary.

"Never mind," said Danny, looking suitably crestfallen. "I've got a train to catch at 5.00pm and I wouldn't be able to make that slot, thanks for your time" and walked off.

He knew that this particular eighteen hole course takes around three and a half to four hours to complete, depending on your skill set. That meant if Anderson was true to form he would be in the pub for about 1.00pm to 2.00pm latest even if he stopped at the 19th hole, Danny would be waiting.

Bang on 1.30pm the confident Giles strode into the Red Lion public house with Councillor Tubbs bringing up the rear and instantly went over to his reserved table.

Danny had watched him pull up in the car park from his position at the bar. The waiter was over at the table like a shot and almost fell into the table in his haste to serve this esteemed fellow and his guest.

Danny was watching all this from his position at the very busy bar and wondered why someone would give such reverence to these men?

There was another man with him that Danny thought looked familiar, the chap from the meeting, thought Danny.

Hadn't the man at the golf club said Tubbs? Yes, that was him, the same fella that had "rescued" Anderson from Danny's ramblings the other night.

The barmaid had noticed that Danny was fixed on the two men; she leant forward towards him and whispered,

"They always came in here following their golfing morning and brag about their prowess and how much money they have won! The others probably let them win! I mean look at the guts on them two," she added, "plus they're about ninety years old each!" she finished conspiratorially.

Danny said nothing; he just smiled and nodded his head in agreement.

This was risky for Danny as she might pop up as a witness in the future, still he had no choice really, he couldn't exactly rock up at Andersons house could he?, No, the risk was worth it and if his plan worked out there really wouldn't be any evidence at all would there?.

Around 2.45pm and following their usual round of shepherd's pie and three pints of real ale the elder of the two gentlemen, Tubbs, got up shook Anderson's hand and left, Danny suspected that they had already had a drink or two at the club before they got here by their manner, he was right of course; they were three sheets to the wind and clearly enjoyed their booze.

Danny was sitting at the far end of the bar in plain sight and was watching the whole thing unfold, Giles got up and approached him, Danny remembered the old man's awareness from the other evening and was banking on what happened next,

"Well, young man, you again? What brings you here?"

"Would you like another pint, sir before the bar closes Mr Anderson?" said Danny.

"The bar won't close while I'm in here, son," bragged the confident Giles while winking at the barmaid, "Will it, love"?

"No sir," said the young girl looking for reassurance from the landlord who was keeping an eye on everything,

"Last orders," boomed the landlord, "we open again at 5.30," he stated while looking directly at Giles. It seemed like the usual ritual to Danny and that the landlord said it for the benefit of others lingering about. People started to leave while a few others decided they would indeed have one last one for the road.

"I'll have a pint of Best, son," said Giles, "now tell me what you want, from our last encounter I recall something about using the galvanizing process at my factory." Danny was impressed, this man was no fool and despite his age and tipsiness he was definitely on the ball.

Danny bought the drinks, a pint of Best ale for Giles and lemonade for himself.

"Shall we sit over there in that little alcove where we can talk a little more privately?" Danny said quietly, "It will be worth your while," he added.

"I don't trust a man that doesn't drink!" laughed Giles, "but you've got an honest face, go ahead you have twenty minutes or so before the wife picks me up," and walked over to the alcove, part one achieved thought Danny and took a deep breath.

Once seated Danny went straight into his pre-prepared pitch,

"Here's the thing," he started, "I have a large order of galvanised bicycle stands and racks with Croydon council that I secured several weeks ago. The orders are approved and I am in possession of the signed contracts and the goods are in the manufacturing process as we speak. I am to supply six hundred individual cycle stands and a further one hundred and twenty cycle racks that will accommodate four cycles for the local schools and hospitals in the first instance, with a further order of the same in the pipeline The problem I have, and being extremely honest here, is that I only have twelve weeks left to get the first order out and my usual galvanising company doesn't have the capacity, moreover, they are inundated with their own work and just can't fit me in! The council are in contract with the fitters and if I don't deliver there will be consequences.

I have most of the metal prepared and ready at my place in Dagenham, but I will clearly not be able to meet the council deadline without some serious help. Your factory as you reminded me a few days ago has the biggest zinc baths in the country and more importantly, the capacity. That's why I came to you, hand on heart here I'm desperate!

If I can't fulfil my contract the council will sue me but more importantly I stand to lose my business! I really need your help; you are my last chance to save the reputation and viability of my company".

Part two achieved, Danny breathed out slowly and was looking straight at the wily Yorkshire man.

Giles looked decidedly unimpressed, at least on the outside. Danny couldn't read him at all and was beginning to think he had blown it! After all this kind of business talk wasn't really his game and the old man had seen right through him hadn't he?

In fact the Machiavellian Giles Anderson's greedy little mind was working overtime! He saw this as an opportunity but wanted to make the boy squirm!

The more he squirmed the more he would pay for the privilege thought Giles. Of course he could help him! He owned the damned factory and could do what he liked.

For now he was just looking directly at Danny who was sitting there bowed head and was wringing his hands. A technique that was alien to him but he felt necessary in this instance.

Giles left it a few more seconds that felt like hours to Danny, and then finally and suddenly it seemed he had come to a decision:

"Right young fellow, by the way what's your name?"

Danny gave him the name of the man who actually did own an iron works in Dagenham, a Mr Graham Allburn, he doubted that Giles would check on it, and anyway he didn't have the time. Tomorrow was Friday, and he would be long dead before Monday morning one way or the other before he could make any serious enquiries.

Danny smiled, his smile wasn't reciprocated, Giles was a serious business man and had dealt with these young whipper snappers before.

He intended to make him pay handsomely for getting him out of the mess he was clearly in, whilst teaching him a valuable lesson and simply said. "I can help you, son, but let's do the maths and timescales. My business charges by the tank time and processing by the hour. We can move five pieces through the process an hour at £100 per hour multiplying by nine hours at that cost means we can galvanize forty-five pieces per day.

Bearing in mind that I have three tanks to which you will only have access to two of them if we agree on something of course. Don't forget, I need to keep at least one going for orders already in the pipeline you understand.

This will give you ninety pieces per day at a cost of £1800 multiply this by around seven working days to complete six hundred number would cost you close to twelve grand. Are you keeping up here son"?

He looked at Danny who said nothing, but nodded his head

"Good, then let me continue, these are just the figures for the individual single stands. I'm assuming from previous items of this sort that the cycle racks are broken down into six- or eight pieces and bolted together once galvanised, am I close?"

Danny nodded again, he dare not say anything as he hadn't given this that much thought, he was staggered by this man's knowledge and to be brutally honest impressed by his mathematics.

"Good!", Giles continued, he was enjoying this. His reputation for being able to summarise costs in the blink of an eye was well earned and respected by most he had come across in this business and the young fella opposite was equally impressed it seemed. He went on, "That means the racks would cost you around a further sixteen grand, A grand total of about twenty-eight thousand, son!"

He exclaimed rather pleased with himself. "Notwithstanding that, it would cost me another ten grand just to push my other orders back in the queue. I would have to upset a few loyal customers to fit you in, plus the "drink" I will expect if you get my drift son? You'll be looking at a bill of over forty grand by the time we are done!, I will expect the "envelope" before we do anything with your goods," he paused and looked straight at Danny without blinking.

First to speak is the loser thought Giles and folded his arms.

Danny was trying hard to think here, one wrong word could destroy the plan he had formulated, just capitulating to his demands could cause him to suspect it was too easy, whereas letting him know he was being ripped off could cause Anderson to get up and leave without a deal.

Danny needed time to think and excused himself to the toilets.

Danny returned and realized that the bar was empty now and the governor had come over.

"Mr Anderson," he said, "would you and your friend here like another drink? My little speech wasn't aimed at you sir, but you know how it is!"

"Well, that depends on my friend here, Albert."

"What do you say, Graham?" said Giles.

Danny had time get his speech prepared whilst in the toilet and, he had watched his uncles negotiate deals before and had learned a lot from them.

"Are we having another drink, son?"

Danny eventually broke his silence, and very calmly said, "Yes please. How about a large brandy for my friend, Mr Anderson and lemonade for me, please, Oh, and get one for yourself and the lovely barmaid over there."

Giles was smiling now, almost smirking, it made Danny think, "And I'm going to enjoy killing you Anderson," while also thinking what a smug bastard he was.

Danny just smiled back and the landlord toddled off to get the drinks while Danny got out his wallet and continued the conversation.

"Mr Anderson," he started.

"Giles, please call me Giles after all it seems like we are going to be doing some business, son, unless I'm very much mistaken".

"Fair enough, Giles it is then," said Danny, he had gotten a lot more serious now and the usually confident and cocky Giles Anderson was looking into the eyes of a completely different person. It unnerved him a little, but he couldn't quite put his finger on it afterwards.

"The truth of the matter," continued Danny, "is your costs are high and over the top compared to other factories and leave me with very little profit, I also think you are taking advantage of my position."

Giles squirmed a little and thought that perhaps he had been a little greedy.

"However," continued Danny before Anderson could respond, "It's my own stupid fault that I'm in this predicament. I have bitten off more than I can chew and realise that I have no choice, but to learn the hard way as it were. I don't particularly like being on the spot like this but hopefully once we have the initial items of concern out of the way we can renegotiate the additional orders to our mutual benefit moving forward".

Giles sat back in his chair and took a swig of the newly arrived brandy.

"Young man, I'm a Yorkshireman you may have noticed and I'll tell you something. I like your candid response. Straight talking is the way it should be, and yes, this deal is going to cost you more than you thought but consider it a vital lesson in business.

Don't ever promise anything you can't deliver and certainly don't sign contracts until you're sure you can deliver what you say you can," he said rather smugly. Danny wanted to tear his face off there and then!

Instead, he just smiled and looked at the condescending prick opposite him. Giles got that feeling again just looking at Danny, but shrugged it off. The money he was going to make from this deal was overriding any sense he may have had.

Giles outlined the deal and demanded five thousand pound in cash as a sweetener.

Danny agreed, but told him that he would have to get the money from his safe in Dagenham and it would have to be tomorrow now, as this was unexpected.

"No problem," said the senior man, "you understand that this is a "drink" for setting this up and would need to be discreet. The rest of the deal we can discuss in my office and make arrangements for a legal payment process.

Meet me at my factory at 6pm tomorrow evening. Everyone will be long gone by then and I can show you the setup we have.

Use the rear entrance, I don't want any nosey parkers knowing my business, how does that sound"?

Perfect, just perfect thought Danny but simply said, "See you at six.."

"Excellent!" said Giles. "Six tomorrow evening, it is! Don't be late! I have plans for the rest of the evening."

I'm sure you have, thought Danny, but I don't think you understand how the evening's going to end you pompous old prick, do you?

Inside his head Danny was playing the scenario, frame by frame, step by step just like a taped recording where you can pause for a moment and savour the moment. Subconsciously, he had licked his lips and was lost for a short time in that moment. His eyes had gone dark and he had this skewed smile on his face that made Giles a little nervous. Just after six the following day, Giles would come to realise what that look meant and seriously regret not trusting his instincts.

He continued nonetheless, the lure of making a quick buck out of this greenhorn had removed any barriers that the protective part of his brain was screaming at him and repeated his earlier instructions,

"To get to the factory, just come up from here along the A22 then turn left towards Uckfield, and then turn right into the Bell Lane industrial park just after the fire station. We are up at the very end next to the scaffold yard you can't miss us, there's a pathway to the right of my building that takes you directly to my offices at the rear. Come that way and rap on the door, I'll be there and don't forget the money."

"I won't," said Danny effusively, all the while thinking but you won't get a chance to spend a penny of it! Danny smiled that crooked smile and left Giles there

His plan was now developed, he knew exactly how he was going to do this but he needed to refine it a little. One thing that concerned him was the old man's car. He was sure that's how he would get to the factory but the plan inside Danny's twisted mind left no trace of Mr Anderson and the car would be an obvious starting point for the inevitable investigation that would follow. He couldn't just leave it there after the job was done. He would have to dispose of it, and he knew just the place and the people who could

210

help him with that. He drove back to Grinstead, gathered his belongings from his room, walked out of the hotel without checking out or looking back and immediately drove to London.

Danny met with his uncles at their flat and told them "almost" everything.

"So, it's tomorrow then is it, son?" said his Uncle Jimmy. "Just make sure you have all your eggs in a basket. The last thing you want is to leave any clues for the filth! Just get the job done, get the car back here and disappear for a few months. As we've discussed our villa in Spain will give you the sanctuary and privacy you need for as long as you want, I reckon four or five months and the case will have gone cold!"

Harry joined in, "Get the car to Jimmy Sullivan's yard straight away. We will let him know you're coming tomorrow night. He will wait until you get there Just flash your lights when coming up the drive and he will open the gates, and don't worry, Jimmy's under strict instructions that there must be no trace of the motor! He won't be able to work on it until Saturday morning, though, when the yard can officially open and start noisy works. However, he will tell the boys not to come in on Saturday, he and his son will get rid of it personally. He's done this sort of thing for us in the past and knows the ropes!" Opening the drawer directly in front of him, Jimmy took out a huge wad of cash and counted out the five grand Danny had asked for and put it in an envelope. "Your new passport is in there and the remainder of your fee will be with Pedro when you get to Spain. Get yourself off to Heathrow early morning on Saturday. The flight will be booked for 10.00am to Malaga. My agent on the high road will have the tickets ready by tomorrow afternoon and I will get them to Jimmy. I'll make a call later to Pedro who looks after our interests over there; he will meet you when you land. You can't miss him; he's a great big fat fuck with a moustache almost as big as his face!"

The brothers burst out laughing; Danny didn't get the humour but laughed along anyway.

Harry continued, "Jimmy Sullivan's scrap yard is just off the Peckham High Road and down a railway arch lane that leads to the rear of a railway goods yard and very secluded. There is only one way in and one way out. The railway goods yard is accessed from the other side of the tracks."

The Parkhurst brothers had used his services on more than one occasion and he was "very reliable".

Jimmy and his "boys" could "strip a tank in under an hour," said Harry," and you would never know it had ever been there.

Danny nodded in that matter of fact way that intimated that he knew the place,

"Good, good," said Harry, "If this goes off as planned, and I've no reason to think it won't, this could be the start of something beautiful and very lucrative son. You wouldn't believe the amount of people who want someone or another "looked after," would you Jimmy?"

The brothers laughed again, Danny just sat there and smiled that crooked smile the brothers had seen before. Privately and even though they had both been involved in serious crime for decades neither of them had come across this level of coldness before, they both shuddered inwardly.

Once Danny had left the two brothers poured themselves a drink and pondered on their nephew,

"He's a cold one all right," said Harry, "I just hope he stays calm, gets the job done and gets away cleanly."

"Don't worry about him," said Jimmy. "There's something about him that tells me he's actually relishing killing this fella and I've no doubt he will do it as he said he would. I mean in the first instance we were just going to have him blow his brains out do you remember?"

"Yes, I do," said Harry, "Danny was the one who said no need, I'll do it my way and came up with his own method. I remember being quite taken aback with that don't you, Jimmy?"

"Yes, I remember the conversation well my son, I had a bout of the shudders if I recall!" he continued ."I knew, when we met him in Maidstone that first time that he was up to this kind of work and even more so now! I think we can safely say we have found the perfect replacement for our dear incarcerated friend. I mean, what he's going to do to this Anderson fella is pretty sick even by our standards, but you also have to say quite clever," he continued, "and Tommy is delighted that's the most important thing. The story he told us about his mother, her descent into alcoholism and her ultimate death makes you understand the man's complete and utter hatred of this fella, and his desire to erase him from the planet in the most painful way imaginable doesn't it?" He chuckled at this and that set Harry off.

They both poured another drink and sat there laughing,

"Don't forget the fifty grand Tommy has paid us!" said Jimmy, that set them off again. An outsider looking in would have thought it's just two fellas having a laugh about some random trip down memory lane or something and not the fact that they had just discussed a brutal killing that was about to be conducted by their own nephew.

Danny went back to his flat, packed his rucksack in preparation for tomorrow, lay on the bed and soon fell asleep. Sometime later the nightmare started. The dream this time was of an old man who looked very much like his father, not that he knew him that well but in the dream he knew it was him. He was screaming at Danny, "It's your entire fault, you little bastard! I'm going to kill you!" while lunging towards him fists clenched and ready to strike out when he got near enough. Strangely, he was talking in a northern accent and was changing in appearance.

One second it was Ronnie, his father, the next it was the old tramp from the derelict house and right now it was Giles Anderson!

Danny was desperately trying to get away, but as in all his dreams there was no obvious way out. Every turn led to a dead end and Danny was terrified. He knew that if this man, whoever it was, caught up with him he wouldn't stand a chance! In the dream he was only a boy of eight or nine and no match for a man of this size! He could smell petrol in the dream and soon realised that the smell was coming from the thing looming towards him. On closer inspection the monster striding menacingly towards him was dripping in what was obviously the source of it. His hair was matted with drops of the liquid running down his face. His white shirt opened to the top of his chest was soaked in the pungent liquid and was running down towards his trousers. It seemed like he had just got out a petrol bath fully clothed. His eyes were glazed over but piercingly blue and staring straight at him. Danny had his back to the wall and was desperately looking for an escape from this madman! It seemed that any minute this creature would be upon him and would consume him.

Suddenly, looking down he saw had a match in his hand, in one quick movement he had lit the match and had thrown it towards the oncoming assailant. Instantly setting him ablaze, he turned into a fireball and almost immediately combusted and disappeared leaving nothing but a charred circle directly in front of him.

Danny screamed and sat up in the bed. He was wide awake immediately, sweating profusely and breathing heavily. He could still taste and smell the fumes and burnt flesh from the dream.

Dreams are strange. Thought Danny, It took him some time to get back to sleep.

The following morning Danny pondered on the dream.

What did it mean? If anything, as with all of his dreams it took him some time to realise that it was just a nightmare and meant nothing, He has had loads of these nightmares over the years and recognised that this was just an overspill of things that had happened in the past, but he found this particular one much more difficult to shrug off, it was almost like a sense of doom or foreboding.

Danny just put it down to "pre-fight nerves" went and had a shower, got dressed and went out for breakfast. There was a nice little café on the corner who did the best fry up around. When he was done he went to the local post office and bought a large envelope and two first class stamps. He would need these items when he returned.

When he returned home, he put on the telly and called for a taxi to take him to London Bridge train station.

No later than 1.00pm he had told the controller. She knew Danny and confirmed the time, she immediately informed one of her drivers and told them who it was for.

"Don't be late!" she had told him.

" I definitely won't," said the nervous respondent, the place was owned and controlled by the twins. Everyone who worked there knew the boys and their nephew. No one wanted to upset either one of them, it never ended well if you did. Danny's taxi was early and got him to London Bridge before 1.30pm.

He bought a coffee and a newspaper and boarded the 2.10pm train from London to East Sussex with plenty of time to spare.

Uckfield station was the end of the line and went no further thanks to the closure of the extended line to the town of Lewes sometime in the late sixties.

It was only a two hour or so journey but he definitely did not want to be late and arrived in the small town carrying his rucksack around 4.15pm

The next train from London was at 3.10 and would have been cutting it fine; no need to stress yourself out thought Danny and got the earlier one. He hated using public transport but in this case it was a necessity, no one paid him a second look.

Coming out of the station and turning immediately right, he started walking up the High Street, it was pretty busy and suited him down to the ground. The more people the better. Besides, they were all just going about their business. The town was expanding mostly due to an influx of Londoners who wanted out of the metropolis and all the crap that went with it.

Danny just blended in. He had an hour or so to kill and walked past the turning that led to Bell Drive and continued up the High Street looking like any other person just out doing a bit of shopping

Looking across the road at the shop with the big red and white sign, he suddenly had a hankering for something sweet and casually strolled into the local Woolworths on the High Street.

He bought a bag of pick and mix; lemon sherbets were his favourite and made up most of the bag. They made him think of his mother who used to get them on payday from Mr Singh's across the road from Durham Buildings.

He doesn't remember much about those days or even the events that took place that fateful night, although the constant nightmares would remind him that something terrible had happened but never quite getting to the nitty gritty of it. Something to be thankful for he thought, by now of course he knew exactly what had happened but thankfully he supposed, he remembers no details.

However, he does remember his mother, Auntie Silvia and of course Corey. He often wondered how they were doing and thought he might pay them a visit when he comes back from Spain?

Probably not a good idea, "let sleeping dogs lie" his mother used to say, she was right of course. No good could ever come of it.

Danny was a totally different person now anyway, and him turning up out of the blue would just stir up memories that were best left as just that, memories.

In that moment Danny felt a twinge he hadn't felt for some time, sadness he supposed it was. A brief look back into his life, and the thought that things could have been so different if those events back in 1972 had not happened.

His mother was a good woman who always provided the love and care any little person could need. Danny adored her, she would always tell him how handsome and clever he was while stroking his hair and kissing him all over his little face. He could still smell the stale tobacco on her lips in that moment and the way she used to wash his dirty face with a hanky that had been spat on by her! Disgusting but Danny smiled at the sweet memory, anyway.

Now here he was fifty or so miles from London about to kill a man for money! He was quite mad but a functioning madman if there was such a thing, Psychologists would probably put him down as a functioning sociopath or psychopath.

Danny just liked to think of himself as an avenger who wanted to kill bad people, in his own logic these kinds of people had put themselves in this position and made themselves targets. If they didn't hurt people they would not be hurt, simple as that really.

Ever since his time in jail and the meeting with Tommy and his uncles, he knew what he wanted to do. He now had the resource and knowledge and not just blindly hurting people for little or no reward and as a consequence doing hard time in prison where you were just a number.

Danny wanted to continue this path and still have the freedom, his path was set, no going back now.

The time flew and when he looked at his watch it was 5.40, the High Street was very busy now and he started the ten or fifteen minute walk down the street to Bell Lane, turning right at the bottom of the High Street and walking straight past the fire station.

He crossed the road into Bell Lane and made the short walk to the factory.

Dozens of people were walking past. All seemingly finished their shifts for the day and were heading home, with some going straight to the pub, he thought.

Most of the units leading to the factory were closed with the odd one still locking up for the weekend. The further up the lane he got, the quieter it became. The main hub of this industrial estate was nearer the front across the road from the fire station and the big Tesco's that had popped up in recent years, with the big factories and workshops towards the rear. He already knew his destination of course was the last unit on the estate.

Danny kept his head down, tucked his hands in his pockets and carried on until he was only a hundred or so yards from the main gate of the works. He could very clearly see that the factory was closed as was the scaffold yard next door.

The turning circle was empty not a vehicle in sight. He was worried now; perhaps Anderson had changed his mind. Maybe something had happened, and he couldn't make it? Had someone already dropped him off? Were they with him?

It was 17.55pm and Danny was letting his imagination run away with him. He continued on anyway, got to the entrance and walked up the right-hand path towards the rear of the building and positioned himself by the bin store just out of sight from the pathway. He unwrapped a lemon sherbet and popped it in his mouth.

The rear of the building was surrounded by trees and no one from the main road that run past the estate could see in. He could see the office windows and staff entrance door from where he was. The glass was opaque and he could clearly see that no lights were on, it was deserted.

Suddenly, and just when he thought Giles had bailed on him, he heard footsteps coming down the rear path that led to the main road. This threw Danny a little bit as it seemed Giles had been dropped off. That meant someone else knew he was meeting him, perhaps a change of plan was needed he thought quickly but to what? Danny's mind was working overtime by the time Giles arrived at the bottom of the path.

"Glad to see you son!" boomed the confident Giles, "and even more glad to see you are bang on time, lad, I like that. I have left the car over the road, lad. If the missus knew I was here she would think I'm up to something," he chuckled "and we can't have that can we son?"

"No, I suppose not," said Danny.

"Come in, come in," said Giles when finally getting the door open.

Straight away a sharp beeping noise could be heard. Giles immediately entered with Danny hard on his heels and went over to a wall panel that housed the factory alarm system.

I hadn't thought of an alarm! Danny immediately thought, I'll have to deal with that on the way out.

Danny watched closely as the older man disabled the alarm. It looks simple enough he thought but without the code he couldn't reset it. Things were changing right before his eyes; he hadn't put enough thought into this had he?

It didn't really change a lot though as in Danny's mind he was still going to kill him, but he would have to rethink his exit strategy, but that's for after the event he thought to himself.

Leading him into a well presented and modern office, Giles sat behind his leather bound desk with an equally beautiful leather bound chair and beckoned Danny to sit in the chair facing him.

"Have you brought my envelope?" Giles said without any further ado, "I'm not a man for small talk, lad. This is strictly business and I don't have a lot of time, I'm meeting someone later this evening if you know what I mean," he said with a wink that made Danny feel physically sick.

What type of woman would lay down with this fat and old prick?! he thought.

Danny said nothing and sat down, rummaging through his rucksack found what he wanted and handed the smirking Giles a stuffed envelope containing the five thousand pound previously agreed.

This was something he had considered. He needed to get the wary Mr Anderson to be confident and relaxed, it was working. Giles blatantly counted every penny in front of Danny, stuffed it back into the envelope and put it in his top drawer locking it straight away and putting the key back in his trouser pocket.

"Now, young fellow" he said getting up, "We have less than an hour or thereabouts to kill. The first thing I want to do is show you my factory before we lose the natural light that shines through the glass roof and windows. Afterwards, we can discuss the finer points of attending to your needs and the costs involved here in my office. I must tell you, however, that the customer I was telling you about during our first meeting is threatening to sue me if I don't get his order out in time but don't worry," he went on, "I have negotiated a deal with him by way of compensation. Unfortunately, this money will have to be met by you, do you understand"?

Danny understood all right, if this was a legitimate deal he would be shafted to the point of bankruptcy by this greedy profiteering and blood sucking leach.

"Yes, I understand," said Danny with a sorrowful look.

Giles got up and walked towards the door, Danny also got up and proceeded in following Giles out onto the shop floor.

Giles was pleased with himself, he was going to take this boy to the cleaners and rightly so. He's the one who put himself in this position by biting off more than he could chew! Serves him right!

Walking slightly ahead of Danny, he started his tour.

"As you can see, son, my factory is huge; over to the left there you can see our stockpile of finished material, neatly packaged of course and waiting to go out next week. Just a bit past that, you will see our external storage yard. Covered from the elements of course! That's where we keep orders to bring in for metal work fabrication and galvanization. Your items will be stored there before we undertake the galvanisation procedure," he continued.

Danny thought Giles liked the sound of his own voice and was imagining putting an end to his droning and annoying voice. Giles continued "Although we pride ourselves on the supply and fabrication of all kinds of metal products to companies all around England the real money is in the galvanization process," he bragged.

"See those tanks over the on the right?",

There were three of them, varying in size with the smallest being around six foot long by two foot wide and the largest one looked like a medium sized swimming pool. In fact, it was twenty five feet long by ten foot. Directly above these tanks were steel cages enclosed with steel mesh and hanging in the air by chains that in turn were connected to a control box for lowering and raising the cages into the baths. All supported by a huge steel beam with runners that moved the cages along when the process was underway. Right at the end were the acid baths used for cleaning the excess off of the finished product.

Beyond that was a lay down area for drying before packaging.

"That's where the money is, lad! The medium sized bath over there is where your goods will go at ninety pounds an hour, whereas the biggest tank at the end will cost two hundred pounds an hour add in the zinc costs of course and you can see it's a pretty lucrative business. The only down side being the constant temperature that we have to keep the baths on., Did you know these baths heat up to around 850 degrees and have to be on constantly? Even over the weekend as the zinc cannot be allowed to cool! It would bugger up the baths!" he exclaimed. "My electric bill is astronomical!" he went on, "do you know how much this set up cost me lad?"

I've no idea thought Danny but I'm sure you're going to tell me, you self-righteous prick!

"Over a hundred grand lad, back in the late sixties! He said before Danny could respond.

"Still, it's all paid for itself fifty times over since then lad, but the bills are still killing me." He moved on, walking down to the smallest tank at the end of the line.

"Even this little tank costs sixty pound an hour and I'll tell you something.... Els.. Those were the last words he ever spoke.

Giles felt strange, he was on his knees. How the hell did I get here? He was thinking, he was groggy but still conscious, but he couldn't focus his eyes. Danny hit him again, this time Giles was out cold.

Giles was slowly coming round, he vaguely remembers falling to his knees and feeling slightly sick but that's it.

Still groggy he could make out wire mesh, but he couldn't move his arms to touch it.

What the hell is going on? Giles tried to speak but was unable. Why can't I speak? For some reason,. His eyes were hurting and he couldn't quite get them focussed. It took him a few minutes to recover and when he did and realised what was happening he screamed into his gag and soiled his trousers.

Danny was waiting patiently sitting in a chair he had found on the shop floor while all of this was going on. The old man had a hard head he thought, he had whacked him on the back of the head with his trusted "leveller", a leather pouch with a lump of lead enclosed within. Lead weapons were more reliable when you only wanted to knock someone out, whereas steel piping could kill someone instantly or tear open the skin and cause a lot of blood, either way, he didn't want that did he? Oh no!, I've got things to do! Danny thought to himself, gleefully.

He had struck him the first time when he couldn't take any more of the old fart's constant chattering and had used this particular method on several occasions over the years

It normally worked instantly, but it needed one more hit with this tough nut though.

"Welcome back to the land of the living, Mr Anderson. You had me worried for a bit there I thought you would never wake up." Danny smiled and in that moment, Giles knew this wasn't going to end well.

He also knew what that look on Danny's face was, and that he had foolishly ignored. It was malicious and spiteful, verging on madness. Giles could feel his bladder leaking, he had never felt smaller, he wanted to say something and talk his way out of whatever this boy was thinking of doing. More importantly, he needed to know why? There was no money in the factory and nothing worth stealing unless you had a huge lorry. Even then, we are only talking about a few hundred pounds in scrap metal. It didn't make sense, but he couldn't speak! He was very aware by now that he was tied, gagged and inside a cage, one of his cages of course... oh God no, not that please God no… he started to weep.

Danny was sitting directly below the caged Giles. He got up and went over to something that was planted on the floor directly in front of Giles and pressed a button. Giles watching from above had to squint his eyes and focus to see what it was, and what he saw horrified him. It was a camcorder and the little red light was now blinking. He tried to scream but nothing came out. He was sweating like a pig and the smell from his trousers was now making him nauseous, not a good thing to happen when you're gagged he thought and suppressed it. He was racking his brain as to why this was happening, he wanted to ask, but he couldn't!

He didn't think the word frightened would do how he was feeling justice. He had literally soiled his underwear, he was petrified.

"Do you know why you're in this position and why I'm here?" Danny finally said.

Giles was furiously shaking his head from side to side indicating that he didn't.

"Well, shall I enlighten you Mr Anderson?" Giles was moving his head equally between yes and no.

He wasn't sure that he wanted to know. I appeared that this boy was intent on hurting him, however, there's always hope I suppose, perhaps there's been a huge mistake and he's got the wrong man?

Giles wasn't stupid though, he knew this lad had done his homework, especially with the way he had made contact and followed it through over several days. No I'm definitely the one he wants thought Giles dejectedly, but why?

"Do you remember a couple of families back in London, Mr Anderson?" Young families that lost their dear husbands and fathers while falling through the roof of your factory, a fall that was preventable wasn't it?.

Only you were too tight to get the roof fixed weren't you? Even then you had every chance to properly compensate these poor people, but no, you decided to cry poverty instead. Using a highly paid lawyer you walked away with a paltry fine all the while laughing at the widowed women and their children Standing outside the court, looking for compassion and compensation for their loss.

One of those ladies was with her young fifteen year old boy. Mr Anderson. His name is Tommy Spillane, does that name ring any bells, Mr Anderson?"

It did, Giles instantly went back in time and could picture the families in his head standing outside the courts, hugging, weeping and comforting each other, while imploring him to do the right thing.

I could have helped them he thought, a few thousand pounds would have been peanuts to me, and I wouldn't now be in this position, if only this boy would let me talk, I would make amends. Giles wasn't stupid, he knew deep down that it wouldn't matter what he said now. This boy was clearly mad and intent on seeing this through, the camcorder was proof of that!.

Giles was openly sobbing now and desperately wanted to take off the gag and offer something to this lad, he would have made any promise at this point, he was furiously shaking his head and trying to utter the words but the gaffer tape covering his mouth just below the nostrils was too tight and he could only get out muffled cries. "Tommy remembers you, Mr Anderson," Danny continued, "It took him quite a while to track you down, over twenty years in fact!, You thought you'd gotten away with it didn't you?"

Giles was shaking his head vigorously from side to side with tears streaming down his face while trying to make eye contact with his gaoler,

"What's that?" said Danny "You're sorry?"

"Mmfph", screamed Giles through the gag, he nodded towards Danny as if to say I am and at this point he meant every word he was trying to get out,.

"I know, I know," said Danny, "and that's all well and good, Mr Anderson, and I'm sure Tommy will appreciate the sentiment but unfortunately for you his dear old mum passed away a few years after that "accident" Mr Anderson, do you know how she died?"

Giles at this point knew the game was up and that he was never going to leave this place alive unless someone came to the rescue, but no one knew he was there did they? He hadn't told a soul, not even his mistress, he wanted to surprise her with cold hard cash when he met her later and he definitely didn't tell his wife.

She was getting fed up with his interference in the business and taking back handers from prospective clients.

She also knew that he had a lover and she also knew that keeping her would cost money. So, Giles never told her or anyone else for that matter about tonight, he moved his head sideways and slowly in complete and utter resignation to indicate that he did not know how she had died.

Danny had now moved below Giles while looking up at his prisoner in the cage, and was removing the steel lid covering the zinc tank directly below his victim.

The blinking red light on the camcorder was still active and indicated that the whole thing was being recorded. Giles started screaming behind the gag but it only came out as muffled sobs.

Danny could hardly hear it anyway as the motor had started to the winch which was slowly lowering the cage with its precious cargo kicking and squirming inside.

230

"Please God, no!" Giles was screaming behind the mask, but Danny couldn't hear him by now as the noise of the motors drowned him out. He had moved behind the recorder and was moving it in line with the descending cage, He paused its movement for a moment using the hanging electrical box inches away from the boiling zinc and said, "She died from organ failure, Mr Anderson, Brought on by years of alcohol abuse, caused by losing her one and only love, George Spillane. You left them and another family in poverty Mr Anderson, and for that Tommy sends his regards."

With that Danny pressed the down button and the cage descended.

As the cage entered the 850-degree boiling zinc solution Danny had moved beside the camera to get a little closer. He wanted to savour the moment. His pupils were dilated and fixed on the descending cage, he had the look of a complete and total maniac on his face.

Anderson's feet were the first things to enter the tank where the liquid metal fizzled and crackled as it accepted the trousered flesh of the screaming participant.

Dancing blue flames jumped out of the tank alongside what looked like molten lava, making Danny take a few steps back, but not far, he wanted to take it all in.

He wished now that he had taken off Anderson's gag and had got to hear him scream rather than the muffled sound that had soon stopped once the molten metal was up to his ankles. The cage was now fully submerged and the tank was bubbling away in protest of this foreign object.

Danny thought, he should wait a while longer but was eager to see what remained.

While waiting, Danny stopped the camcorder, removed the tape and put both back into his rucksack alongside the keys he had extracted from Anderson while the big man was unconscious.

After about fifteen minutes the bath was still making rumbling noises as if to object to what was happening. Danny raised the cage anyway and was disappointed to see that there was still evidence left of the big Yorkshireman. Not much but enough to identify that it was a person. Molten flesh, bone and clothing were hanging through the mesh dripping back into the zinc bath, causing flames and boiling spits of molten metal to fly up in the air, he lowered the cage again.

This time, he left if for half an hour while he went to Anderson's office and got his five grand back from the desk drawer. There was a kettle on the side and a fridge just under the counter. so He made a cup of tea, popped another sweet in his mouth, and then he very calmly sat back in Anderson's chair and reflected on what had just happened.

To Danny it was wonderful! The dancing flames were the highlight for him; it reminded him of the old tramp who had stupidly robbed him all those years ago. Danny's got his spark back! he thought and laughed out loud. The maniacal grin in his face, would have been terrifying for any watching person, anyone witnessing this would have certified Danny immediately.

When he returned to the tank it had stopped bubbling, and was now just humming like all the other tanks.

He raised the cage, it was almost empty, the only thing remaining was what looked like blood staining on the cage So he lowered it again and had a clean-up around the tank and put the chair back, fifteen minutes later Danny raised the tank again, it was empty now but just to make sure nothing was left he simply moved it along the line with the control panel and dipped it in the acid solution at the end of the track for a few minutes before finally placing the cage back into its original position No one would ever know what had just happened here!

The tape was for Tommy, a little gift and surprise bonus as it were and he's not going to show it to anyone is he?

I hope he likes it thought Danny who was still grinning manically; he picked up his rucksack and walked away.

He didn't bother with the alarm. He didn't want to accidentally set it off did he?

He had cleaned up around the tanks as best he could, but he could still smell burning flesh. It was in his nostrils alongside the equally pungent smell of molten metal, he savoured every breath.

It had grown dark outside, but he quickly found Anderson's car in the car park across the road, a very distinctive red Jaguar.

It was risky driving the car from here all the way to London, but he had no choice, in any event it wouldn't be reported missing until at least tomorrow so it was a small risk as long as he drove sensibly and some over eager policeman wasn't lurking around some blind bend trying to catch some poor unsuspecting or speeding motorist out. As it turned out the journey was uneventful, and he had soon dropped the car off with Jimmy back in south London. It was 10.30pm by the time he had finished dropping the car off. He caught a black cab from Peckham highroad and went straight to his pad in Southwark

Once he arrived He took the tape out of his rucksack, put in the video recorder and pressed rewind.

Very shortly after he was watching the horror movie that he had laughingly titled "Boiled Bastard." He sat back in his comfiest chair and admired his handiwork.

Tommy's going to love this he thought, after watching it for the umpteenth time. Danny eventually put it in the jiffy bag he had purchased several days ago alongside two first class stamps and put it in his rucksack, it was addressed to a Mr John Pritchard, 112 Tottenham Court Road, London, an alias and postal address used by his Uncle Jimmy, he would collect it a few days later, Danny would post it from the airport.

Danny had met the substantially moustachioed and rather large Pedro at the airport as planned; he spoke really good English and gave him a running commentary all through the journey along the dirt roads of Malaga. They soon arrived at the substantial and magnificent villa provided by his uncles, less than thirty minutes later. Pedro let him in, gave him a brief tour of the "Hacienda" gave him his telephone number and a set of keys, and promptly left with the comment, "I will see you tomorrow afternoon, Senor Danny."

Danny slumped into the beautiful leather sofa adorning the very large lounge and let out a huge sigh. Life was good .His uncles had delivered his first "real" job, and Danny had executed it, literally and he could not wait for the next one.

He needn't have worried though; it would not be long in coming. Malaga was full of ex pats and criminals, there would be work here he thought.

It was huge, Danny had never seen anything like it, he thought it was going to be a pokey little place with a small swimming pool and views of the beach.

Only this villa was further inland and about two miles from any beach, at least that's what had formed in his head while on the flight.

He wasn't prepared for this! There were six bedrooms four with en-suite bathrooms The master bedroom, which Danny had already decided would be his room, had a TV and a bedside phone sitting on a marble side table, with a patio directly outside the room accessed through triple sliding doors and furnished with sun loungers and a marble coffee table.

The loungers were facing outwards towards the sun that was just beginning to set and the view was incredible.

He walked outside, to his left was an orchard that was clearly fruiting oranges and to his right was an equally impressive swimming pool that wouldn't have been out of place at the Olympics. This, too was adorned with sun loungers separated by magnificent palm trees.

To the rear of the property was what looked like a vineyard.

This was Danny's first ever trip abroad and he could never have imagined that it would be like this.

He went back in and found the kitchen. Like the rest of the place it was outstanding. It had a five burner gas cooker hob with built in and stacked ovens, a massive double fridge/freezer with built in water dispenser and ice maker.

In the fridge were dozens of cans of Pepsi alongside a similar amount of bottled water. To the right of the cooker was a double cabinet that appeared to have every bottle of spirits ever made!

The kitchen island was thirty millimetre thick Carrera marble surrounded by six leather bound foot stools and the floor was laid using huge porcelain slabs that were cool underfoot.

Danny found this out the following morning when he woke up dripping with sweat after yet another nightmare to get a glass of water.

"Don't drink the tap water unless it's boiled," he heard his Uncle Harry say in his head; "Pedro always keeps the bottled water in the fridge, oh and make your own ice with the bottled water and don't trust the fridge dispenser either. There've been a couple of "unfortunate" accidents hasn't there Jimmy".

Danny remembered and helped himself to a sealed bottle of spring water from the fridge and went out onto the veranda. It was already scorching hot at 7am and he wondered what he should do.

He was already feeling a bit lonely and isolated, it had only been a day but he wasn't a patient man and needed excitement! He did wonder how he would kill at least three months stuck here on his own! Still, it could be worse he chuckled and settled down on one of the sun loungers to watch the world go by.

Pedro turned up later that afternoon. Danny soon learned that you would never see him before 2pm local time, it was just their way.

"Come, Senor Danny. I'm going to drive you into town. Your Uncle Jimmy has asked me to show you the sights of Malaga.

It is a beautiful place and I am happy to escort you around anytime you want, starting today if you wish?"

Why not? Thought Danny. It would be his first visit to a foreign town and he was as excited as a six year old!

"Come on then, let's go!" he said a little more childishly than he would have wanted.

Pedro was delighted and giving his most benevolent smile, beckoned Danny to follow him.

Pedro showed him the sights all right.

He started with the Picasso Museum. Danny had never seen such beautiful paintings and sculptures.

"There must be hundreds of them!" exclaimed the excited and enchanted Danny.

"Over two hundred individual items I believe, senor," stated Pedro. "Do you know he was born here in this very town over a hundred years ago?"

Danny didn't but wanted to know more.

Pedro continued, "It is said that Picasso was a founder member of the cubism style."

"What's that?" asked Danny.

Pedro replied almost instantly as he enjoyed imparting information about Malaga's most prestigious son.

"It's a form of work where the artist takes an object or a person to paint and reformulates it into an abstract form a bit like that one," he said pointing at a portrait named *"The Weeping Woman"* hanging behind a glass protective shield.

Danny was dumbstruck; he had never seen anything so beautiful in his life and strangely started crying quietly, gentle tears bathing his face.

Pedro took him by the shoulders very gently and led him out of the museum.

"I don't know what came over me! I'm sorry," Danny said.

Pedro didn't understand it either but simply said, "No need for apologies. Beauty sometimes has a way of stirring deep emotions inside a person, my young friend. Perhaps you have lost or are missing someone that you considered beautiful?"

He wasn't far off thought the now under control Danny, but he doesn't need to know my past.

"It's all good now, Pedro. Don't worry about it. Where shall we go next?" he asked excitedly.

Pedro was a man of the world and moved in circles that Danny hadn't yet experienced. He knew better than to probe. He also knew what Danny was and he wasn't about to make the mistake of digging.

"That's good, Senor Danny. Shall we go to the city port? I know an excellent little restaurant down there by the sea that serves the most succulent seafood platters, are you hungry?"

Danny was and said, "Let's go, Pedro!" he laughed at that and so did Pedro, even though he had heard it at least a thousand times!

Some things never changed Pedro thought darkly. Bloody foreigners!

The restaurant was everything Pedro had said it was and Danny was the happiest he'd ever been.

They finished the day just walking around the famous port town before making the short drive back to the villa.

It was the worst part of the day for Danny, he would need to go back to the museum on his own and see what had unsettled him. He had an idea but to just start crying like that had unnerved even him.

He wanted to make sure what it was that had induced such emotion.

Pedro drooped him off and reminded him to call his uncles that evening.

"They said call them at 7.00pm but I didn't ask if they meant Malaga time or London time"

"What do you mean"? Enquired Danny.

"Malaga is one hour ahead of British time, senor, but being only an hour I doubt if it makes much difference? Do you need anything else, Senor Danny? There's plenty of food and drink in the fridge but if you need anything else just let me know".

"It's all good, Pedro," he replied, "see you tomorrow and thanks for today, it was really great."

"Buena's noches, senor. Hasta manana, see you tomorrow," said Pedro with a small wink before driving away.

It was nearly 7.00pm now, According to the clock on the kitchen wall. He made himself a drink from the extensive bar in the kitchen and made his way to the lounge where there was a further telephone.

He dialled the number and waited. A few short rings later his Uncle Harry's unmistakeable voice was booming down the line.

"Danny, my boy, How are you settling in to our humble, little shack? And why are you calling me an hour early? It's only six o'clock here, I'm sure I told that fat prick, Pedro, 7.00pm?" He was laughing so Danny knew it was just his uncle being stupid and having a laugh.

"It's fantastic here, Uncle Harry! Why do you and Uncle Jimmy want to stay in boring old London when you have a place like this is beyond me."

"You'll soon realise why, son, give it two weeks at the most and I guarantee you'll be begging to come home," Harry said laughing. "It's all sun, sea and sangria for the first timers, but even the most die-hard sun worshippers and Pina colada sippers want to come home after a while, you mark my words, Danny. Anyway," he said with a more serious tone, "lets' get down to business, did you post that envelope from the airport and did Pedro give you our envelope when you arrived"?

"Yes to both, Uncle Harry".

Danny didn't like his uncle referring to Pedro as "the fat prick" as he seemed like a nice fella.

"The parcel was posted when I got to the airport. Pedro met me like you said he would and handed me the envelope almost immediately when I met him. He has looked after me brilliantly since I got here! He even took me into town earlier. We went to the Picasso museum and had lunch by the port. It was fantastic," he sounded like a child and he knew it but he had never been treated like this before and wanted to let his uncle know.

"That's good, son, very good but don't forget why you're there. We will keep an eye on things over here and let you know if there is any development. If you did what you said you were going to do, I can't see an issue; you should be able to come back within a few months tops."

Danny didn't like the tone of his uncle's words, and said very quietly and darkly,

"I did everything I said I would, Harry," he said quietly, deliberately missing out the uncle part. "When you get the tape you will understand," then promptly hung up the phone before his uncle could respond.

"Bloody hell!" said Harry. "That boy of ours has some serious issues. I merely said if you did what you said you were going to do, for fucks sake!"

"He's sensitive," said Jimmy, "I told you I should take the call! You are too accusatory, sometimes. The boy needs kid gloves. I'll call him back tomorrow and put his mind at ease."

Harry wasn't happy and Jimmy being his twin knew this straight away.

"Don't worry, Harry," said Jimmy. "If the kid gets too leery, I'll do him myself!"

With that, they both laughed which broke the tension and went back to watching the telly.

By 1989 the progression and development of DNA profiling had improved so dramatically that literally thousands of criminals were getting "their collars felt". Cold cases were reopened and specialist teams of detectives attached to various crime squads were sieving through them meticulously and making almost daily arrests with the new evidence provided.

This mostly had an impact on lower levels of criminality but had also caused the more serious villain to consider their past "indiscretions", had they left something behind that the police could use to come at them? Had they been careless? Wearing gloves on a job was one thing but leaving trace elements like hair and fibres was another. These policemen were determined and in some cases delighted, that they had this new found resource and could finally pin something on their much sought after quarry. Some of the big boys were extremely paranoid and were considering their options.

Those villains who had the resource thought the best plan of action was to "disappear" for a while and the favoured destination of this time was the Costa Del Sol in the region of Andalusia on the mainland of Spain. Better known to most as the "Costa Del Crime" it had been and still is to some extent a safe haven for criminals from all over the world.

This was mostly due to the non-existent extradition laws and gave criminals a place to recharge their batteries as it were and consider their options. This changed somewhat in later years, for more serious crimes committed in the perpetrators home countries and more and more villains were sent back to their country of origin to face justice. However, at the present time of 1989, it was still extremely difficult for the United Kingdom and other countries to get their quarries back to answer for their crimes and the criminals knew it.

Not only that, the authorities and those in powerful positions amongst the Spanish hierarchy in the region welcomed the influx of cold hard cash that was flowing into the ever-growing towns and local amenities. At the time, it was felt that it wasn't in their interests to comply or agree to any extraditions requests.

This meant that the place was buzzing with criminal gangs from all over the world, including Mafioso from Italy and the United States. Although there were fewer in number, there were Albanian mobsters and the great British criminal who felt relatively safe and secure in their newly found paradise. The only downside to this seemingly idyllic life choice was security.

The Spanish authorities basically left them to fend for themselves and rival gangs would often attack each other with no warning. Vicious beatings, stabbings, shootings and even murders were committed almost every day and the chief of the Malaga police had directed his officers that as long as this was between themselves and that no "civilians" were involved, they should turn a blind eye and let them get on with it, in addition to this the average police officer at this time was only taking home about 30.000 pesetas a week, the equivalent to around £250 English pounds and corruption was rife, it was better to let them police themselves.

Danny had spent the last few weeks just walking around the province. He was fascinated by the culture and the many different nationalities that were living here. His un-travelled mind had not considered that there would be so many different people from all parts of the world living here as in his mind it was purely Spanish with girls dancing around in Flamenco dresses and the men playing maracas and fighting bulls while wearing silk shirts and silly hats, at least that's what the TV had shown him! How wrong he was. He was amazed as although he was a Londoner, he had never experienced anything like this in his short life and he wanted to be a part of it. His uncles were certainly living up to their promises and at this moment in time he would do anything for them. He never wanted this feeling to end.

Danny was taking a short afternoon nap as had become the norm for him these, past few weeks and was sleeping soundly and dreamlessly. Strange, but the nightmares had all but disappeared and Danny had never slept so well in his life, The midday sun was too much and like everybody else he knew in the area had taken a much needed siesta to escape its rays and the inevitable day sweats it gave you, when he was suddenly awoken by the bedside phone ringing. It was his Uncle Jimmy.

"We have a job for you, son."

Immediately awake, Danny listened intently to what his uncle had to say.

"Pedro will be over to you in a few hours with all the details. We need you to act on this as a matter of high importance Danny, do you understand?"

"Yes, I do, uncle! Anything you need, he replied,

" Good lad, Danny. Just take instructions from Pedro. He will give you all the resources you need to get this done. Listen to him, son. He knows the target better than anyone. He might be a fat prick but don't mistake that for stupidity. He's been around the block and has looked after our interests over there for years and knows what he is doing".

"OK," said Danny, "but why do you keep calling him that? He's a nice bloke and I don't like it! Yes, he's a little overweight, so what? He's been very good to me these past few weeks and I like him."

"All right son! If it makes you happy I will stop calling him a fat prick, happy now?"

Jimmy was looking at his brother sitting right next to him and throwing his eyes up to the sky. He put his hand over the mouthpiece and whispered to Harry.

"Told you he's a sensitive little fucker, didn't I?"

Harry just nodded in that I told you so manner that he had and went back to reading his paper.

"Yes, I'm happy uncle. I'll wait here for Pedro to come over and fill me in with all the details", said Danny in a much happier frame of mind.

With that, Jimmy put the phone down without so much as a goodbye and that was that.

They had already given their man Pedro the "job" through a secure line and would leave the method of the undertaking for him to work out with Danny.

Around 6.00pm, the rather rotund Pedro came to the villa. They both sat on the outside patio where he told Danny all about the job, who the target was, where he was and what he was to do immediately after it was completed. He handed Danny a .22 calibre Beretta pistol with silencer.

Danny gave it the once over and checked the magazine, it was full.

"I will be waiting for you across the road at the bottom of the Hacienda on a scooter. Don't mess about! This is a very dangerous man and would not think twice about killing you if you give him a chance. Just get in and get out. When you've done it, just walk down the drive as if you had visited and he wasn't home. Hop over the fence on the other side of the road where I'll be waiting. Jump on the scooter and we will leave via the dirt road that leads to the main road, we will come back here, pick up your things and I'll drive you to the airport in the car. Comprende?".

Danny had never seen Pedro in this way before and was looking at him with a new found respect. Pedro had gone "dark" and had a look about him that was unnerving. He had seen this look in his uncle's eyes and other dangerous men when they were discussing something serious.

"Yes, I understand," he finally said equally seriously, although he was thinking to himself "How the fuck are both of us going to fit on a scooter?" but said nothing further.

The following morning Pedro pulled into the drive of Danny's bolt hole riding a Vespa! The first thing that went through Danny's mind was how the fuck can that little thing carry the two of us?

Pedro must have read his mind.

"Don't worry mi amigo! This little motorcycle can manage us both."

Danny felt a little guilty at the thought of Pedro reading his mind but said nothing. He just hopped on and away they went. Fifteen minutes later and after a rather bumpy ride through dirt roads and off the beaten tracks they were in the north Malaga hills, adorned by beautiful countryside with the occasional villa scattered along the hillsides.

They arrived at the bottom of a rather splendid looking driveway that led up to a sumptuous looking hacienda with its low-pitched roof and red clay tiles with a grandiose arch entrance. Danny got off the bike and Pedro rode away. Walking up the drive in his light blue tracksuit, dark sunglasses and baseball cap, Danny looked just like any one of the locals who frequented the Malaga pubs and bars that had "infested" this once glorious farmland.

Pedro had told him that his quarry was married and it was usually just them in the house at this time of the day. They were having some renovations done and the labourers would not arrive until just after ten am.

Only he and his wife would be there. She was in fact the sister of a serious player back in England and if possible she should be left alive. It was him and him alone that needed to pay the reaper..

Danny understood, he hadn't killed a woman before and didn't want to start now. He would "do his best" he had told Pedro.

When he reached the entrance a pretty good-looking woman for her age stepped out to meet him.

"What can I do for you young man, unfortunately we are not hiring at the moment," she said while smiling at him.

"Oh, that's ok, Missus. That's not why I'm here. I have a message for Freddie that I've been told to give him directly and in person," he said while attempting his best smile.

"Who's the message from young man?"

Danny was expecting this as Pedro had told him the best way to approach it.

"It's from your brother, Roy, Mrs Wilson," he said matter of factly.

"Oh, my Roy, That's good, how is he?"

Danny just shrugged his shoulders.

"Oh! Never mind," she continued. "Freddie's having a swim right now, just follow the path up there," she said pointing to the side of the house.

"Would you like a drink? I usually make him one about this time of the morning".

"No thanks, Mrs Wilson I have to get back to work in an hour, I won't be long, but thank you anyway," he said while starting the journey towards the rear of the house,

"Just give me a shout if you need anything," she shouted after him. "By the way, what's your name?" she said while walking back inside.

Danny wasn't really listening and never responded he just had his head down and was halfway up the path. She just thought he hadn't heard her and went back into the house.

Freddie Wilson was somewhat of a celebrity in and around Malaga. He was known to everybody that was somebody and was friends with some serious players, some of whom were residing in town on the "Lam", as it were. Unfortunately for him he had been a rather naughty and greedy boy and had helped himself to part of a parcel of cocaine that was destined for England. At this time Freddie was running out of money. His usual business back in "blighty" was a middleman for robbery takings that involved gold or jewellery and was too hot to handle. He would take it off their hands and pay a percentage. His usual means of disposal was the Middle East where no one asked questions and cash was king. He was well known to always deliver for his "partners". However, work had dried up these past few years as most of his friends in that world were doing serious time for well-known heists.

Following the Brinks Matt bullion robbery in 1983 the largest heist of its time in England, he had come to Spain. The authorities knew he was a fence big enough to handle that much gold and thought he was somehow involved. They had him under almost constant surveillance from 1984-1986 and no one would touch him with a barge pole now. The money was almost gone and he had to do something to live. He made his last and subsequently fateful error by getting involved with drugs. The money that went with this new enterprise would be the downfall of not only him but many a good (or not so good) man in the years to come.

Danny was approaching the swimming pool. Freddie was just about to get out when he saw the looming shadow of a person in his blurred eye line, looking up at Danny. His last words were "What can I do for you, son?"

Danny just shot him straight in the head without any preamble and put another one in him just for good measure. The pool was almost instantly turned crimson red as Freddie drifted face down and floated away.

Danny just walked back the way he came; He had just reached the bottom of the drive when he heard the hysterical screams of Freddie's wife but didn't look back. He simply hopped over the fence on the other side of the main road, jumped on the back of the Vespa where Pedro was waiting as they had planned. Pedro kicked it into gear and rode away with Danny clinging to the rear bars; back the way they came and avoiding the main roads. They were back in the villa fifteen minutes later. Danny quickly had a shower, changed his clothes and put them in a bag with the gun.

They were on the road in less than ten minutes after that. The police wouldn't be at the Wilson place for at least another hour and by that time Danny would be on a plane. He would be sad to leave this place, but business is business and a little part of him wanted to touch English soil again. His uncles were right, it did get a bit tiresome just sitting around in the hot sun, although he had enjoyed his time here he wanted to feel good old British rain on his face, plus he really wasn't the type to just sit around. He wanted the hustle and bustle of home. The bars and clubs of Malaga were just not the same.

Mrs Anderson had reported her husband missing on the Sunday afternoon. She had gone down to the local police station around 2.00pm, just after lunch and told the desk sergeant that her husband hadn't come home. The bored and disinterested sergeant took down the particulars and informed her that the police would look into it.

"We will send someone round your house to take further information in the next day or so," he said dismissively. "We need to wait for twenty-four hours before we can make proper enquiries, madam. He's not a child, is he?"

Phillipa Anderson was furious but knew this was the protocol and walked back to her car.

The following day a rather green and similarly disinterested police woman called Sandra Bates visited the Anderson family home and asked for further details from Phillipa.

She told the P.C everything she knew, including the fact he was having an affair. The young police woman raised her eyebrows at this and almost yawned. "Perhaps that's where he is?" she said rather awkwardly. "This kind of thing happens all the time you know, maybe he's taken up with her and decided to make the situation permanent?" she said, not unkindly.

Phillipa was having none of it!

"My husband's indiscretions are just that," she said snottily. "My husband couldn't! No! Wouldn't survive without me! Besides, he loves our boys and grandchildren and would never have missed a Sunday lunch with us all! No!, something's happened and I want, no, I demand, that you look into this and find my husband, I know it looks bad what with the other woman and all that but my gut feeling is that something's wrong, and I implore you to take this seriously!!

The young police woman although only in the job for a few months still thought that it was more likely that he was with his lover but as was her duty she began to ask for a few more details.

"Do you know where other party involved lives, Mrs Anderson? I need to pay her a visit just to confirm if he's there or not there, you understand? Does he drive a car? When was the last time you saw him and what was he wearing?",

The questions were coming thick and fast while the young policewoman looked intently at the distraught Mrs Anderson.

Phillipa gave the young woman all the information she had, including the name of Giles' lover, a certain Veronica Jones and her address.

The young policewoman wrote it all down and finally said, "Do you know of anyone that would wish or do your husband any harm, Mrs Anderson?"

"No, I most certainly do not!" she replied. "My husband is a pillar of the community and has only done good works since we relocated to this town."

"How long have you been in Grinstead, Mrs Anderson?"

"Nearly twenty years, young lady," she replied.

"Just one more thing then before I leave, where were you before, if you don't mind telling me?" Sandra enquired.

"I'm not sure what that's got to do with anything, but if you must know we came down from London around 1969, Southwark, in fact."

The young policewoman got up, folded her notebook and told the clearly distraught woman that she would pass this information onto one of the detectives at the station, before she left she added, "Try not to worry so much, Mrs Anderson. I'm sure he's just hiding away somewhere and probably too embarrassed to come home. We usually find people within a few days and they reunite with their families with their tails between their legs."

Phillipa didn't think that was the case, she knew her husband well, "I suppose I have to follow the protocol and see where it leads," she said on seeing the young policewoman out.

Sandra merely nodded, got in her light blue police panda and drove back to East Grinstead police station.

On arrival, Sandra reported to her direct superior, the similarly disinterested desk sergeant who had dispatched her earlier this morning and told him everything she had heard. He merely laughed, "Bloody hell girl! Another bloke who's gone off with his lover and the old woman thinks he's on the missing list? Do you know how many of these I've dealt with over the years?"

Sandra had no idea but said, "Nevertheless, Sarge, we need to hand this over to CID upstairs and let them take it from here."

"A complete waste of police time if you ask me," he added before walking off muttering under his breath. Sandra turned on her heels and walked the short trip to the investigators office on the first floor. She didn't really know the protocol when dealing with detectives and simply stood in the doorway watching two men typing away at their desks.

Eventually, one of them glanced in her direction, got up and came over.

"Can I help you? P.C," he said.

"My name's Detective Inspector Lenny Smith and I'm assuming you want to talk to a detective. Please come and sit with me and tell me what you're working on."

Lenny smith had been with the Sussex constabulary for the past fifteen years, he had previously been with the Met in London under the now Chief Superintendent Peter Thomas but had transferred when his wife got pregnant and wanted to move out of the dangerous metropolis.

"You're very lucky young lady, I'm between jobs at the moment, I've just wrapped up a rather brutal murder case down in Brighton," he added braggingly.

"Now tell me everything about your case."

Your case, thought Sandra. Yes I suppose it is!

She eagerly proceeded to give the well-worn and experienced detective all the details, when she had finished Lenny gave her explicit instructions. He knew who Giles Anderson was immediately and knew all about his connections and standing in the community around here. "The very first thing I want you to do is visit this "other" woman. If, he's there then case closed but if not we need to escalate this to the highest level.

This man and his friend Councillor Tubbs, quite often play golf with the Chief Superintendent and believe me when I tell you young lady, you don't want the shit that will come with a botched investigation! You need to give this your full attention. If you establish that he's not at this other woman's place and you can't locate him anywhere, I will assign a detective to work on this with you. No, sod that!" he said changing his mind rather quickly

"Come on I'll take you there. The Super won't like it if it's simply a case of him hiding out with his lover but if something has happened to him we need to get a head start."

They arrived at "the other woman's" house less than half an hour later, she was in and invited the officers inside and sat them both in the lounge,.

Lenny had already noticed that the distinctive red Jaguar was nowhere to be seen, maybe he's already left? He thought.

He hadn't, Veronica told them both that she was due to see him on the Friday night but he hadn't showed up. She had just thought he had a family issue which had been the case on previous occasions she declared. However, it was strange though that he hadn't called her she added..

"When was the last time you saw him, Veronica, and did he tell you of any concerns he had?" said Lenny, He was nervous now. This was looking a little suspicious, if Mrs Anderson and Veronica were to be believed.

"I last saw him on the Tuesday afternoon for a few hours," she replied. "He had been playing bowls with some friends just down the road, and I'm sure you've noticed I only live a few hundred yards from the club, and no he never mentioned any problems to me. I mean, why would he? I'm only his mistress after all!"

Lenny had noticed the bowls club just on the corner before they turned into Veronica's cul-de-sac.

"Yes, I know the bowls club," he said, "and what time did he leave here, Mrs Jones?"

"It's Miss Jones just for the record, Inspector, I've never married. Veronica stated rather tartly.

"Apologies, madam. I just assumed, please forgive me!"

Lenny had deliberately asked that question as it would establish if there was any Mr Jones to consider. "He left around 6.00pm," she continued, "and told me he would see me on Friday evening around 7.00pm, but like I said, he never turned up."

"Thank you , Miss Jones. Before we leave I have one final question and please excuse my directness but do you have any other lovers or interested parties that would be jealous of your relationship with Mr Anderson?"

"How dare you!" she proclaimed, outraged, "Who do you think I am? I am not a whore!"

"Again, please accept my apologies madam but we have to ask, I meant no malice with it. We are just trying to ascertain the facts."

With that Lenny and Sandra got up.

"Like I said, Miss Jones, I have to ask these questions. If something has happened to Mr Anderson I need to know if there are any suspects. I'm sure you understand."

She did and said "I love him inspector although I'm sure you don't believe that, after all he is married, but I always thought that someday he may leave that awful woman and be with me!" She was crying now and the watching Sandra thought at that point she probably had nothing to do with his disappearance and told Lenny her thoughts when back in the car.

"Don't be so naïve, Sandra!" Lenny had said.

"Keep an open mind, in my experience, it's the ones you least expect who are the most dangerous. If it's worth anything, I too don't believe she has anything to do with Anderson's disappearance, but as with all these things I'll wait until I can discount her with any certainty. Let's get over to Mrs Anderson's before she marches into the station demanding to see the superintendent, I have a few questions she needs to answer."

Sandra drove and made the relatively short distance in fifteen minutes, "He didn't crap far from home did he, sir?" she said pulling into the drive

"No Sandra, I am rather afraid he didn't".

Phillipa had seen them coming up the drive and wasn't impressed. They had sent her the greenhorn girl again in a marked police car, although there seemed to be a gentleman in plain clothes with her. It's something I suppose, but haven't they heard of discretion? They could have used an unmarked car she thought!, "Welcome back, young lady," she said from the porch "And who is this with you?" she asked rather sternly.

"My name is Detective Inspector Leonard Smith of Sussex CID, madam, He explained, showing her his ID badge.

"PC Bates here has informed my department that your husband is missing and this at first glance appears to be an unusual and an out of character disappearance, am I right in assuming that, Mrs Anderson?"

"That's right," she said. Phillipa noticeably relaxed and invited the two officers into her home; she was satisfied now that a senior police officer was taking this seriously. They walked through the impressive hallway, into the rear of the building through the very well-presented reception room and out into the conservatory. The house was adorned with art deco and modern art. It was obvious to both police officers that there were no money issues here, but looks can be deceiving thought the wily Inspector Smith.

He already had Mrs Anderson down as a suspect. He later told the naive P.C Bates that, "It was usually the last person to see them alive and had reported them missing who had something to do with it! Get all your facts together and assume nothing until you have the evidence that either excludes them or otherwise."

Sandra understood and was excited to be working with this senior man. She could learn a lot from him, not like those other "bone heads" at the station!.

"Let me start by asking you when you last saw your husband, Mrs Anderson," said the inspector, "I know you told PC Bates during her previous visit, and I have seen her notes, but I need to hear it again if you please."

Phillipa replied, "I last saw him on Friday around 5.30pm, he told me he had some appointment to keep and probably wouldn't be back until the next day, I knew what that meant of course or at least I thought I did. Am I to assume from this question that he wasn't at "Her" house"? she asked bitterly, all but spitting the words.

"I'm afraid that's right, Mrs Anderson. She hasn't seen him since the previous Tuesday and doesn't know his current whereabouts."

"Are you sure, inspector? Was his car anywhere to be seen? It is very distinctive you know, a brand-new red Jaguar, there's not many of them on the roads at the moment."

I've read PC Bates' notes, madam and know about the car, did he leave here in it?"

"Well of course he did," she almost shrieked, "how else would he have gone?"

"I'm sorry, Mrs Anderson. To you these questions may seem mundane and even a little bit obvious, but we need to know the exact circumstances in order that we get the facts right," he said rather sternly looking straight at her.

"I don't like your attitude, Inspector. Do you know who my husband is? I won't be subjected to an interrogation in my own home! Just do your job and find my husband before I call your superiors and get you replaced!"

She was almost in tears now, and the experienced detective very softly said,

"That's your prerogative, of course Mrs Anderson, but I'm merely trying to get the full facts here and to establish a timeline. I know its uncomfortable and distressing for you, but that's my job. I'm definitely not accusing you of anything; I'm merely asking questions that any detective worth his salt would. You do want me to find him, don't you?"

"Of course, I do," she said while blowing into a hanky provided by the nearby PC Bates.

"I'm sorry for threatening you like that. I know you will do your best but I'm so worried, believe me, when I tell you, something's happened to Giles, I just know it."

"Thank you, Mrs Anderson, we understand your distress and I have just few more things to ask before we leave. Can you give us Giles' movements leading up to Friday, there may be something there we can work with."

She told them all she knew about his regular golf outings and included that Giles had an office at their factory in Uckfield,

"Have you spoken with the factory today Mrs Anderson"?

"Yes, of course I have. I spoke with the foreman, Jim Scroggins, earlier this morning and he told me that no one had seen Giles there since last Wednesday." She suddenly leapt up, "Oh my God!" she said, "He may have gone to the office for one of his dodgy dealings or something and might have collapsed there and be in his office. Jim doesn't have a key or access to it!"

"Don't worry, Mrs Anderson, we will get over there straight away, but what dodgy dealings are you referring to?"

Phillipa gave them a quick rundown of Giles extracurricular activities while searching for her office key, found it almost immediately and gave it to the already on their feet officers who duly left with siren blaring heading for Uckfield.

"Dodgy dealings? PC Bates," said Lenny from the passenger seat. "The plot thickens!" They sped off towards Uckfield.

On arrival they were met by the factory foremen, Jim Scroggins. He had been there from the beginning in 1970, and had served the Andersons without ever taking a day off.

"I open the factory every morning and lock it up at night," he had proudly informed the officers leading the way through the factory floor.

Lenny asked him if he had known about Giles perhaps meeting people here to arrange dealings outside of the "norm".

"Oh yes," said Jim, "I've known about Mr Anderson's under the carpet dealings for some time. Indeed only a few months ago, I came into the factory on a Saturday morning to pick up my lunch box and flask I had left behind, and there he was bold as brass giving some gentleman a tour of the factory, he pulled me to one side, gave me a tenner and said, "Keep this to yourself Jim!"

"I thought nothing of it really. I mean, it's his business and what he does is his own affair. I was just grateful for the tenner as I only came in for my bits!" he laughed. All this was established while walking through the factory; the two police officers had entered through the front and were unaware of the rear entrance.

Lenny took the key given to him by Phillipa and cautiously opened the office door. He had seen dead bodies before when he was a patrol officer in the Met, but he knew the young and inexperienced PC Bates had not.

"Stand back, Sandra," he said, "I'm going in." Stepping through the now open door, Lenny instantly ascertained that there was no Mr Anderson in the room. It was fairly small and anybody in there would have been obvious.

"He's not in here!" he exclaimed and Sandra walked in.

The office was spotless and looked like it hadn't been used for some time, however, on further inspection; Sandra noticed a small piece of paper under the wheel of the sumptuous leather chair and informed Lenny.

"It looks like a receipt, sir. It appears to be from Woolworths for sweets and has Friday's date on it."

"Bag it, Sandra, you never know it may be something but it's clear that our man is not here."

"Well, that's a relief," said Jim "I was worried for a moment."

"Tell me," said Lenny, "when you opened up this morning was there anything unusual or odd that springs to mind?"

"Well, now that you mention it, Inspector, the alarm wasn't set," he said. "I always set the alarm out in the hall by the rear door and leave through that exit. Friday was no exception and it was almost 5.15pm after everyone else had left."

"Anything else?" said the now suspicious policeman. His experienced nose was tingling, even the greenhorn PC Bates was starting to think that something wasn't right about all this.

"No, nothing that springs to mind sir, everything seemed in order. Do you think something's happened to him?" Jim asked quizzically.

"No mate, I can't make that assumption without any hard facts, can I? Besides you could have easily forgotten to turn the alarm off, couldn't you?"

Jim was outraged and told the officer such.

"Not a chance inspector!" he stated rather indignantly. "The alarm is right on the wall beside the door and you have to walk past it, it bleeps constantly once you set it until the door is closed. It's impossible to ignore!, This morning it didn't bleep, and I assumed that Mr Anderson had been here and simply forgot to set it before leaving, although that would be strange as like I said, he's been here before and always set the alarm.

"Show me," said the inspector. Jim did and walked out into the fresh air beyond.

Immediately to the left was the bin stores where the ever alert and observant PC Bates had found something else.

"Sweet wrappers sir, shall I bag them as well?"

"Yes, bag them PC Bates, you never know?"

It was clear to the wily police inspector that someone had been in Anderson's office on the Friday of his disappearance as the date on the receipt would prove, but how are the wrappers connected? He thought they were, to his mind someone had waited by the bins, possibly for Anderson to arrive, and they had gone into his office, but where were they now?

On the way back to the station, Lenny had made a radio transmission for an all points search of Anderson's car. He gave the description, registration and who to look for should the car be found with a driver inside.

He turned to Sandra, "This is not good, Sandra, it appears that Anderson has just disappeared from the face of the earth, if you believe his wife. He could still turn up, of course, laid up in a hotel and telling us it all got too much for him and he needed to get away, but something tells me there's more to it. Get that scrap of paper and the wrappers to the lab boys straight away when we get back. There may be something in it you never know."

A few days later, the lab technicians reported that it was in fact a receipt for "pick and mix" bought at the nearby Woolworths in Uckfield at 4.25pm on the previous Friday and it was impossible to get prints from it. The wrappers were also confirmed as coming from Woolworths and again it was impossible to get prints from them, however, the receipt did appear to have a stain on one corner, and did the inspector want more analysis done, they questioned.

Definitely he had told them. He had heard all about this new DNA technology that law enforcement were now using and thought it may lead to something.

Lenny rang Mrs Anderson almost straight away, when she answered he simply asked her if Giles would eat pick and mix from Woolworths, she laughed.

"No inspector! Not only was he more of a savoury man, his false teeth couldn't cope with anything like that!

Definitely not! I've never known him to even go into a Woolworths!"

Three weeks later the lab boys came back again, they had a profile from the stain but it could take months before they get a match. The database was still in its infancy and even then, if any potential suspect had not had a sample taken there was little hope of matching it to anyone. All they could tell him at this stage from the analysis was that it had shown the blood type left on the receipt was blood type O and one of the more popular ones. in fact it was probably the most common he was informed.

Lenny called Mrs Anderson again,

"Do you know your husband's blood type, Phillipa?"

"Oh my God! Have you found him?" she shrieked down the phone.

He kicked himself mentally, not exactly tactful there were you son?

This poor woman has just spent the last four or five weeks wondering what's happened to her husband and you lead with that!.

"No Phillipa, I'm afraid not," she had insisted that he call her by her first name in recent weeks. "We tested a sample of this new thing called DNA profiling and we can now be certain of the blood type found on the receipt we found in your husband's office, do you know his type?"

"Yes, I do," she said, he's A positive."

"Are you sure, Phillipa?"

"Yes, I am," she said, "Giles had a minor operation under anaesthetic several years ago and there were complications, I remember, it well he needed a few pints of blood, and it was definitely, A positive, I can check with the doctor for confirmation if that helps?"

"Please do," said Lenny, "and come back to me." She confirmed it less than an hour later.

Lenny and Sandra, had retraced all of Anderson's movements in the week leading up to his disappearance and had taken statements from all those known to have seen him or spoken with him during that time. One thing that popped up the most was this young fella who had first been seen talking with Giles at a reception on the Tuesday preceding his disappearance, and was seen again at the golf course on the following Wednesday morning, where he had enquired about a round of golf. The attendant remembered him well as he wasn't a member and found it strange that an individual would just rock up on his own looking for a tee time. He also remembers telling him about the esteemed councillor and his party including the well-known Giles Anderson's involvement, and their intentions for the following day.

Lastly, but more significantly he had been seen at the Red Lion public house on the A22 talking with Mr Anderson about what appeared to be business on the Thursday afternoon.

The esteemed Councillor Tubbs had confirmed the Tuesday evening meeting and vaguely remembered the young man being in the pub on the Thursday afternoon.

The pub landlord and the barmaid had also confirmed his presence on the Thursday and had given very similar descriptions of this mysterious young man.

Six foot plus with dark wavy hair, muscular build with "beautiful hazel eyes" the bar maid had added. All circumstantial Lenny speculated, but he would present his evidence to the chief inspector nonetheless and hopefully start a murder enquiry as he now believed that Giles Anderson was dead.

There was no trace of him anywhere. The car had not been found and more importantly his bank account had not been touched in this time since his disappearance.

Lenny's intention was to form a murder squad to hunt the mysterious stranger down.

If they can identify him they may be able to find out his blood type. He may already be on the DNA database, Lenny thought hopefully and we may be able to match him. Although proof of blood type wouldn't be enough to convince his superiors he still thought that there was enough to form a team. He wrote up his report as the lead investigator in this missing person file and with some input from PC Bates presented it to his superior officer for consideration.

Detective chief inspector Robert Stevens of the Sussex police force had gone through DI Lenny Smiths recent report and called Detective Inspector Smith and PC Bates into his office.

"I want to start by firstly saying well done with your intensive detective work and the thoroughly professional way you have presented your case," said DCI Stevens. Sitting behind his desk with all of his commendations from the police commissioner laid out neatly in a row behind him, Lenny knew where this was going already. He was a seasoned detective and could read the DCI like a book, he continued,

"Essentially and on the record this is still a missing person's report, there is no real evidence of any wrongdoing here despite Mrs Anderson's protestations and some circumstantial evidence. I understand that the man has completely and mysteriously disappeared from the face of the earth but where's your evidence of foul play?"

"If I may interject sir," said the senior investigator,

"Go ahead Lenny, we are all friends and colleagues here. I'm interested if you have something else to tell me that is not in your report? he said while peering over his glasses like some university professor waiting on a chance to pour cold water on the student's argument, "I'm all ears."

Lenny wasn't that stupid, he knew he couldn't present or say anything that wasn't in the report. If he had, the Chief Inspector would have hauled him over the coals, no, he had put everything he knew about the case in it already.

"No sir, I have nothing further to add that is not in the report, but I would like to say the following, and I believe this whole heartedly sir as does Sandra." He looked over at her and she nervously nodded her agreement, "This mysterious well-built and good looking man with dark hair and hazel eyes has been identified by three separate individuals, and if I could interview him I think we could get more information. In my opinion his presence on three separate days leading up to Anderson's disappearance is more than just coincidence. Further to that we have a small piece of evidence from what I believe is the crime scene. This has turned up a blood type that is not Giles Anderson's. No one else had access to that office in the timeframe and could only be someone unauthorised and as yet unknown. We're also aware that Mr Anderson has not used his bank account since his disappearance, there are significant funds within it, and we are incredulous that he would not have needed it should he be on the lam as it were. Finally and more importantly, and if I may say so sir, you haven't met Anderson's family. They are convinced he would not go off like this. He has three small grandchildren that he idolised and would never miss at least three days a week with them. They are as certain they can be that some harm has come to him, as am I and our colleague here. PC Bates, sir"

DCI Robert Stevens had made his bones on murder squads, serious crime squads and other various squads that were formed for particular individuals. Indeed, he had worked with the renowned Jack Slipper of the Yard, when they had formed a special squad to catch the great train robbers in 1963. He had also played a big part in arresting the infamous Charlie Wilson on his return to England in 1968.He had been around and knew the score. He was made a detective inspector by 1972 and promoted to his current role after transferring from the Met in 1980.

Born in 1938 he had joined the Met in 1959.He was close to retiring aged only fifty and wanted to retire to his villa in Malaga and grow oranges. He definitely didn't want a fuck up in this case, besides, he didn't want a murder enquiry, and he had his reasons.

"You make a compelling argument, Detective Smith, and I totally understand your frustrations, but the facts remain unchanged. There is no firm evidence of murder here. You don't have a body in the first instance. You know better than anyone, Lenny, despite having lots of circumstantial evidence it just wouldn't be a good case to prosecute. I have already run this past the director for public prosecutions and they won't touch it with a barge pole without a body or at the very least substantial evidence of death."

No, I'm afraid that without the aforementioned evidence we just cannot proceed with any certainty. The risk to the tax payer just isn't justified and unless you can find something else to add to the file, like a body, I'm afraid, we are where we are, I'm sorry but there it is." He stood up.

Sandra and Lenny took this as their dismissal, shook the chief inspector's hand and were walked out. "Inspector Smith," said the DCI from within the room.

"Yes sir," said Lenny turning around.

"We have another murder case with an actual body down in Eastbourne. I'm sending you down there to assist with the enquiry, DCI Pangbourne at the Eastbourne station house will fill you in with all the details, I've told him you will be there first thing tomorrow morning"

"Yes sir," said Lenny and off he went.

The case was put on ice but would remain as one of the many unsolved cold cases in Scotland Yard's files, it would be another seven years before anyone looked at it again.

Danny arrived at his uncle's place in London, just after 3.00pm the same day and was greeted like a returning king! His uncles were ecstatic with the work he had done for them and had given him a holdall containing fifteen thousand pounds. Danny was delighted of course but it was more the acceptance of his family that really gave him the best feeling, money was secondary.

"Go and have a rest now, son and keep your head down for a while, we will be in touch," said Harry when the time came for him to leave. They both hugged him, that was unusual for them but Danny embraced it with all his heart, that's all he's ever wanted, he almost skipped out of the house he was so happy.

The twins really were "made up".

"I'll tell you something, Jimmy lad," said Harry to his brother, "You were right on the money! That boy is ruthless!, No fuss, no mess, he just gets on with it, you were also right about his temperament too. He just needed a hug!" They both laughed.

It would be some time before Danny killed again. Work of this kind was scarce but they just kept Danny on a retainer of five hundred pounds a week to look after the brothels and clubs. The foot soldiers they had were being managed by him and Danny seemed to have the knack of controlling these men without the need for unnecessary violence. This surprised the twins more than anything but they were delighted with him nonetheless, less violence meant less visits by Mr Plod, things were looking good, but that was about to change.

Present day

Following the twins informing Tommy of the rats in his kitchen, Danny was called to a meeting at the brothers' house in south east London. When he got there, Tommy Spillane was sitting in the lounge with his man, Albie. Danny knew who they were of course but was surprised nonetheless to see them sitting there as the twins very rarely had visitors to their auntie's house.

Danny was introduced by his uncles to his great aunt Rene, his grandmother's sister way back in 1988 when he was released from prison. They never spoke about her husband, Bertie, for some strange reason and Danny never asked. All he knew through the usual gossip mongers around town, is that he disappeared quite some time ago under suspicious circumstances back in the sixties and as a consequence his uncles had inherited the business. Now, it was 1995 and his place in the family was cemented. His auntie adored the boy and although she was now in her late 70s, she was bright as a button and was an amazing woman. Danny loved her like no other woman, apart from his mother of course, she had welcomed him into this house with open arms and a whole lot of unconditional love, something that Danny had very little experience of. He would have died for her.

"Danny," said Uncle Harry, "I think you know Tommy and his business partner, Albie."

Danny walked over and shook both their hands.

"Of course, Uncle Harry, I know Tommy well from prison, and I know Albie through what Tommy has told me and his formidable reputation precedes him." Albie nodded his head in appreciation but said nothing. Danny took his seat opposite the esteemed guests and waited for Tommy to speak. He hadn't seen him since 1988 and wondered what he wanted with him?

However, it was Jimmy that spoke first.

"Tommy has a small problem, son and asked for us to sit down with you personally and not go through the usual channels. Tommy being a good friend and all, we obviously agreed to it although, it has to be said we resisted at first as we cannot and should not all be seen together. That's why Tommy arrived a little earlier. He's been here for over an hour, Danny and Albie's been here slightly longer We know most of what Tommy's got to say, but the room's yours, mate," he said nodding in Tommy's direction.

Tommy began, "Danny, you did me a great service back in the day, and I'm extremely grateful, although I have to say the way you completed that bit of work and the tape you made was highly unusual and if I'm really honest pretty gruesome even for my taste, but each to their own son. I'm not going to dwell on that as you got the job done and that's that."

The twins were looking on a little nervously now as they didn't expect Tommy to come out with that and wondered how their nephew would take it.

Was Tommy calling him deranged? If so he wasn't far off, but wondered how the volatile Danny would read it?

Danny just smiled and said nothing.

Tommy cleared his throat and continued, "The reason I brought that up, son, is that this other job we've planned, this time on your own patch just down the road in Wandsworth. I cannot stress highly enough that this time there can be no cameras, videotaping or anything of that nature. I don't need that kind of proof, not that I did with that other fella, I trust you to do a job and when you tell me it's done that's it, I don't need anything else, do I make myself clear, Danny?"

"Absolutely, Tommy," said Danny, "I was a little green back then and wanted to impress you, it won't happen again."

The twins were visibly relieved and so was Albie, his boss had balls of steel talking to a killer like Danny in that manner but the boy took it well.

Tommy continued, "The fella we are talking about has done me a terrible wrong son although without him, I would never have met you. However, that being said he's still a grass along with one other who we will deal with sooner rather than later and needs to get what's coming to him. As you know, his name is Billy Saunders and back in 1984 around two years before I met you, he conspired with

277

a bent copper, and one of my trusted lieutenants to get me put away for reasons that are only known to them."

Danny interrupted, "I don't need to know all this Tommy, if you say he's got to go that's it for me, I'll take him and his muggy minder out tomorrow night as planned and that will be the end of it."

Tommy put his hand up as if to say hold on, "If you let me finish, son, you'll understand. I intend to try and find out that information tomorrow night, Danny, and want you there with me and Albie. Now don't take this the wrong way son but your penchant for the gruesome shall we say may be invaluable to me, I don't have the stomach for torture but I'm sure that you do, will you help?" Danny was taking all of this in, and Tommy was definitely digging him out, wasn't he? Still, he wasn't far away from the truth was he really?

"Just tell me where and what time, Tommy and I'll be there," he finally said.

"That's settled then," said Tommy, "I'll see you at my lockup in Kings Cross tomorrow night at 6.00pm sharp! I and Albie will be there. Now let's get down to this other fella, his bent copper friend."

"Hold on a minute," said Harry, "with all due respect, Tommy. There are a couple of things we need to discuss with you first before all this goes down. Now we know about that rat Saunders and have already agreed a cost and time frame, but we haven't discussed anything concerning your other rat, Darren, or indeed the dirty copper. As you well know Tommy, "doing" a couple of "wronguns" is one thing, but doing a copper, well that's another thing altogether! This needs proper discussion."

Tommy sighed and continued, "That's why I'm here, Harry, just let me finish and all will be revealed." Albie was in awe of his long-term friend, he had solid steel balls, he always knew that, but sitting in the house of another dangerous firm and their hired killer dictating the conversation, well that takes some gonads.

"Fair enough, Tommy," said Harry, "but you've blindsided me a little here. We will listen to what you have to say but don't be offended if we don't agree."

"I totally understand," continued Tommy, "and please accept my apologies if I have offended any one of you. I merely wish to outline the whole thing in its entirety for your consideration and thought it best just to get it all out in one hit so to speak. The reality is that we don't know if anyone else is involved do we? We need to find out or the consequences could be horrendous. It may be that we have to call off the whole thing depending on what we get out of Darren."

The whole room including Danny were impressed by Tommy's politician-like statement and all nodded their approval.

The relieved Tommy continued, "Saunders we've talked about and his dancing monkey boy Karl Green, they have to be done tomorrow night but as I said that depends on what we get out of the rat. Danny are you ready?"

"Yes, I'm ready, Tommy."

"Good boy! If you get this done cleanly we can forget about you fucking up my Clapham safe house!" he said with a grin.

They all laughed although it was a little muted.

"All jokes aside, tomorrow is my preferred day as this has been around for far too long. I don't want to leave it any longer. The pain this prick has caused me, and my family must be repaid and quickly. However, we have to be sensible; steaming in without full knowledge of who knows what would be stupid! We get everything out of Darren that he knows and make the final decision there and then. If it's a no go you simply deliver the parcel, Danny, collect the money and leave then we rethink the whole thing. Hopefully, we get what we want to hear and the fucking Gypo and his goon are gone tomorrow! As you all know, I'm supplying him with quite a large parcel of his favourite white powder tomorrow, or so he thinks, and you all know he's had the nerve to continue buying from me knowing what he's done!"

"He's done that to deflect your interest elsewhere, Tommy," piped up Jimmy. "He knows you would have suspected him, and by his buying from you these past few years has taken the heat off him, or so he thinks."

"Exactly!" continued Tommy, "and that's what he needs to think, that Friday night is just another routine drop. I am going to call him later tomorrow and tell him that Darren can't make the drop as he's indisposed; I think it would be better than you just turning up Danny. You might not even get through the door, and the key to this going the way I want and that is that you need to get into the house without any trouble, you can't kill him on the doorstep, is that clear Danny?"

"I know what I need to do, Tommy, we've been over it several times now," Danny said a bit too aggressively for his uncle's liking.

Tommy ignored the tone, "Good son, now let's get onto tomorrow night. Harry and Jimmy, I'll pay you both five grand each for Danny's time if that's all right with you?

They both nodded in agreement, "And Danny, you'll get ten large just for tomorrow night if you're in agreement.

Danny also nodded.

"Good, good," continued Tommy, "we've already agreed the fee for Mr Saunders and his monkey boy. Danny, you can keep the holdall he's got there for my goods as a bonus. There should be sixty grand in that bag son and it's all yours, just get the job done and don't forget to leave a little something for the sniffer hounds! Moving on to our bent copper, Harry, when you met up with him you took photos and a video recording as we discussed. I've seen the tapes, but don't worry I have no intention of killing a working police inspector. I won't even bother with him later when he retires as I know the heat it can bring down on all of us. However, Danny's going to place a few photos from that meeting inside Saunders house and don't worry, there won't be any that has any of you in them."

With that he produced five photographs of the bent copper in various poses just sitting below the pub sign and on the back of one of them was a name, date and address. The date was the same date that Darren was arrested back in 1984, and the address was Wandsworth Police Station, the name was that of one Lenny Smith who had been DS Thomas' partner in crime back then and was still a serving officer as was Thomas. The room was quiet, the twins, Danny and the ever-faithful Albie were in shock and awe at Tommy's brilliant plan. "So the copper gets investigated and more than likely would lose his pension. That's brilliant!" said Harry.

"Only one problem though, he will suspect that we set him up for those photos and he would be right of course, that might cause me and my brother some issues moving forward.

"I very much doubt that, Harry," said Tommy. "He will be a spent force by the time the inquiry is over. Besides you never really had any connection to him either did you? No, he will crawl away into disgrace and obscurity I guarantee it, if he doesn't, then we have a re-think don't we."

"One final thing gentlemen, this other copper, the esteemed Detective Chief Inspector Stevens, have you had a chance to talk to him, you need to find out what he knows? I don't want any of this coming back to any of us."

"I'm calling him tomorrow," Tommy said, "as funnily enough he left a message at my London post box earlier today for me to call him."

"I wonder what he wants?" said Jimmy, "Well, we will soon find out, my son won't we!"

"Keep me in the loop, Harry. I'll be interested to know what he actually knows about all this, if anything." Tommy said getting up, "Danny you know the score, get yourself back to Bridie's and make your final preparations. I'll see you tomorrow night at the lockup and if there are any changes or issues I'll let you know. There shouldn't be as Saunders will want his parcel by Friday night. He flies out the following day to his little place in Spain and will want his "goods" in place before he goes, the good thing is, Darren should be able to give us a little more background knowledge as to his movements and nuances when we see him tomorrow. Knowledge is power, my friends," he said finishing with a wink.

"I'll leave first fellas, if that's OK," said Danny, "I'll do a quick scan of the area and if there's anything suspicious outside or in the local area, I will come back and let you know."

No one minded and Danny left. Albie left ten minutes later and made the same commitment, only this time he would pick up the car and drive around for a few minutes and pick Tommy up from the end of the road. There was nothing to report and the two north London men drove home unmolested or followed.

"They're right to be paranoid," said Jimmy when they had all left, "You never know these days what those filth know and if they're watching you do you?"

"No, you don't," said Harry, "and come to think of it, I think I might call our friend DCI Stevens down in Sussex now. I'm curious as to what he wants to talk about? It can't be anything to do with this little caper though, give me that pay as you go mobile phone, Jimmy. I'll do it now."

Jimmy was in shock, all the blood had run out of his face and his demeanour was one of someone who had been told he had a terminal illness

"You can't be serious, Bobby?"

This was the name he used for Detective Chief Inspector Robert Stevens, formally of the Metropolitan Police and now with the Sussex constabulary.

"Harry, get over here! Bobby, say that first part again so that my brother can hear!"

Harry came bowling over; he had noticed Jimmy's demeanour and the tone of his voice had startled him. "What's going on, Jimmy"? What has he told you?"

"Say that again, Bobby, my brother is next to me now and needs to hear this," said Jimmy.

DCI Stevens began, "I had a DI here in Sussex called Thomas back in the late 80s. I believe you had some dealings with him back in the day when he was a PC working under me with the Met, he assisted me in that little problem you had in the sixties, do you remember?"

"Yes, we remember," said Harry, "we also met him a month or so ago," continued Harry, "where he offered some information relating to a certain friend of ours across the water and another gentleman in Detective Thomas's old stomping ground of Wandsworth in exchange for some serious money. Twenty five grand, in fact."

"It must have been some info!" replied Stevens, a little more cagily now.

Jimmy responded, "Not worth twenty-five grand, mate!"

Jimmy wasn't sure what Stevens knew and even if they were still "working together" in that way.

"That's of little consequence to me," said the chief inspector, "If he has something on this person or persons. I know nothing about it. he's working alone."

Jimmy was relieved to hear it.

"Indeed, I haven't worked with him in that way since the early seventies. He moved into the serious crime squad, and I moved onto CID at Scotland Yard, then on to Sussex. I hardly saw him after that and the next thing I knew he had transferred to Sussex and was under my command in the Criminal Investigation Department as a Detective Inspector. Even then it was odd as we never spoke about our time in London, as brief as it was and just got on with the job in hand. However, I do remember back in 1988 he came to me with a missing persons case involving the disappearance of a prominent member of the community, a certain Mr Giles Anderson."

At the mention of that name the blood had also drained from Harry's face and he was visibly shaken to the core.

"Anyway," continued the senior detective, "there was no real and solid evidence of any foul play despite

285

numerous coincidences, mostly surrounding a mysterious man seen on several occasions before the man went missing and the case was put on ice, until recently."

"Why until recently, Bobby, and why are you telling us now"? Piped up Jimmy, Harry thought he knew the reason but didn't want to believe it.

"Well, as you may well know, Thomas no longer plies his trade here in Sussex but the officer who first reported the missing man still does. She's a Detective Sergeant now, in the regional crime squad and is currently up for inspector! She's a real go getter; her name is Sandra Bates and took this all rather personally back then if I remember rightly. In fact she bagged and tagged a few items of interest while conducting the investigation which have apparently now thrown up a DNA match. She has her profile, lads and brought it to me so that I may reopen the case. Of course, I had no choice and referred it to our District Commander who concurred that the case should be re-opened. It's currently with the cold case squad here in Sussex, but so far there has been no match to the DNA from our data-base."

"Then where's your problem?" said Harry.

"Well, I have done some digging around myself, son," he continued, "I went through the old case files as is part of my duties and after a few laborious hours of scrolling through mug shots of men a certain age back then, and believe me, there were hundreds who matched the description of this mysterious fella. Want to guess who I eventually came across?"

"I've no idea," said Harry, who knew only too well what this fucker was going to say and was dreading hearing it.

"Well, I can't say with any certainty, Harry and I'm sorry to tell you this, but it sure fits your nephew's description. He was released from prison in 1988 where you two visited him seven times between 1986 and his release early 1988. I was able to get this from prison records, boys and so will any other "gum shoe" worth his salt that does even the slightest leg work and will quickly match you up with him. I reckon if we had his DNA we would be able to confirm he was involved with it in some capacity. Fortunately for him, when he was last in prison the authorities were not taking samples. They do now as a matter of course as you both know; everyone arrested these days has to give a DNA sample voluntarily or otherwise."

"Us visiting our own nephew has no significance," said Jimmy jumping in.

"Strange how you didn't deny his involvement Jimmy," said the shrewd old detective.

Harry's face was a picture. He was staring at his brother as if to say, "For fucks sake think before you open that big fucking mouth." Jimmy just stood there mouth open, but had nothing to say.

Harry continued on, "OK, Bobby. What's our next move? I'm not going to mug you off, you clearly know it's our nephew that's involved and to say otherwise would just make monkeys out of us all."

"It's a tricky one lads, you know I can't interfere with a potential murder inquiry, and if I know this Detective Sergeant Bates like I think I do, she will follow the evidence and DNA profile to its inevitable conclusion. She has clout now and the backing of a cold case board who I think will now open a murder file. I believe it will lead her and the team straight to your nephew and inevitably you two. Don't forget the witnesses are still around and a quick look at your nephew's mug shots will confirm who he is. She will have him in custody within months, if not weeks!"

Harry and Jimmy were stunned, they really didn't know what to say or do. There was an awkward silence for a few moments and it was Stevens who broke it, and said what they were all thinking.

"When they catch him and not if they catch him, he could lead them to you. What will you do then boys?, I can't help you with that, you're on your own!" he said in a triumphant fashion.

Harry was already hatching a plan and suspected Bobby wasn't telling them everything. He asked to meet with the slippery old detective,

"Risky," said the suspicious Stevens. "I definitely should not be seen with you two at the moment. I retire in a few months and can't risk being involved with any enquiry and I don't want my pension nicked from me, I'm sorry but that's out of the question."

Harry was furious, "Listen to me you, fucking parasite. You will meet me later this evening! No ifs, no fucking buts about it! Just get your scrawny little arse over to my house, toute fucking suite and don't ever forget we could bring you down with us as well! We have more than enough on you, not just to fuck up your pension, but to get you a prison sentence as well, are you following me inspector? You've had a good fucking run with us, Sunshine, and made plenty of money! You owe us and we want paying!"

It was Stevens' turn to have all the blood drained from his face. He knew the brothers well and had heard all the stories over the years including the rumour that they had murdered their own uncle in cold blood back in the sixties and knew they were not bluffing. He was seriously scared. He knew the twins wouldn't think twice about murdering him or at the very least causing him serious discomfort this close to retirement. He had no choice really and said, "OK, Harry, calm down, I'll leave now and should be with you within the hour, we can talk this through."

"That's better!" said Harry, "See you in an hour," and promptly hung up the phone.

Danny had arrived at Bridies place. He had been going through the conversation they had at his uncle's place on the drive to Mitcham. It was simple really. He would go to the lock up in Kings Cross tomorrow, extract a bit of info from that fucking grass, Darren, kill him, then hopefully head off to see another piece of shit across the water and his phoney crony. That statement made him laugh out loud and anyone watching him in that moment would have thought he was mad. It wouldn't be far from the reality though as Danny couldn't wait to ply his trade again.

The thought of killing those men in Wandsworth had him near to the point of salivating, he was looking forward to it, and he slept soundly that evening.

"It's on, son," Tommy was on the phone to Darren. "Get your arse over to the lock-up at 6.15pm.Pick up the parcel and get it over to Silly Bollocks over the water! Albie will meet you there; he's bringing it to the lock-up himself."

There was nothing unusual in Tommy's request, they had done this numerous times over the years and Albie sometimes did the drops to the lockup. It was never Tommy, not since that time he had been nicked anyway.

Darren always felt a pang of guilt when he thought of that time, he hadn't done anything wrong in his mind but he supposed he should have told Tommy about Saunders the night he was nicked but how could he? Tommy wouldn't have believed him; he was in the nick for far too long. Over six hours in fact and Tommy would have suspected him of grassing or at the very least saying something that could harm him in the future, especially as, he had walked out scot free and the drugs were placed with Saunders.

What did Saunders aim to gain from it all and who was that fucking copper? Darren couldn't work it out. His freebasing habit had certainly played its part hadn't it? He couldn't think straight at the time and all he knew was that Green was there to pick him up outside the police station and take him to Saunders. Darren wasn't that stupid though, he knew Saunders would want something in return, but in fact he had never asked for anything ever had he?

Indeed, he even let me have his caravan up in Norfolk for the weekend and gave me a copious supply of drugs to enjoy myself. Was it a coincidence that Tommy was nicked that same weekend? Darren knew the answer, but it was too late to do anything about it now. I mean, Jesus, if I went to Tommy and told him all that he would cut my bollocks off! Nah, best to let sleeping dogs lie he thought. It's been nearly eight years now and it's all forgotten.

Arriving at the lockup just before 6.00pm Danny rapped on the side entrance door. The place was an old railway arch that went right back under the train track and was one of many, along a cobbled street that were mostly used it seemed for car and motorcycle repairs. The noise from the passing trains overhead were horrendous and made the whole unit shake, especially at this time of the day. It was the main route into Kings Cross station and very busy.

Tommy's lock up was at the far end, right next to a café that was now closed and had been for several years. Beyond that was a huge gated arch that led to the railway lines. It was locked up at this time of the evening; Tommy had bought the lease to the café some time ago, but had kept it unoccupied since. Albie opened the door,

"Come in son, he's not here yet." He was referring to Darren, as Tommy was standing just inside a little office overlooking the large expanse of his lockup. He gave Danny a nod and that was it. There was a chair situated directly opposite the office that seemed to have been placed there intentionally, it had.

Detective chief inspector Robert Stevens arrived at the twins' house an hour later as promised, and was shown into the kitchen of the magnificent house by Jimmy.

Harry was already in there sitting on one of the comfortable stools that adorned the kitchen island. "Sit down, son and make yourself comfortable, this won't take long," said Harry.

Jimmy pulled out a chair for the nervous Chief Inspector and sat directly beside him.

Stevens felt a little intimidated, but tried to hold himself together and attempted to get the conversation started on his terms.

"Listen fellas."

"Shut the fuck up Bobby and you listen to me!" said the already angry Harry cutting straight across him and leaning over the island while pointing his finger in the detective's face. "You're going to sit there and tell me and my brother every fucking thing you know about this case and don't leave anything out! We will know if you're holding out on us. Don't forget we know what happened down there in Sussex and we also know you were holding something back in our earlier phone call."

Stevens' heart was beating at a hundred miles an hour and he was now seriously regretting agreeing to this meeting. He wasn't prepared for the twins admitting any involvement in the case and was thrown off guard. "Harry, we go back a long way! I've never held out anything on you or your brother. What I told you earlier was all I know."

"Bullshit!" said Harry, "You're the chief inspector of the squad investigating this case, and I suspect you know more than you're saying! That's why we wanted you here, now tell me everything you know, including the bit you have conveniently left out."

Stevens was trying to think, if he told them what he knew would he even make it out of this house? The twins were volatile and would not think twice about killing him.

Harry was reading his mind and said, "Listen son, if you've got something to say just say it, we are not going to hurt you although we could," he said with that crooked smile of his that seriously unnerved the now sweating detective. "No one knows you're here, son. I very much doubt that you reported or logged this visit with the station house, did you?"

Stevens, as with all other senior policemen were always on duty and was obliged to let the station house know if he wasn't available for any reason. Harry was looking at him intently.

He was right, of course. There was no way he would have told anyone about this visit, not even his wife. Stevens was shaking his head in agreement with Harry and finally said,

"OK, lads, I'll tell you everything, I know, but try to understand that I couldn't get involved. I'm too close to it all and they would know if someone was giving information out on the case."

Harry and Jimmy were furious!

Jimmy jumped in, "So you would have let us be dragged into a murder case and not told us you slimy fucking prick! After all the business we have put your way? You would never have made traffic duty if it wasn't for us!"

Bobby thought Jimmy was going to attack him at that point until the calmer Harry stepped in. "Calm down, Jimmy. Let the Chief Inspector tell us what he knows."

"Thanks, Harry," said Stevens. "Look, I told you there was an inquiry, didn't I? If it wasn't for that, you would be oblivious to it all and locked up with your nephew. It's up to you now, what you do with this information but I can't get involved moving forward, you understand don't you fellas?" he said pleadingly.

"Just tell us what you know, Bobby, and we will decide what to do next," said Harry.

Detective Inspector Bates knows who Danny is and has already set up a murder squad.

She also knows that you two are his sponsors and suspects your involvement. You haven't exactly been shrinking violets these past years have you boys? Half the Met knows what you do for a living but mostly due to me, you haven't had your collars felt, at least give me that!"

"Continue," said Harry, coldly.

"The way I see it, boys, is that they don't really have that much on any of you. Not even Danny, they can place him at the factory office on the day Anderson went missing but they can't prove foul play, there's no evidence of that and more importantly, no body!

Although the circumstantial evidence is strong, Danny could just say he was visiting on business, and when he left Anderson was alive and well. It's a hard case to prove murder, that's why, I decided back in 1988 not to proceed with any further action. The case is weak, but this DI Bates is determined to find out what happened to Anderson and her eyes are set firmly on you two and Danny."

Harry was listening intently whereas Jimmy just wanted to blow this fucker's brains out, he could have told us this much sooner and said so.

"Jimmy, you've got to understand, I can only tell you so much! The squad is small at the moment and any heads up on this case could lead back to me, at least I'm telling you now and at great risk! I mean what would it look like if I was seen talking to you, I would be drummed out of the force and possibly doing a prison sentence, you know, what prisoners do to ex coppers in there! I wouldn't last a week!" Stevens was seriously panicking by now.

Harry had been thinking throughout all of this and said, "What else, Bobby"? There's something else, I can feel it!"

Stevens was also thinking although mostly about a way to end this "interrogation", get the fuck out of here and end his association with these psychopaths. He was seriously regretting ever getting involved with them, although they were right about one thing, he wouldn't have got where he was without their information over the years. They had put away quite a few villains in their time with he himself making most of the arrests, I suppose, I owe them he thought and telling them the next part was the least he could do.

"The serious crime squad are also involved boys and you're top of the list. The powers above have decided that "firms" like yours need to go. They suspect you're involved in more than just the villainy that they know about and are working closely with the murder squads and cold case review teams across London and the home counties, that's why I didn't want to be here tonight., You are possibly under surveillance, although, I doubt it at the moment as the task force has just been formed and will probably take a few days to get everyone together, but when it does you need to be careful boys and cover your tracks. They know who you are and won't stop until they have something on you!"

The men were stunned, but not surprised. Times were changing and they knew this could happen one day. Even with their contacts like Bobby and others.

Time for a change me thinks, thought Harry. It was Harry that spoke next,.

"Bobby, we do go back some years and have helped each other throughout that time, but as with all things the end is near. When you leave here tonight we won't bother you again, however, before you go, I want to give you something," and walked over to the safe in the lounge while continuing to speak, "I suppose what you've just told me and my brother was inevitable in some ways and we really appreciate the heads up, however, what I'm about to give you may just take the heat out of the situation and give us time to make our own arrangements and extract ourselves from suspicion while giving you the evidence you need for your Detective Bates in the Sussex case."

He was putting on gloves which seemed strange and for a moment Stevens thought he was going to pull a gun and shoot him. However, he just produced a VHS tape.

"This was recorded back in 1988 while Giles Anderson was being murdered and is the final piece in the jigsaw," continued Harry, "It categorically proves what happened to him, by whom and why, it will not have any DNA trace on it as it is a copy. Danny sent it to us just before he got on a plane to Spain following his murder, and I copied it, the original went to a certain Mr Tommy Spillane over the water in north London, I'm sure you're familiar with the name, but I very much doubt he has kept his copy".

Stevens was flabbergasted, "You mean that Danny recorded the murder? Jesus Christ lads, this is dynamite, but why on earth would he do that?" asked the open mouth detective.

"He's a psychopath, Bobby, simple as that," said Harry, "He seems to take great pleasure in his work and was extremely proud of this one. He's our nephew and our blood, of course, but me and my brother are not going to spend the rest of our lives in prison down to him. The evidence on that tape and what you already know should be enough to keep the serious crime and murder squads busy for a while. You take all the credit, get one of the biggest gangsters in London off the streets and we walk away, for now at least. The only thing I ask is that you raid Danny's flat next week. Where you will find this while acting on information you have received or at your recommendation we will put it there by Sunday evening, if you promise that, you can have it. The alternative to not agreeing this, is not worth talking about," he said menacingly.

Stevens knew what that meant and would have agreed to anything at this point. He knew the boys would not let him leave this house if he didn't.

"You have deal boys," he finally said, "but why must I wait until next week, Harry?"

"That's my business, Bobby and its non-negotiable, do we have a deal?"

"Yes, we have a deal, Harry," said the much-relieved detective. "Good luck boys, it was great working with you," he said unconvincingly while getting up to leave. The twins rose almost simultaneously and walked him to the door.

"Oh, by the way, Bobby," said Jimmy, "Don't forget that we still have a few things on you, I'm only telling you that just in case you decide not to honour our agreement, do you understand?"

"Don't worry lads, I'll stick to our agreement, I mean why wouldn't I?" With that he left into the cold and dreary evening, a very relieved man.

Once Stevens had left, the twins went back into the kitchen. It was Jimmy that had all the questions,

"What the hell are you doing, Harry? You've just given up our own nephew and a good friend; our name will be worthless after this!"

"Don't be so fucking naïve, Jimmy. It's a small price to pay! Besides, they will find the tape at Danny's and it will look like it was part of their investigation, our names will almost certainly be mentioned, but with no evidence they can't pin fuck all on us!"

"Two things you haven't thought about my old son," said Jimmy, "Tommy and Danny! Especially Danny, he will know it was us who planted it in his flat and Tommy will know shortly after! Do we really want a war with that mob across the water; we don't have the firepower anymore whereas Tommy does, and not only that, once the rumours start, we won't be able to fart in London anymore our name won't mean shit!"

"Danny's never going to know," said Harry darkly with that strange look on his face.

Jimmy instantly recognised it and almost as instantly knew what Harry was planning,

"Absolutely fucking genius brother, if Danny's never lifted they can't get his DNA! Not only that but the filth will be too busy investigating that little lot over the water! Do you want me to call Pedro or do you want to do it?"

They both started laughing, "You do it brother," said Harry," That fat prick seems to like you!" They both started laughing again.

A little after 6.15pm, Darren let himself onto the lockup. He immediately saw Albie and a strange looking big fella he hadn't seen before standing right beside him.

"How's it going Albie and who's your friend?" he asked amiably.

"This is Danny, son. He's going to be helping us for a while this evening aren't you, Danny?" said Albie while walking towards the lockup door and slipping the bolt into place.

"No need for that, Albie," said Darren, "The door locks itself."

"Let us worry about that," said Tommy walking out of the office.

Darren was surprised to see him there. He hadn't noticed him when he entered the lockup and now had a sudden and unexpected knot in his stomach. "Watcha Tommy, what are you doing here?" he said nervously while looking all around him. Danny had gotten a lot closer and so had Albie.

"Take a seat, son," said Albie

"What's going on, mate? said Darren, "I have to leave in a minute, you know what matey boy's like if I'm late with his parcel!"

"Let me worry about that, son," said the now looming Tommy. He had a look on his face that Darren didn't like and was making him feel a little uncomfortable.

"Take a seat, son. Funnily enough that's who I need to talk to you about, our dear old friend in Wandsworth, that fucking Pikey prick Billy Saunders."

Darren was pushed down into the seat and knew almost straight away that something was wrong, "You have a bit of explaining to do, Darren," said Tommy quite calmly, "and I'm not going to beat around the bush. I know about you getting yourself nicked over the south back in 1984, and I know that Saunders was behind it. What I don't know is what your part in it was Darren. Now, don't be scared! I just need the facts and have no doubt about your loyalty towards me. However, it's a bit strange that you didn't tell me all about it at time or up till now in fact? Now is your chance to put the record straight son, and don't leave anything out, please."

Tommy was standing directly over Darren now with Danny and Albie no more than two paces behind and beside him.

Danny thought this was funny as it reminded him of his meeting with the governor of Maidstone jail some years earlier.

"Do I look like a screw?" he thought to himself and almost laughed.

"Tommy, please mate, I never told you because it would have looked bad!" said the now seriously frightened man. "I'll tell you everything but please listen as it's the truth I promise, Tommy!"

"Get started, son. We have a drop to do once we have this out of the way, and I don't want that prick on the blower, especially now that he's learned to use a mobile telephone, the backward fat prick!" said Tommy reassuringly.

"It was strange, Tommy. I was just over the water and in Wandsworth when I got a pull. I can't even remember the coppers names now but it was unusual. They didn't search the motor or ask me anything when they stopped me. They just shoved me into their motor and took me to Wandsworth police station and that's where it got stranger.

They booked me in at the front desk, but never said what for."

"Didn't you ask?" said Albie incredulously.

"Of course I did but they just ignored me and threw me in a cell! I was a little out of it if I'm honest, Tommy," Darren continued, "as I'd had a couple of liveners before I left. It's not something I'm proud of."

"It was more than a couple of liveners Darren," said Tommy. "From what I've heard , you were washing my fucking powder into crack and smoking it! No wonder you were out of it for fucks sake!"

"I know Tommy, I know, but I promise, I don't do that anymore, it was a one off and after that I've never touched it again!"

That was a lie, thought Tommy and from what he had heard it was still a regular occurrence but merely said, "Go on son."

"Well, like I said," Darren continued, "I was just thrown in a cell and about five or six hours later they released me without any charges. I just thought they hadn't found the drugs and were simply letting me go."

"BOLLOCKS!" shouted Tommy directly into his face. "Someone picked you up outside the station didn't they son?, It was that Irish Dickhead, Karl Green ,wasn't it?"

Darren knew the score. Tommy knew all about it and the only chance he had now was to tell him everything that happened,

"All right, Tommy," he said now crying.

"It was the Irishman who picked me up. I was seriously surprised to see him but he told me that Billy had a bent copper on his payroll and he had sorted out my release and he drove me to Billy's house, that's the truth Tommy, I swear!"

Darren was openly sobbing now while the two other men were just looking at him in disgust.

"I know what you're thinking, Tommy," he said through sobs, "but I promise on my mother's life he never asked me for anything. I wouldn't have given him anything even if he asked, I swear to God, Tommy! Please, don't do this!"

"What about the day I got nicked, son? said Tommy who had got himself back under some semblance of control.

"You were in a caravan up in Norfolk, whose caravan was that son? Was it Billy's?"

"Yes it was, mate," continued Darren, "but I thought nothing of it! If you remember, I said, don't do the drop and I'll sort it when I got back, Jesus Tommy! If I thought he was going to set you up I would have warned you, I just thought it was a coincidence, honestly!"

"If you say so, son, but what about when I got nicked? Why didn't you tell me then what had happened if you're so innocent in all this?"

The frightened man was now visibly shaking and sobbing so uncontrollably that he could barely get the words out.

"I was frightened, Tommy, I knew what you would think! But I promise you this; I had fuck all to do with setting you up! I would never have betrayed you or the boys, if you give me the chance I'll drive over and kill that fat fucking cunt and the Irishman right now," he said more in hope than expectation,

"Don't worry about him, Darren," Tommy said softly, "Our man Danny here will take care of him. You could however redeem yourself a little here and explain to him how it usually works when you do the drop, following that you can get out of my lockup and never darken my doors again, I'm done with you."

Darren was relieved and gladly told the nearby killer everything he knew and had done on previous occasions. Danny knew most of it anyway; it was just the little detail of first entry and the usual protocol that he wanted.

Once he had finished, Tommy said, "Thank you, son but just before you leave I just want you to know that my wife and daughters send their regards." With that he swung a baseball bat directly into the head of the still sitting man, knocking him off the chair and rendering him unconscious, he continued the assault until it was clear Darren was well and truly dead.

"Albie, tidy that filth up when Danny leaves, I want no trace of that fucking rat ever found!"

With that he dropped the bat and went back into the office and took his gloves off. No one had even seen him put them on, let alone pick the bat up! Not even Danny and Albie!

"Ok, now let's get down to business, said Tommy, "It's on, Danny! Get yourself over to Wandsworth, our friend is expecting you by 8.00pm I called him yesterday and told him that Darren is on another bit of work for us up north and can't make the drop. I also told him you're one of our trusted friends and have worked with us for years and that your name is Mickey. He seemed to accept that, but be careful son this fat cunt is a wily bastard! Don't turn your back on him, ever; I want that Pikey and his monkey dead by tonight. When it's done call your uncles and not me. Albie will give you the parcel and final instructions before

305

you leave. Don't forget to leave some of the Charlie behind and the photos tucked somewhere discreet, this has to look like a drug deal gone wrong, are we clear?"

"Crystal clear, Tommy," said Danny, "we've been through this numerous times I know what's needed here!"
"Good," said Tommy, once again ignoring the boys apparent exasperated tone, "and for fucks sake, no videos Danny!"

With that Tommy left the lockup and went home. The two men stayed behind and went through the final few things.

Both men put their gloves on and got started.

"In this bag is three kilos of super prime self-raising MacDougal's flour! Once the bag is in his hands it will feel like the usual weight. In this bag is an ounce of Columbia's finest marching powder, according to the late Darren."

They both looked at the lifeless body just outside the office. "The Irishman doesn't check the goods until you're in his room on the first floor. If you need to, you can give him a sample from this bag, but we've done this so many times before with him it's become almost routine.

However, it's there if you need it, this is the bag that's left behind of course. Hopefully by the time he decides to check it you will have dealt with him, but don't forget he doesn't know you and things may be different, from what I've heard the man is a prick so you never know. It's imperative that Billy doesn't get wind of anything. I know Tommy has already said this, son, but Billy Saunders should not be taken lightly! We know he's armed and the last thing anyone wants is shootout! The element of surprise should eliminate that issue!"

"Don't worry," said Danny, "The last bit of info obtained from our late friend over there has really helped. I know the floor layout and the access and egress route. I'm all good mate, Look, I better be going, time's ticking on."

"Fair enough, son, just remember, once the Irishman's dealt with you come down the stairs as if you're leaving, then head towards Billy's quarters, hopefully, he will just think its Karl."

"Honestly Albie! Stop worrying I've got it covered!" Danny picked up the holdall, took out his gun, this time it was a 9mm Glock 17 with added suppressor, it wouldn't be completely silent but it would certainly reduce the noise to that of a popping noise, and left the lockup.

Albie had no doubt the boy would do what he said he would, he had seen that tape several years ago and knew Danny was more than capable but he couldn't help feeling a sense of unease, he just couldn't shake it. He turned with a weary sigh to deal with what remained of Darren, shaking his head and muttering.

Danny arrived in Treport Street Wandsworth just before 8.00pm.

He was lucky, there was a parking spot just before the alleyway that led to Billy Saunders' back garden and on that side of the road. He got out of the car, went to the boot, took the holdall out and walked back towards Alfarthing

Lane and the front door of Saunders address, only a few doors down the road.

Danny knew the front of the house like the back of his own hand. He had spent a few evenings in the pub opposite, the Lord Palmerston, when he was using the Clapham safe house. It was risky but well worth it and he had watched Billy and Karl come and go from the house several times. He had analysed both men intently and surmised Karl shouldn't be a problem. He was overweight and didn't carry himself very well, whereas Billy was a different animal. He was big and broad and carried himself with the swagger of someone who was confident in their abilities; I won't give this man an inch thought Danny.

Karl watched Danny walking up the path from his first floor window, bang on time he thought, not like Darren who almost always was late.

Karl was pissed off with Darren missing this delivery as he usually brought him a little sweetener and between the two of them used to "cut" the goods a little bit and share the profits. It was risky because if Billy had found out he would have cut their fingers off but such was the pull of this drug it was worth the risk and only took a few minutes to do while Billy sat downstairs watching his stupid programmes.

Let's see if this boy wants to play?

Danny had reached the front door and was about to ring the bell when it opened and there stood the Irishman with a big grin on his face, "Come in, come in," he beckoned. "Straight up the stairs and first door on the right," he proclaimed while scanning the outside of the street before closing the door.

Danny made his way up the stairs and straight into Karl's room. It was neatly arranged and quite spacious., The telly was on in the corner and ironically, *"The Bill"* was just starting with its familiar theme music. Just inside the door was a reasonable sized dining table with only two chairs. In the far corner was Karl's king size bed covered in what can only be described as a leopard print quilt cover.

Danny almost laughed, the thought of this fat prick rolling about on his "love nest" almost made him throw up!

Karl came in shortly after, "Plonk that bag on me bed son," he said in his broad Irish accent.

Danny complied, "Sit here, mate and let's have a quick chat," he said conspiratorially turning up the TV a little.

Danny didn't say anything; he let the Irishman talk, "Do you fancy a cheeky little line? My old son," Karl said getting his own bag out and racking up a couple of lines,

"Not for me, fella," said Danny, "I've got to drive back over the water in a minute."

"Suit yourself, mate," said Karl and leaned forward in his chair to snort his fist line of the evening, unbeknown to him it would be his last.

Karl lent back in his chair and was trying to work this fella out; he certainly wasn't a Darren and didn't seem like the type to want to get involved in his and Darren's usual activity. Shame he thought to himself but still it's probably only a one off, and there's always next time isn't there?

He got up and walked past the sitting Danny and went over to the bed, leaning over the holdall with his back to Danny. He didn't hear Danny get up put his gloves on and creep behind him. He was just opening the bag when the last thing he ever heard was a "pop", he slumped forward and began to saturate the leopard print quilt cover and pillows with his brains and blood.

Danny pushed the dead Irishman aside and casually picked up the holdall, collected the bag of money that was clearly just sitting there in front of the bed, turned and let himself out of the room.

Closing the door rather noisily behind him while saying a little too loudly, "Cheers mate, see you next time," whether Billy downstairs could hear him or not he didn't know but proceeded to walk down the stairs.

He could clearly hear the television blaring out from somewhere downstairs. It appeared he too was watching *The Bill* as Danny could hear the sirens in the background, he opened the front door then slammed it shut.

Billy was engrossed in the episode about teenage prostitution and was therefore oblivious to what was happening upstairs. He had heard the man arrive of course and had heard him leave. Karl would be down soon with his parcel but not before the usual protocol, at least five minutes!

Any attempt by anyone to gain a surprise entry including the police would be met with a front door that was heavily fortified. Billy was facing the rear French doors and could see all the way down to the rear gate which was also heavily fortified and padlocked from the inside. He knew that the most critical and obvious time for a raid or a rival attack would be directly after the courier had left.

He was a man of experience and always followed the same routine following a drop; he was therefore surprised when the door to his parlour opened. Turning around in his mother's old leather winged armchair, he said "What the fucks going on Karl! Have you checked the front door?"

The sight that met him was not of Karl but of Danny standing in the doorway with a silenced gun pointing straight at him.

Billy was only a few feet away, he stayed surprisingly calm and just said, "Who the fuck are you and what do you want?"

Billy had been in many tricky situations before including having guns pointed at him, it took a lot to make him unsteady but there was something about this fella,.

That look in his eyes not only told Billy that he was serious; it also told him that he had done this before. Billy knew people like him and for the first time this evening was genuinely worried,

"Just sit there and don't fucking move!" Ordered Danny.

"I have no problem with killing you where you sit, and I think you know that but I'm not here to kill you Billy otherwise you would be dead by now. I just want some information."

Billy was desperately trying to think, his own weapon was in the bureau only a few feet away but he wouldn't make it would he? This kid was half his age and would kill him in a second. No, he's right if he wanted to kill me I'd be dead already. He relaxed back into his chair and calmly said, "Fair enough, son, but please tell me who you are and what you want?" He was staring straight at Danny and not blinking. Danny wondered where his weapon was, he thought, he saw a very quick glance towards the bureau. It's probably there he thought, I'll deal with that in a minute.

"I'll tell you everything Mr Saunders, but first you're going to put these on." He produced the handcuffs and threw the first pair into his lap.

"Do your ankles first, Billy, and don't fuck about!"

Billy was outraged, "I'm not putting those fucking things on, son! You'll just have to kill me, and then you won't get your information, will you?"

"Billy," said Danny quietly, "if you don't put them on I'll shoot you in the knees first and you'll still tell me what I want, have you ever been shot in the knees Billy? I've heard it's quite painful."

Billy red with anger now knew the kid meant it

"Fuck you, you little prick! I'll do it but mark my words when this is over I will hunt you down like a dog and rip your fucking head off, personally."

The old man's got balls, thought Danny but simply said, "Good choice Mr Saunders, I will worry about you coming after me later."

Billy reluctantly shackled his own ankles,

"Just one more click, Mr Saunders, if you please," said Danny when he noticed that they were not quite closed.

"You fucking prick!" said Billy, "They're tight enough as they are!"

"One more click, Billy, and I need to hear it, or I promise you that I'll do both your knees after I've finished counting to three," said Danny. "One... two..."

"All right. All right!! Said Billy leaning forward and clicking them into place.

"That's good, Mr Saunders. Now the bracelets," he said throwing the last pair into his lap.

Billy looked at him with utter contempt and sheer hatred.

Danny recognised that look of course and smiled that crooked smile that always seemed to unnerve people. Not this fella though. he looked right back at him and kept the stare going with unwavering eyes.

"It's up to you, mate," said Danny, "but the same rules apply with the bracelets. If you don't put them on I'm going to shoot you in the knees. Please believe me when I tell you I will and you'll still tell me what I want, is it really worth that much pain, this stubbornness? I don't really want to hurt you, but I've heard you're a dangerous man and I'm not going to give you the chance to get your weapon out of that bureau over there."

Billy automatically looked over, confirming Danny's suspicion, Danny smiled, Billy was furious that he'd been tricked like that.

"Now," continued Danny, "put the first one on your right wrist and click it into place, do it now," he said while pointing the gun at the knees of the caged animal before him, Billy complied, he had no choice really did he?

"Good, good," said Danny moving into position behind the chair while pointing the gun at Billy's head. "Now raise your arms above your head and keep facing the window, stay sitting and put your hands together, please don't try anything, Billy, I really don't want to kill you." Before he knew it the second clasp was snapping into place, Billy was harmless now.

Danny walked over to the bureau and removed the gun, "Nice piece," he said casually tucking it into his waistband. Billy didn't respond, he merely put his shackled hands into his lap and waited for his gaoler to start talking.

Danny had pulled one of the footstools towards the patio doors, closed the curtains and sat down with his gun pointing directly at Billy Saunders stomach.

Billy was trying to make sense of all this, he knew it wasn't about the money or drugs otherwise it would have been done by now and this fella would be long gone, no, there's something this kid needs to know, but what?

It was Danny that spoke first, "Do you know why I'm here, Mr Saunders?"

"Not a fucking clue son if I'm honest, but I'm interested to know who you are and what the fuck you want? It's very clear to me that Tommy Spillane sent you, that's the only reason you're in my house but as to the reason for all this," he said while looking down at his shackles, "I've no fucking idea."

Danny was impressed. This guy was far from stupid, it was obvious of course that Tommy had sent him but his acute awareness and total disregard for the situation he was in induced a little more respect for him.

Danny was wise to render the older man incapable, however he still couldn't take any chances, where there's life there's hope thought Danny and started laughing.

Billy was angry now, "What's so funny you little prick? Just take the goods and money, ask your stupid questions and get the fuck out of my house!"

Danny stopped laughing immediately, got up and belted the shackled man just above the left eye with his gun causing a deep gash that immediately started bleeding profusely, "Shut your fucking mouth!" he said, "I'll ask the questions and I'll leave when I'm done."

It was Billy that was laughing now, blood was running down his face "You little cunt!" he said laughing, "Do you think I'm scared of you? I've eaten little boys like you for breakfast! You're just another hired little thug doing his masters bidding. Just do what you have to do; I'm tired of looking at your muggy little face!"

Billy had by now realised that this wasn't going to end well, Tommy was a serious player and this man in front of him was not a novice and meant to do him serious harm or worse. He straightened up his body the best he could, puffed his chest out and continued, "Well sonny, are we getting on with it or what?"

Danny didn't say a word and just shot him in both kneecaps, pop, pop!

Billy screamed and immediately fell forward out of the chair and onto the floor desperately trying to grab his knees and stop the excruciating pain he was feeling. He was never going to walk again, he thought in that moment. "You fucking psycho!" he said through gritted teeth. "What the fuck is this all about? I've never done anything to Tommy, he's my friend."

"That's not quite true, Mr Saunders," said Danny, "You remember Darren don't you?, Well, he's given you up, Billy, and Mr Spillane wants me to let you know."

Danny was laughing again, Billy now laying on the floor looked up and saw nothing but madness in this boys eyes. At that point he knew this wouldn't end with just a knee capping. Danny was hovering over him with the gun pointed directly at his head.

"Wait, wait," Billy managed to say through the excruciating pain, "don't do this, I can set you up for life, whatever he's paying you I can double, no triple, just tell me what I can do to get out of this?"

Danny sat back down on the stool and just looked at the stricken man lying on the floor. There was blood everywhere and the mere fact that this man hadn't passed out yet was impressive, he finally said, "There's nothing you can pay me Billy. A contract is a contract and I'm well known for completing them and this job is no different. You could offer me a million pounds, but it wouldn't matter."

Billy was resigned to his fate now; he could feel himself drifting away. The blood loss was making him drowsy and he knew the end was near.

"Who are you, son? I know Tommy well, and I know he uses outside parties to do his dirty work, at least give me that before you kill me"

Danny considered it for a moment and thought there would be no harm in letting him know,

"I work for Jimmy and Harry Parkhurst, Mr Saunders and my name is Danny Mason."

Through the excruciating pain and substantial blood loss, Billy suddenly realised who Danny was; he was Lizzie Lane's son! He knew the Parkhurst boys as well of course from back in the fifties, they had lived just around the corner in Delia Street and Lizzie was their half-sister, they moved away when they were teenagers.

He also knew Danny's father, that no good piece of shit, Ronnie Mason who had robbed him back in the sixties. He never did catch up with him, did he? He remembered the murder of Lizzie back in the seventies and recalled the murder had taken place in front of the boy now standing over him, it was all over the papers, at this point and through his pain he suddenly saw a way out,

"Listen son," he said through gritted teeth.

"I knew your family, in fact your mother Lizzie stayed here while your father Ronnie was in prison back in the sixties, 1964 if I remember, I looked after her, in fact you were only a baby, and I let her have a room upstairs for free until your dad got out! That's got to count for something right?"

Danny was a little taken aback by this news and hearing his mother's name for the first time in a while. It made him a little sad, but it didn't really change anything did it? he thought. She's gone now and has been for some time.

Billy was staring up at him pleading with his eyes and waiting for a response.

"I'm sorry Billy, but none of that matters now," Danny finally said. This is why he hadn't killed him straight away. He wanted him to beg, he wanted to break him.

"I've got a job to do, and like I said earlier I always deliver." He loomed over the stricken man and cocked his weapon.

"Before you do it son, you need to know one thing" said the now resigned Billy looking at Danny through blood soaked eyes.

"What is it?" said Danny,

"Your mother used to suck my cock for the rent money and she loved it," he said through gritted teeth. Danny emptied the Glock into him, Billy's body jumped with every round until all Danny could hear was a clicking noise from the empty magazine.

He went back upstairs and placed the photos Tommy had given him in Karl's bedside cabinet, picked the bag of flour up and scattered the ounce of cocaine over Karl's table, went back downstairs and walked back through the parlour, stepping over the lifeless body of Billy Saunders, Danny didn't give him a second glance.

Hooked on the patio doors were a set of keys. Danny thought they would be for the rear gate padlock, he was right of course and walked into Treport Street with no problems, got in his car, drove off and headed straight to the airport, the twins had arranged his flight to Malaga for that evening.

It was 9.00pm and the flight was for 11.40pm from Heathrow, he had plenty of time and would leave the money, gun, gloves and his clothes in the long stay car park, where good old Uncle Harry would collect it the following day and destroy any evidence.

"Your money including the "bonus" from Tommy will be wired over to Pedro in due course."

His uncles had thought of everything, thought Danny fondly and he actually felt love for them.

This was something alien to Danny, but it made him feel good, plus he couldn't wait to see Pedro again, he really liked him.

.

Harry and Jimmy Parkhurst had popped open a rather nice bottle of "Moet and Chandon" champagne and were toasting their manipulations.

"Cheers, brother!" said Harry.

"And cheers to you brother!" said the smiling Jimmy.

"It's a shame really," continued Harry, "I got to like the kid when all is said and done and as for Tommy, well he's just another casualty in this war we are constantly fighting I suppose."

Both brothers laughed.

"It is what it is, brother, said Jimmy, "rather them than us, we couldn't do a twenty stretch or more at our age could we?"

"Not a chance, Jimmy, I wouldn't even want to do six months in any of her majesty's shit holes, fuck that! Tommy's used to it though, isn't he? The only problem now is that he will probably die in there; still he knew the rules and must have considered this could have happened. I liked him though so let's have a toast." They both raised their glasses and simultaneously said, "Absent friends!" and burst out laughing.

Arriving at Malaga airport, Danny was met as before by the rather large and moustachioed Pedro.

Danny was really pleased to see him and was looking forward to relaxing for a few weeks, no doubt his uncles would find something for him to do, but he'd cross that bridge when he came to it. For now he was just looking forward to sitting by the pool drinking Pina Coladas, and the odd trip into town to take in some more of the culture. He wanted to see that painting again, for some reason it reminded him of his mother and recent events had brought her back to the fore. Pedro drove the relatively short distance to the villa but was quieter than usual. The last time he had been here Pedro was a lot more talkative. Danny thought this was strange, but simply put it down to the time of the day, it was late and perhaps, he was tired. yes, that's it he thought.

Pedro pulled into the drive, got out and opened the villa's front door, "Get some sleep Danny, I'll be back tomorrow around 3.00pm perhaps we can go to lunch?" he said walking back to the car.

"That sounds like a great idea, Pedro! I look forward to it, see you tomorrow."

Danny walked to the previous room he had used before, everything was the same and he suddenly felt at home. Maybe, I could live here? he thought yawning, However, it had been a long day and he just wanted to sleep. He would give it more thought tomorrow, he slumped on the bed fully clothed and was asleep in minutes.

He was dreaming, this time it was two men searching for him. They reminded him of someone or something, but, he couldn't quite put his finger on it. He was at his Aunty Rene's house back in London. It was dark and none of the light switches worked.. He knew the house like the back of his hand of course, but couldn't for the life of him work out what room he was in? Suddenly and out of nowhere one of the men came lunging towards him, what was that in his hand? Was it a gun?

Danny couldn't make it out and while trying to, the other man was just as suddenly behind him and had got him around the neck and he was powerful. Danny was no lightweight, but couldn't free himself! He could smell the powerful aroma of molten metal and horrifyingly realised that the man holding him was Giles Anderson! He smelled of lemon sherbets! The other man was now a lot nearer and Danny could see through the gloom what he was holding, it was a camcorder and the man brandishing it was his Uncle Harry!

He had this strange grin on his face and was saying something but all Danny could make out was "Fucked up" and "it's time son."

Danny was screaming now and just as suddenly he was wide awake! Standing at the end of his bed was Pedro with another man he had never seen before. Danny sat up and wondered if he was still dreaming, the men had guns pointed at him. He wasn't dreaming, this was real, but before he could react, the men shot him from point blank range straight into his chest killing him almost instantly, Danny was dead, he was thirty one.

The twins had left specific instructions with Pedro, "Danny's body can never be found son, do you understand?"

Pedro did. It wasn't the first time he would be acting on behalf of the twins, he knew what they wanted and more importantly why. Without his body the police would never be able to connect him to the Anderson murder. They didn't have his DNA did they and without it couldn't prove a thing and although the brothers would come under investigation the police wouldn't have enough and they would walk away from this scot free! Clever! thought Pedro.

They buried Danny in amongst the orange groves at the far end of the Hacienda. He would make great fertiliser he chuckled to himself while digging the hole with his "assistant", Mickey Grover.

Mickey had landed the previous morning and had been sent by the twins. He had only been out of prison for a month and was going to work for them in the business.

"All we ask is for your loyalty son. Everything else comes with that," they had told him.

The twins had arranged for Danny's flat to be thoroughly cleaned on the Saturday.

There would be no trace of Danny there whatsoever. The firm they used for this were extremely professional; it took them two days and was finished by Sunday evening.

Harry arrived to pay them and lock up, before he did he put the tape in the bottom drawer of Danny's bedside cabinet and walked out. He didn't know about his "secret" flat in Putney or the fact that he had a son; Danny had never told them about either. The police would discover the tape, the following Tuesday.

Tommy was arrested a short time later and charged with conspiracy to murder. He was acquitted the following year at the Old Bailey after serving eight months on remand. The jury only took four hours to reach their verdict, the evidence was flimsy and without any actual proof of his involvement he was released.

He had immediately got in touch with the twins, they had visited him in Wandsworth prison while he was awaiting trail and were horrified that Danny had kept a copy of the tape. They assured him that they would hunt him down as he had mysteriously disappeared from their villa in Spain and "deal with him" appropriately, Tommy suspected they knew more than they were letting on but from his position there was very little he could say or do, he would wait until all this was over then make his own enquiries, something didn't smell right.

Detective chief inspector Robert "Bobby" Stevens retired to his villa in Malaga following the trial. He knew Tommy Spillane would be acquitted, the case was too fragile.

Tommy's defence had merely said he had no connection to the man responsible for this heinous crime and the crown had not proven any such connection, in addition to this, the mere fact that this brutal killer had mentioned Tommy's name while undertaking this brutal crime also proved nothing. It was malicious slander and in the absence of this man and any other proof of association the crown could not with any certainty prove their case, the jury agreed 12-0, and that was that.

Win some, lose some! Thought the wily inspector as he walked out of the court, He also suspected that the twins would have known this and that their nephew would never be found, clever boys. This past year had the serious crime

324

and murder squads concentrating on the north London boys and barely bothered the twins, they were away and scot free, for now. He would meet up with them the following week at their villa in Malaga very close to his one and crack a bottle or two.

Detective Inspector Sandra Bates, now attached to the serious crime squad from her usual cold case review team was furious at the acquittal and vowed to continue the search for Danny Mason; she suspected he was dead as there was absolutely no trace of him anywhere despite a huge international manhunt involving Interpol and the Spanish authorities.

"He is either dead or hiding out on the Costa del Sol!" she had confided in her team, either way this isn't over, we need to find Danny Mason or his body, I aim to bring Tommy Spillane and his "friends", the Parkhursts, to justice if it's the last thing I do!

The End